PHYLOMANCER
AERDA ONLINE VOL. 1

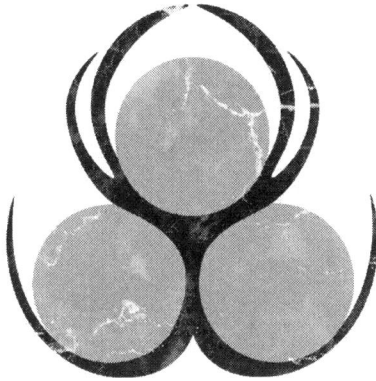

Jack Bryce

Sign up to my newsletter, and you will be notified when I release my next book!

Visit jackbryce.nl for more information.

To the One.

CONTENTS

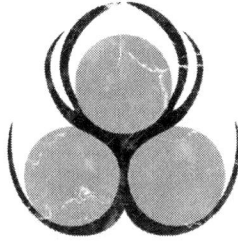

CHAPTER 1

I was born into my new life screaming and crying, torn away from warmth and safety.

Through my pain and panic, I saw a sphere of light grow in a mass of darkness. Text appeared, black letters against the light. They were blurry at first, but they grew sharper with every second.

Mortal, you are Awakened.

The letters faded.

My mind swam. It took a while for coherent thoughts to form, but when they came, I remembered where I had been and what I had been doing.

I had sat behind my computer, counting down until my preload of Aerda Online activated. With three weeks off from work and a supply of my favorite junk food, I was going into a game-a-thon with a few of my old guild buddies, each one as hyped—or even more so—to play Aerda Online as I was.

The last thing I remembered was the countdown timer reaching 00:00:00.

Shapes swam into view, and I narrowed my eyes to make them out.

A limber face peeked over a ledge to look down at me.

What the... am I in some kind of pit? I tried to move, but my body was unresponsive.

Fuck... Is this the game?

I blinked a few times, forcing the face to stay within its lines and grow clearer. He had a fine face, firm jaw and aquiline nose with piercing blue eyes under an unruly mop of long black hair that made his face seem pale. He wore rings of a reddish material in his ears—copper, brass, or maybe bronze.

The world around me took shape. A tingle in my muscles told me I was gaining control—that I could soon move. The image cleared up, and I recognized the face.

It is me.

I was looking at myself in the reflecting surface of a babbling creek.

The smell of a forest, crisp and earthy, made its way into my nostrils. In the background, a bird chirped a merry song.

My muscles were slow to wake, but I began feeling my weight pressing down on my hands. I pushed up, a groan escaping my lips, and sat. Rubbed my head, I blinked down at my body. I wore strange clothes—a gray wool hose and a dirty dun tunic with a leather belt—but the body was mine, the dirty hands moved at my command and resembled my own, except they were more callused and had more grime under the fingernails.

This is *the game...*

***

I studied the surrounding forest. It was springtime—the air carried a gentle, humid warmth, and the leaves hung green and fresh from the trees. The creek in front of me babbled along its rocky bed. If I had not been just transported into a game, I would have thought it peaceful.

Two icons manifested in my view—one a stylized knight's helmet, the other a yellow question mark.

Shit.

Even as I looked around, the icons followed my view, staying fixed at the top. The icon with the question mark began flashing, and a text appeared.

Mortal, open your quest journal by focusing on the relevant icon and willing it to open.

This is unreal. I fixed my gaze on the flashing question mark and a text box popped up. It was transparent, and I could by sheer force of will make it more or less so.

Your Awakening
Challenge level: 1 (easy)

You are Awakened, Mortal. Born unto this world with limitless potential. Unfortunately, you cannot return to your old world—not now and perhaps never. Here, in the world of Aerda, you must thrive or die. Put your questions aside and gather power, for only the powerful may learn the truth.

Fear not, Mortal: the Game Masters shall accompany you on these first few steps, which are always the hardest.
Follow the creek to learn more.

Objective: Follow the creek downstream.
Reward: 100 XP

I chuckled—more a shock reaction than anything else. My legs trembled as I clambered up. I tried to focus on the icon of the knight's helmet, but it was grayed out. This had to be some kind of joke. I looked around, trying to find anything that would let me glean the truth.

When I saw two suns in the sky—one half eclipsed by a blue-green moon that dominated the horizon—I knew it was no joke.

I had seen this sky in trailers for Aerda Online; I had been one of the people to speculate on the forums if those two suns and that gigantic, earth-like moon would have any in-game effects or if they were just cosmetic.

My heart raced as I looked around. My body was real, albeit sluggish, as if I had slept deeply and was roused suddenly, and the springy turf of the creek bed under my feet was real too. The wind on my face, the crisp air, the chatter of birds, the scuttle in the undergrowth; it was all lifelike.

I had dreamed of this... My life in the real world was not too bad. I worked as a corporate lawyer with a large firm. They had tucked me away in an ivory tower where I slaved for long hours with other associates, but the money was good: I made my way through life without missing a payment on my student loan, which was more than most of my generation could say. The mentality at the firm was to work hard, play hard: on Fridays I got drunk (and sometimes laid), rinse and repeat on Saturdays. Sundays were for recuperating and playing games.

Yet despite the comfort and luxury, it was dreary and monotonous. I came alive when playing games, and I sometimes lay awake wanting to be the Mages I played in RPGs.

But this...

I swallowed, took another deep breath. It did indeed feel like an awakening. I looked at the creek. Ahead, it meandered out of vision between stout trees and several large boulders.

Maybe it is a joke, maybe it isn't real... Maybe it is just a game. I took a deep breath, raised my chin. I was going to play along... for now.

***

My walk along the creek was actually pleasant. The forest took me back to my youth, before I traded the sheltered village life in Oregon for the Seattle hustle and bustle. I realized it had been more than a year since I had been in a forest.

I closed my eyes for a moment, focusing on my other senses. The suns warmed my skin, and I reveled in the vibrant scents of the forest.

This is not too bad.

When I opened my eyes again, I was looking straight at some sort of creature.

It stood half hidden behind a tree, spying on me. Its eyes were large, completely black, and set deep in a brown-green face with round features similar to those of a deer: a broad, flat nose, long ears, and a pair of branching antlers. The creature had hoofs, and its legs, hips, and groin were covered in coarse fur that reached up to its belly button. It was no taller than a child, but it gave me a wicked grin, revealing yellow pointy teeth.

My stomach churned when I felt its hostile intentions. Black text appeared in front of me.

You have encountered a foe, Mortal. Focus on it now to learn its stats.

I felt a need to turn and run. I had encountered fantastic enemies in games before, but never... well, *for real*. Still, I was not going to be swayed. I stood my ground, heart pounding, and looked at it.

Faun
Level 1
Stamina: 8, Health: 4, Mana: 6, Sanity: 3

The creature chattered something that sounded like a warning. It stepped out from behind its tree and brandished a mean-looking spear roughly the length of my arm. It had a jagged iron tip.

Another block of text appeared.

Foes may physically attack you, and you may respond by parrying, dodging, or blocking their attack. Each of these actions is governed by a skill and resolved with a Check. Checks consist of adding your score in the relevant skill and your relevant attribute to a randomly

generated number between 1 and 100. If your opponent beats or equals your result, he wins. Otherwise, you successfully parry, dodge, or block his attack. Since you have no weapon to parry or armor to block with, we recommend dodging the incoming attack…

Incoming attack?

With a feral shriek, the creature ran at me, leveling the spear and aiming it straight at my groin.

Fuuuuck!

Dodge Check result: (28 + 6 Agility + 5 Dodge =) 39 versus opponent's 48.
You receive 4 Physical damage (piercing)!

A green status bar appeared at the top of my vision, going down from 8 to 4, but there was no pain. I frowned at that. Despite my low result, I had apparently ducked out of the way and did not receive an actual wound, even though my 'dodge' was not exactly graceful. A text popped up as the Faun watched me, panting, hesitating.

Damage is subtracted from your Stamina first. So long as you have Stamina, most regular attacks will not draw blood. Only when your Stamina is depleted, will you receive damage to your health and suffer wounds. However, dodging has cost you an Action. If the Faun had not hesitated, he could have followed up with another attack. Now is your chance to take the initiative!

I had some difficulty with that… I stood there, watching the feral little thing, unable to act and unsure what even I could do. The Faun responded by shrieking and stabbing at me again. This time, I was a little more ready and braced myself.

Dodge Check result: (81 + 6 Agility + 5 Dodge =) 91 versus opponent's 31.

I deftly dodged out of the way. It was a lot more graceful and not as exerting as my previous attempt. The Faun charged past and came to a stop a few steps away. It studied me some more, doubt in its large black eyes. Its grin had faded.

This time, I was quick, I jumped forward, steering clear of the spear, and gave the Faun a kick like I would a soccer ball.

Unarmed Check result (untrained): (23 + 6 Agility =) 29 versus opponent's 48.

The Faun raised its spear and brought the haft between me and itself, and my foot painfully struck the rough wood. Still, I saw its Stamina bar go down by 1 to 7.

Unlike dodging, Parrying does not cost an Action. However, parrying costs 1 Stamina per Encumbrance of the item used to parry the attack. If you have no Stamina remaining, you may also parry using Health, straining your muscles and wounding yourself through overextension.

With a grunt, the Faun tried to spear me again, but I slipped out of the way, getting an 88 against his 41. This body was a lot more dexterous and limber than my real one; I had not been so quick and graceful since High School, when I had played on the soccer team. I smirked, enjoying my newfound youthful agility.

Again, the Faun hesitated, and another text block appeared.

You are unarmed and thus at a disadvantage. However, since you chose Phylomancer as your class, you have magic available. Your only offensive spell is Flame Sprout. Try gathering the power of fire in your fingertips and projecting a gust at the creature.

Fuck… now we're talking.

An incantation that felt as natural to me as breathing came from my throat as I extended my right hand and tensed the muscles, willing flame into it. Somehow, I knew it would work. A moment later, a jet of what looked like liquid flame spurted from my hand at the Faun. It shrieked and tried to get out of the way.

Elemental Check result: (15 + 7 Cunning + 5 Elemental =) 27 versus opponent's 16.

You deal 12 Physical damage (fire)!

The Faun shrieked in pain as its Stamina and Health burned away at once, its fur catching fire. I was served the horrible sight of its skin boiling and peeling away, blisters popping, as it collapsed into a smoking ruined corpse.

Holy mother of fuck...

You receive 100 XP.

***

The spell had cost me 3 Mana, and I had 9 left. Even as I watched the Faun burn away, I felt my breath return to me; my Stamina bar refilled. A moment later, my Mana bar followed suit.

> **Stamina and Mana regenerate out of combat. You may also spend an Action in combat to regenerate 1-6 Stamina or Mana. Health and Sanity do not regenerate on their own and require medical or magical attention to restore.**

Okay, thanks game.

After the corpse stopped burning, leaving a patch of scorched grass and a pile of charred bones, I proceeded downstream of the creek in a daze, mind reeling at what I had just done.

How often have I dreamed of this? Arcane power at my fingertips, elements mine to control... I found no joy in watching a creature burn to death, but the immense power of being able to cause that type of suffering was intoxicating. I was still dwelling on it when the creek led me to a small clearing. There was a handcart here, as well as a pitched tent and the remains of a campfire. A corpse lay in the grass on its stomach. There were several crude wounds in its back; deep cuts that could have been made by a spear.

I hesitated for a moment, then stepped closer, curious if this was what I had been looking for. A new objective appeared.

Search the corpse.

I looked around. A game path led up to the clearing and trailed off into the forest. At the edge of the clearing, the canopy grew so dense that hardly any light filtered down. Keeping a wary eye on the trees, I approached the corpse. I gave it a nudge with my foot, then turned it over.

It was an Elf, slender and tall and dressed in a—now blood-soaked—green tunic with brown wool hose underneath. From his belt hung a dagger, and he was clutching a book in one hand and a small pouch in the other.

Instinctively, I reached for the pouch. Text appeared.

You have acquired a Vault. Vaults are soul-bound items, which means you cannot lose them on death. Each Vault has several inventory slots that you can use to store items in. This Vault has 8 such slots. You may access and store items in your Vault as an Action. It is recommended to wear items you may need more quickly, such as weapons and potions, on your body, so you will not need to waste an Action in combat to acquire them. Now, reach mentally into your Vault.

I focused on the item, and a box popped up with two rows with four slots each. The Vault was nearly empty, except for three slots. One slot displayed an icon of biscuits and nuts with the number 4 in the top-right corner; the next one held a symbol of a waterskin with a 2 in the top-right corner. The final slot showed an earthenware flask with a stopper. I focused on each item in its turn. The biscuits and nuts were trail rations—nothing special—and the waterskin was what it said on the cover. For both, the numbers indicated how many days' supply of the item was left.

The flask, however, was a healing potion. Drinking it took an Action and would restore 1-12 Stamina.

Probably good to have one of those, even if it does only restore Stamina... That spear took down my Stamina quick enough.

Next, I took the dagger from the corpse and studied it.

Dagger (Shoddy)
Level 0
Skill: Daggers
Damage: 1-2 + Strength Physical damage (piercing)
Encumbrance: 0.5
Description: A dagger is a common sidearm of many warriors and a frequently used tool.
Special qualities: Due to its size, parrying an attack with a dagger incurs a -5 penalty.

Well, that's nothing special.

Still, I took the small scabbard that the Elf had carried the weapon in and fastened it to my belt, right next to the Vault. The Healing Potion had a cord that allowed me to tie it to my belt. The rations and waterskin I kept in my Vault.

I looked the corpse over and pried the journal from its cold hands.

It took a while to read, but it was a clear account of how the Elf, a traveling tradesman, had come to this forest from a city named Alonsby to purchase pelts from hunters. He mentioned his apprentice—a young, orphaned Human from a village near Alonsby. Apparently, they had stopped here for the night, unable to find the hunters...

I closed the journal and gave the Elf a last look. There was something familiar about him, as if he came from a memory that was not... well, mine.

Quest completed: Your Awakening!

Description: You have found your old master's corpse. You were once an apprentice tradesman. No more, however, for you have Awakened to limitless potential. Put the past to rest and come unto your birthright!

Reward: 100 XP

I had actually been someone else... This body was home to another before I came, and I pushed them out when I... Awakened.

I looked down at my hands again, noting the calluses, and I knew how it had happened—I saw it unfold in my mind as if it were a cutscene: the apprentice had seen his master fall before the spears of several Fauns. Not a warrior, he had fled. A single Faun gave chase while the others pilfered the trader's camp. Despairing, the Human had cowered behind a bush on the creek bank, hoping the Faun would not see him.

And he had Awakened.

Poor guy… Or is it poor me? It has to be a—

"Did you kill that Elf?"

I veered up, turned around, and was blinded by beauty.

***

The woman that stood before me was tall and willowy. Her smooth limbs betrayed a grace that was inhuman, and her long, pointed ears confirmed that suspicion.

I sat next to the corpse, open-mouthed, as my gaze trailed up her long legs, to her flat and smooth midriff. She wore a black skirt that clung to her luscious curves and a chest armor of black-dyed leather that was more a bra than anything else, revealing her inviting cleavage. Her face was perfect: a cute snub nose with full red lips underneath; large, almond-shaped eyes of a deep green color; and all of it framed by long, blond hair that she had braided back. The sight of her caused a stirring underneath my wool hose.

Well, it seems all of that *is functioning in this game world too…*

She held a sword in her right hand—it looked worn and scuffed—and she had a wooden shield with an iron rim slung over her back.

I cleared my throat, then focused on her.

Anuina Willowsdaughter (Elf)
Level 1 Ranger
Stamina: 8, Health: 4, Mana: 12, Sanity: 6

She gave me a bold look, appraising me the same way I had appraised her. "Well?" she demanded, her voice firm and clear. "Did you kill that Elf?"

"Uhh, no," I said. My voice in Aerda Online was much like my own, only a little deeper. "He was... he was my master."

She frowned. "Master? Are you a thrall?"

"A what? Oh no, I'm just... an apprentice?" That did not sound very convincing.

Deception Check result (untrained): (32 + 7 Cunning =) 39 versus opponent's 104.

Anuina shook her head and raised her sword. With a supple shrug, she rolled her shield off her back. A green willow tree stylized in Celtic knots was painted on it. "You're no apprentice," she said. "You burned a Faun with magic. Speak the truth!"

I raised my hands. "Woah, woah, calm down," I said. "I was an apprentice. Something happened... and now I'm... *something* else." I gestured at the dead Elf. "But he was my master. We were here to buy pelts. Fauns killed him."

She relaxed her stance somewhat, deep green eyes still mistrustful. "What is your name?"

"Oram Ludwickson," I replied and frowned. That was a far cry from my name, but it had rolled off my tongue intuitively.

That's the name I chose at character creation... the name I use for most of my game characters.

I remembered the character creation screen with its many options; I had chosen the Phylomancer class, a type of mage that channeled magical knowledge from creatures willingly bound to him... People speculated that it was the most powerful class, provided you could collect enough bonds. It was also a special for early Kickstarter supporters, unavailable to anyone who had not bought one of the highest support tiers. There were about 1,000 such accounts, and some had been sold on clandestine markets for as much as 2,000 dollars. I had stuck to mine, curious to see this fabled class.

Right now, Barbarian may have been better.

Anuina frowned at me. "You are Awakened?" It sounded like a question, but it really was not.

I nodded, unsure what the ramifications were. "Yes," I said and, deciding to own it, I rose to my feet.

I may not be a Barbarian, but I have enough arcane power to defend myself. Once again, my eyes roved over her enticing body. *It would be a damn shame if I had to, though...*

The effect of my confirmation was neither good nor bad. She just narrowed her eyes. "Do you serve Athagort?"

"Who? No. I serve no man."

Her sword arm dipped a little lower. "Athagort is not a man."

"Well, I'm not in the habit of serving anything else either," I said.

"If you are no servant of Athagort's, what are you, then?"

"Confused," I said. "I think that's my one defining feature at this moment."

A faint smile curled her full lips, and the simple beauty of it made my skin prickle. We looked at each other in silence for a while, until I cleared my throat. "What is this Awakened thing?" I asked.

"It is when the Gods decide to imbue a Mortal with greater power and the potential to ascend to godhood."

Godhood? Fuck, yes. "Hm," I said. "And when do I get to ascend?"

She chuckled. "When you have accumulated enough power." She looked me up and down. "If I judge things correctly, you may not altogether be there just yet."

I looked down at my dirty clothes. "Appearances deceive," I said with a grin.

Anuina pressed her lips into a line and shook her head. "True, but rarely so."

"Are you Awakened too?" I asked her.

She nodded, and something melancholy appeared in her expression.

"So you're from Earth?"

"I am of the earth," she said with a confused frown. "Aren't all Mortals?"

"That's... not what I meant."

She's either a roleplayer or an NPC... I thought for a moment. *'NPC'... should I still call them that? She seems about as real as any person. Even more so, in fact, everything about her is... vibrant.*

She sheathed her sword and gave me a last glance. "Well, Oram Ludwickson, be sure to give your former master a burial in accordance with the rites of the Misted One." She nodded in the corpse's direction. "It is only proper." She turned, and although my body tensed at the sight of her full backside, I felt a need to keep her here.

"Hold up," I said. "I don't know those rites."

She frowned at me over her slender shoulder, but her gaze immediately softened.

"Very well," she said. "We'll do it together, then."

***

An hour after we entrusted the Elf to whom I had once apprenticed to the flames, Anuina and I sat by the remains of the campfire. I had difficulty keeping my eyes off her as she sat there, knees drawn up and wrapped in her slender arms as she stared wistfully at the fire.

We had said little, but I didn't feel the weight of the silence as I used to. She was not much of a talker, I could tell, and I knew with a wisdom that I had not had in real life that respecting that was valuable. I leaned back on my elbows, long legs drawn out, and ate some of my rations.

I had seen plenty of pixel Elves before, but the real thing was something else. This melancholy beauty that was normally conveyed in text descriptions or roleplayed— often overly edgy, angsty, or just altogether poorly—was a palpable thing. It gave her an unreal quality, something other than human, and it pulled me in like a magnet. The connection between us was almost painful, and a deep need to draw her back to this world and out of her daydreams mastered my thoughts. I wanted to see her smile, laugh, to make her eyes sparkle.

To make her chest heave with passion, her lips burn, her skin tingle, her—

"It is time for me to be on my way," Anuina said, shattering my fantasies. She looked at the suns above. "I have work to do while there is still light."

"What kind of work?" I asked.

She studied me for a moment, returning to the here and now. Her green eyes were inquisitive. "I came to these woods to slay Athagort."

"Athagort? Who is he?" I asked.

"Athagort is a Two-Headed Ogre… unusually intelligent for his kind. I have tracked him and his Fauns to

Vaskhule, a series of caves in these woods. It was difficult to find them, but I am sure they are holing up there."

I sat up. "So you're on a quest?"

Her emerald eyes turned cold. "Revenge," she said. "Two days ago, Athagort's minions killed my sister. She was... traveling from Alonsby to Wealdhaven."

Traveling, hm? There was more to it; but this was hardly the time to go on a fishing expedition. I raised an eyebrow and moved away from the topic of her sister. "You're going at it alone?" I had seen Anuina's stats. They weren't particularly impressive.

"Yes," she said. "I am. I must."

For the briefest moment, I held her eyes. The coldness in them gave way to her unearthly and delicate beauty. She blinked and looked down, and I was enraptured by her lashes, the fine features of her face, even the slight pull of a muscle in her cheek.

"I will help you," I said. The words came out before I knew it; they came from the heart.

She looked up, and a shimmer of hope kindled in her eyes. "You would do that for me, a stranger who offers nothing in return?"

"I would," I said.

Anuina smiled—the first true warm smile I had seen her give, and it almost made me melt. "Very well, Oram Ludwickson," she said. "We will do it together, and I will be in your debt."

Athagort Bone-Mangler
Challenge level: 3 (difficult)

Anuina Willowsdaughter has told you of a Two-Headed Ogre by the name of Athagort

who makes his lair at Vaskhule, attended by Faun servants. Accompany her to the caves and slay Athagort to relieve the lands around Alonsby of this scourge.

Objective: Kill Athagort Bone-Mangler.
Bonus objectives: Slay at least ten Fauns; do not let Anuina die or suffer grievous wounds.
Reward: 500 XP and 200 XP per bonus objective completed.

This is it, then. A real quest.
A text box appeared.

Mortal, your tutorial is herewith completed. You may now access your character sheet and set out on your first quest. May the Gods of the Tribunal guide you, for the Game Masters will not...

Great...

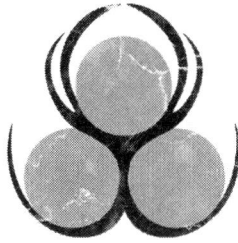

CHAPTER 2

Strange enough, Anuina understood what I meant when I told her I needed a minute to access my character sheet. Apparently, she had one too.

I focused on the icon of the knight's helm, and my sheet appeared.

Oram Ludwickson (Human)
Level 1 Phylomancer

Attributes: Strength 3, Agility 6, Endurance 4, Intellect 7, Cunning 7, Power 6
Resources: Stamina 8, Health 4, Mana 12, Sanity 6
Skills: Dagger 2, Dodge 5, Elemental 5, Illusion 5, Intuition 2, Perception 2, Psionic 5, Staff 2, Ward 5
Abilities: Phylomantic Bond (0/1)
Spells: Ghost Touch (0), Light (0), Fire Sprout (1)
Equipment: Healing Potion, Dagger (Shoddy)

XP/XP needed until next level: 100/1,000

I remembered assigning the scores on character creation. A tooltip had told me 5 was average for a Human on all scores and, being Awakened, I received three additional points to spend. Since I was going to play a mage class, I stuck my bonus points in Endurance, Intellect, Cunning, and Power, and I even cannibalized some Strength points to make sure I had decent Agility—dodging is always a good idea. Reviewing them now—with the knowledge this was not just some heap of pixels on a screen but *actually me*—I was not so sure about my decision to be a glass cannon.

No point dwelling on that, though...

Curious, I focused on the spells to see their descriptions.

Ghost Touch was a level 0 telekinesis spell that cost 1 Mana to cast. It allowed me to manipulate a small object within a short range, so long as the object wasn't worn or carried by someone else. What piqued my interest was that I could use that object to attack others. I pictured myself fencing with my foes from a safe distance using a telekinetically controlled arsenal—it matched up nicely with my meager melee stats.

The next spell, Light, was pretty much what I expected it to be. You cast it on an object and—*boom*—light for an hour at the cost of 1 Mana.

Finally, Fire Sprout was my damage dealing spell. I expected I'd be using it a lot, so I studied it with great care.

Fire Sprout
Spell level: 1
Mana: 3

> Skill: Elemental
> Element: Fire
> Description: A gout of flame bursts from your outstretched hand, dealing 1-6 + Intellect Physical damage (fire). Flammable objects that are not worn or carried will burst into flame when hit by Flame Sprout.

It also turned out that every spell could be upgraded at the cost of Mana to increase the range, duration, damage, or some other metric. However, you could only upgrade a spell to a level you were proficient with. That meant I could upgrade a level 0 spell to a level 1 spell—since I was allowed to cast level 1 spells—but I could not (yet) upgrade a level 1 spell to a level 2 spell since I hadn't mastered level 2 spells yet.

Okay... a pretty basic repertoire of spells. So how do I learn new ones?

I checked out my abilities.

> Phylomantic Bond (Phylomancer): A Phylomancer gains arcane knowledge and abilities through engaging others in a deep bond of phylomancy. Subjects must be willing and engage in the Phylomantic Bond freely and without deceit. Subjects must also be compatible; a strong, mutual attraction will signal such compatibility.
> The arcana a Phylomancer unearths from a bond depends on the creature they have bonded with and the intensity of the relationship. Both the Phylomancer and the bonded one may at any time end the

Phylomantic Bond; arcana and abilities granted through the Phylomantic Bond will disappear 48 hours after a Phylomantic Bond is ended. Currently, 0 out of 1 Phylomantic Bond slots are occupied.

This is going to be tricky. I glanced over at Anuina as she sat by the charred remains of the fire, waiting.

The attraction I felt to her might be a sign of compatibility, but it also might be simply because she was beautiful.

I haven't told her I'm a Phylomancer... and I doubt she'll be in the mood to 'bond', whatever that might mean. In fact, I'm pretty sure asking her would unlock the 'Slapped by a She-Elf' Achievement... I think I'll pass for now.

I mentally willed the text box away and looked at Anuina. "All right," I said. "I'm ready."

She gave a firm nod and nimbly darted to her feet. "Good. Let us make haste. We need to reach the Vaskhule Caves before sunset."

***

The hunter's trail snaked among the trees. Doubtless, I would have been lost without it. I had been a Boy Scout in a distant past, and I was supposed to have some skill at navigating the great outdoors. However, I was about as lost as I had been when I first set myself loose in the streets of Seattle.

I wondered if Anuina fared any better; Elves were by most tropes kind of woodsy. She took the front, following the path wearily, and I did not mind looking at the gracious motions of her cat-like step as she stalked ahead, hand gripping her scuffed sword.

I was still focusing on her perfect backside when a sharp whistle pierced the silence of the woods, followed by a heavy thud. Anuina fell and sprawled on the path and lay there motionless. Before I could open my mouth, two Fauns charged out of the undergrowth, shrieking their hate at me.

Fuck.

They were like the one I had faced before: quick, small, and deer-like. They wore nothing but a loincloth and a spear. A quick glance revealed they had the same stats. However, half-hidden behind a shrub by the roadside was a meaner-looking Faun in fur armor with a short bow.

Faun Archer
Level 2
Stamina: 16, Health: 4, Mana: 10, Sanity: 5

For now, my eyes were on the charging duo. They were almost upon me, and so I raised my right hand, focused fire on it, and sang my incantation, causing a gust of flame to leap forward. I misfired, rolling a 31 against the Faun's 37. The liquid fire shot past my mark and started a small fire in the undergrowth.

Smokey's gonna hate me for that one.

The next moment, a Faun jabbed its spear at me. I braced myself and tried to jump out of the way. I knew it was stupid; dodging cost me my Action, but it was better than taking a spear to the groin. I rolled a 55 against the Faun's 23, nimbly sidestepping the attack.

A black text popped up.

You may use any weapon you have to parry attacks. Parrying an attack costs 1 Stamina per Encumbrance of the weapon you are parrying with, but it does not cost an Action. If your opponent cannot equal or beat your result, their attack will miss.

Another timely tip…

As I stumbled back, I quickly drew my dagger. It was a piece of shit for offense and even worse for defense, but it sure as hell beat dodging until the Fauns would inevitably overwhelm me. Since I had no Action left, the Fauns attacked me again, and my dagger was up just in time to parry the first attack.

The second attack, unfortunately, came through. I half-stumbled out of the way, taking 4 physical damage. That left me with only 2 Stamina since my parrying attempts had cost me 1 Stamina each.

This was going great.

The only lucky break was that the archer held his fire as he tried to peek past his allies to get a clean shot. Thank whatever gods ruled this world that strategy was not the Fauns' strong suit.

Dagger in hand, I spent another 3 Mana on Fire Sprout. The Faun faces in front of me lit up in fear as flames burst forth from my outstretched hand. This time, I got an 88 against the Faun's 42, and the flames caught.

You deal 13 Physical damage (fire)!

Fuck yeah, max damage! I couldn't suppress a morbid sense of satisfaction as I watched a Faun catch fire. It gave a shrill shriek as it fell, kicked a few times, and lay still. I looked up from the burning mess at the remaining Faun and grinned. "You're next."

Furious, it attacked. I raised the dagger, experiencing a sudden dip in confidence in my ability to parry a spear thrust with a flimsy dagger that I wouldn't use to spread butter on a sandwich.

Dagger Check result: (75 + 6 Agility + 2 Dagger - 5 Equipment =) 78 versus opponent's 99.

Shit.

The spear buried itself in my thigh, and I suffered my first Health damage.

I'd been mangled before—I once broke my pinkie finger in a drunk bar fight—but nothing I'd ever felt prepared me for the pain and suffering of a wound inflicted by a jagged spear thrust at me with the intent to kill. It was another 3 damage, which combined with my Stamina loss from parrying to bring my Health down to 2.

My leg gave out from under me, and I sank to my knee, shrieking with pain. The Faun gave a satisfied grunt as it pulled out its spear, large black eyes burning with the lust to kill as it licked its pale lips.

"Fuck you!" I shouted at the Faun, just before I heard a heavy thunk and an overwhelming, glaring pain radiated through my face. I had a moment to look up to see the feathered shaft of an arrow sticking out of my forehead.

Looks like the Faun Archer got his shot...

Everything went black.

You have died…

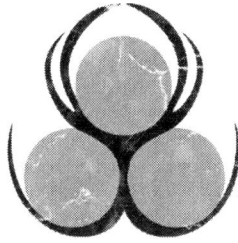

CHAPTER 3

Death does not need to be the end for an Awakened. Whenever an Awakened falls, they lose all their experience and are reborn at their last set Home. They also lose 1 of each attribute, recovering such losses at a rate of 1 per level gained.

However, once any attribute drops to 0, even an Awakened shall pass for good. Please note that all equipment that is not Soul-Bound is dropped on death. For decency's sake, you will always receive a set of clothing upon rebirth.

Since you have not yet been able to find a Home, you will be reborn at your starting location.

Even though my mind was still thick as syrup, I sensed a minor jab in that last one. For a moment, I lamented my deteriorated attributes and wondered if death would be the way back to Seattle… Somehow, I suspected it was not.

Slowly, the world around me materialized, and I heard again the calm babble of the creek—as if nothing had happened at all. As before, it took me some time before I gained control of my muscles, and my mind was still slow.

Anuina…

I pushed up from the wet turf as fast as my muscles let me and began running. It had been light when I died, but it was darker now. One sun had set, and the other was close behind.

My heart pounded away as I jogged, stumbled, and fast-walked, still fighting through the murky experience of death. I passed the dead Elf, already catching a whiff of rot as I passed him, then continued down the game trail.

Eventually, I found two patches of scorched earth—one with a burned-up Faun at its center—and bloodstains on the soil. I looked around, frantic, but I saw nothing else.

She's gone.

And so was I… my corpse was no longer here. I forced myself to take deep breaths—in for four seconds and out for eight. Rinse and repeat, and I slowly got control of myself.

Some of the weakness I had felt on respawning was permanent; my body had weakened, mind slowed: the effect of the drop in attributes. Strength was my dump stat to begin with, and this ordeal had lowered it to 2. I could only die once more. The death after that would be the last, and I still doubted that death would mean waking up in my desk chair.

In fact, I wasn't even sure if that desk chair would still be waiting for me at all, and if so, that I would ever find it again.

I did another breathing exercise, then looked around. Okay, calm down. Try to look and see what has happened. Stooping low, I tried to find any traces or trails. Soon enough, I found a small puddle of blood—most of it already soaked up by the earth—where Anuina had lain. Ruts in the earth showed that her body had been dragged away, but I wasn't enough of a woodsman to follow the trail once it went into the undergrowth.

She might still be alive... But I had no idea what Fauns did with or to their captives... Although I expected it probably wasn't good.

There were no such trails around my corpse, which made me believe my body had just disappeared.

You have unlocked the Tracking skill! Congratulations, you may now invest in it upon gaining a level.

That would be too late.

Panic gripped me; I almost ran into the forest to follow the general direction of the trail. But it would be useless; I'd get lost, ambushed, and I'd die... again. If I really wanted to help Anuina, I needed help myself—I couldn't handle three Fauns alone, let alone a whole series of caves full of them.

I clenched my fists and looked down at the game trail as it meandered through the trees. Thankful for my Light spell, I made my way down the path.

***

By the time complete darkness set in, I was still following the forest trail by the light of my spell. From time to time, I caught a glimpse of two moons—one pale like my world's Moon; the other red like Mars. The earth-like moon I had seen during the day had set.

Behind the two moons stretched a purple-blue nebulous galaxy, and I stared at this alien vista, transfixed by its beauty, whenever I gleaned it through the canopy. But every time, some strange chirping or the creaking of trees swaying in the wind brought me back to the dark forest, and I continued on my way.

Still, Aerda was a beautiful, mystical place, and I felt a deep connection to it—one I never had with the world back home.

Soon, however, more earthly matters presented themselves: my stomach was grumbling, and my throat was dry from the long hike. Of course, I had nothing on me except the clothes on my back. I was beginning to despair when raw laughter drifted to me, coming from a little off the side of the trail. The voices sounded a lot like Fauns. Fear broiled in my stomach when I remembered my death at the nasty little creatures' grimy paws.

I dismissed my Light spell and waited in the total darkness, listening.

Perception Check result: (75 + 6 Cunning + 2 Perception =) 83.

That did it; sure enough, the laughter rang out again, and this time I pinpointed it by ear. I stalked over in its direction.

Sneak Check result (untrained): (6 + 5 Agility - 10 Darkness penalty =) 1 versus opponents' 22 and 38.

I was clumsier than I would have been in real life, and I stumbled on a root I had not seen in the dark. Air escaped my lungs with an "oomph". There was a sharp hiss, then silence.

Great, I roll a mage and the first thing I do is stalk through a forest like some half-assed Ranger... I sighed and slipped behind a tree, hoping I could hide myself and escape their notice—at least until I had spotted *them*.

Sneak Check result (untrained): (64 + 5 Agility - 10 Darkness penalty =) 59 versus opponents' 47 and 98.

You have unlocked the Sneak skill! Congratulations, you may now invest in it upon gaining a level.

It felt a bit meta, but from the Check results I knew one had seen me while the other had not. I spotted movement through the low-hanging branches: two black silhouettes. The one in the front was looking away from me—I could tell because its long, crooked nose pointed in the opposite direction. The other one started just as it spotted me.

I turned around the trunk, extended my hand, and focused fiery death on the Faun that had not seen me. The dark forest lit up with my magical flames, and it caught the Faun unaware.

You deal 10 Physical damage (fire)!

The Faun shrieked in pain, jumping back as the flames made his skin crackle and singed his fur. The other Faun cried out a fell curse and came at me. He tried to charge, but the tree was in the way, which caused him to end up next to me but unable to bring his spear to bear.

Now or never!

I did the same trick, focused pure flame into my hand, and I set the Faun alight. He yelped and tried to dodge, spending his Action, but I still got a 52 against his 37, making him fumble his dodge and costing him all his Stamina. The little hot-coal dance he did would have been amusing had I been in my desk chair behind my monitor with a bag of Cheetos and a bottle of Mountain Dew.

Here it was not.

Shrieking fury, the heavily wounded Faun I singed earlier came after me. As with his fellow, the tree stopped his charge short, and he wasted his entire Action just getting to me.

That one is wounded... he's hobbling and weak. In a split-second decision, I focused my fire on the one closest to me and got a 57 against his 54—close call. He burst into flame for 7 damage, dropping his spear and hitting the forest floor with a cry, leaving a burning corpse.

The other one howled in fury and attacked me with his spear. If I dodged, it would force me on the defensive, and so I did nothing and risked his hit.

You receive 6 Physical damage (piercing)!

Fuck... My Stamina was down to 0, and my Mana to 1... *If I cast another Fire Sprout, it'll cost me Sanity.* Panic clawed at me for a moment, almost making me waste my action.

Wait… I spotted the spear. *Fucking Ghost Touch!*

I focused my psionic powers on the spear the dead Faun had dropped, and it floated up under my telekinetic control. With a lunge, I directed it to stab the Faun. He shrieked with surprise and tried to jump out of the way.

Psionic Check result: (26 + 6 Cunning + 5 Psionic =) 37 versus opponent's 11.

Fuck yes! The spear took the Faun in the flank and dealt 7 damage. For a Faun with 0 Stamina and 4 Health, that was enough. The spear buried itself in the creature's flank, and I twisted it for good measure as I directed my telekinetic powers to pull it out. The Faun grabbed his flank as blood spilled out. He whimpered and collapsed, hoofed leg jerking one last time.

"Fuck yes!" I screamed. "Take that, you fucking pieces of fucking shit!"

You receive 400 XP.

***

I stood over the charred and mangled corpses of my foes, heart racing, chest heaving.

I did it.

It felt like payback. Of course, these were not the Fauns that had killed me—they looked different—but I was pretty damn sure they belonged to Athagort's crew and, as such, were vicariously responsible.

I kicked the Faun I had offed with a telekinetic stab to make sure it was really dead. Like the others, these Fauns wore loincloths and short spears and nothing else. However, I was sure they had been sitting somewhere nearby when I heard them laughing, and I resolved to find their hangout while trying not to lose track of the trail—maybe I'd find something of value.

After my Stamina and Mana recovered, I picked up a spear, cast my Light spell, and headed in the direction from which the Fauns had come.

My efforts were rewarded at once. There was a small hunter's shelter of branches and leaves hidden among the trees, with the remains of a campfire and some supplies strewn about. There was also a burlap sack that seemed much too big for a Faun to carry.

> **Congratulations! You have found a Container. Containers always contain class-appropriate loot that is more valuable than regular loot.**

Now we're talking. I ignored the other stuff and greedily tugged the Container open by its drawstring.

A staff.

Heart racing, I focused on the weapon.

> **Pyromancer's Staff (Common)**
> **Level 1**
> **Skill: Staff**
> **Damage: 1-4 + Strength Physical damage (bludgeoning)**
> **Encumbrance: 1**

Description: A simple iron-capped staff wrought of fire-hardened wood, decorated with flame patterns.

Special qualities: Serves as a Focus; +3 Mana; spells with the Fire Element deal 3 more damage.

Oh, yes… I suppressed a desire to do a victory jig. I had some skill with staves, so this thing meant I could parry with some success. It also meant one extra Fire Sprout with its 3 bonus Mana and increased damage on all my Fire Sprouts.

I rose, tested its weight, and gave a satisfied nod. I double-checked the Container, but this was all.

The other stuff strewn about comprised four trail rations and a jug of water that held three servings. There was also a scruffy pouch with some disgusting contents: a dead mouse, some tiny bones, and teeth that looked disturbingly human, but also seven copper coins and one silver one. They were stamped with a crude face and text that read, "Jarl Warner Warnerson Spear-Eater of Histerborg".

I shrugged, then emptied the pouch—except for the coins—and tied it to my belt. I kept the sack, too, just in case, and stuck it in my Vault with the rations and the jug.

Heartened, I found my way back to the trail. I even whistled a tune to myself as I went on, admiring the moons from time to time.

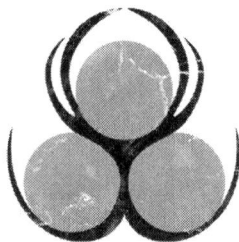

CHAPTER 4

The building stood at the edge of the forest on a hillock that looked artificial. A palisade with platforms with a parapet for archers circled the base of the rise. The building itself was long and low. Smoke billowed up from a hole in the thatch roof, and the welcoming orange glow of fire shone behind its shuttered windows.

At least, I hoped it was welcoming.

I made my slow way to the palisade. Before long, I saw people on the parapet. Moonlight glinted on spear tips and chainmail, but I went on anyway. Once within earshot, a man called out: "Who goes there in the night?"

I leaned on my staff, trying to be a bit like Gandalf: a wise wizard. "I am Oram Ludwickson," I replied. "A weary traveler. I'm looking for a place to rest."

"Are you a mage?"

Shit, the Light spell... I mentally facepalmed. *No point in lying now. Here's hoping they don't hate mages.* "Uh, yeah," I said.

A short silence followed; the man conveyed with another. "Approach the gate," he called out.

I swallowed but took the chance.

Lucky for me, they cared little that I was a mage. The guard that opened the gate—he had a rugged and weathered face with piercing blue eyes in a mail coif—only asked if I had coin, and I showed him the pouch. He let me in and sent me up to the longhouse, barring the gate behind me.

Like a dumbass, I did a full lap of the longhouse before I found the entrance. Laughter and song filtered out through it, and I took a deep breath before I opened the rough plank door.

The sour and dank smell of ale and sweat hit me, a thousandfold worse than the dampest watering hole I had ever frequented in my life. It was a mead hall: straw covered the floor, and several simple but sturdy wooden tables with benches lined the walls. At the far end stood an earthen dais with a throne of wood with elaborate carvings. A wizened, fat man in colorful clothes and furs sat on it, sleeping, with beautiful women in white, slightly translucent dresses on either side of him.

Men and women occupied the benches around the hall, drinking, eating, and singing. Most were warriors—both men and women—muscular folks with crooked bent noses, missing teeth, and scarred hands and faces. They were a rough crowd, jostling and cursing, laughing and roaring. Among them moved buxom maidens with fair skin, carrying platters of meat—sausages, pork roast, and venison—and fresh bread. Both the platters and the women—young and curvy, healthy and in their prime— made my mouth water.

As I closed the door, the warmth of the many fires already settled in my bones.

I looked around, feeling that awkwardness distinctive of coming to some place of revelry alone.

"Welcome, sir!"

I almost started. A short, slightly overweight blonde had come up on my side unseen. She was delicious and gave me a promising look. "May I help you?"

"I, uh, I just came out of the forest," I blabbed, unsure where I was or what the customs were.

She smiled, broad and generous. "Then you must be thirsty."

"I am… is this—where am I?"

She raised a light eyebrow. "You are in the hall of Jarl Vitek Warnerson Spear-Eater."

"Ah," I said, recalling the coin carrying the semblance of his kin. "Of Histerborg."

She smiled. "Yes, that is this hall's revered name. All are welcome if they leave their troubles at the door. The Jarl asks a contribution for food, drink, and lodgings. If you are an adventurer, speak with his steward in the morning; the Jarl is always in search of capable men… and women."

I nodded. Well, this was easy. "I will," I said. "How much is the contribution?"

"A silver coin, sir."

I had no idea if it was good value, but I decided this was not the best time to discover this game's bartering mechanics. I reached into the pouch and handed her a silver coin. She looked me in the eye as she made it disappear in her ample bosom. Something stirred in me—something I had forgotten in a mess of death and scorched Fauns. "Take a seat, sir," she said. "I'll bring you meat, bread, and ale."

"Where should I sit?" I asked, looking around.

She brought a finger up to her plump lips, then pointed at one of the smaller, round tables tucked away in the corner. A cloaked and hooded person sat there alone; two stools stood empty. "There is room over there, sir."

I nodded and headed to the shadowed corner. When I reached the table, the cloaked and hooded person looked up. To my surprise, it was a woman: a tall redhead with a fine face that had something elfin—almond-shaped eyes that reminded me of Anuina. Her piercing blue gaze—cold as ice—took me in top to bottom and back, then rested a little longer on mine than I was comfortable with.

"Uh, do you mind if I sit?" I asked.

She waved a hand. "I don't," she said. "Stand, sit, lie, die: it's all the same to me."

Great... A crazy Viking party and I find the psycho chick. I had a knack for that; most girls I dated ended up going totally berserk.

Still, something about her intrigued me. She pulled me in—reminded me at once of the fascination that overwhelmed me when I had first met Anuina.

I gave her another look and saw chain mail under her cloak. Two long legs stuck out from under it; they were wrapped in skin-tight leather. The rest of her was covered, but those legs... *Damn.*

"I am Oram Ludwickson," I said as I sat down.

"Good for you."

I laughed at that. I didn't know why; normally, I would have considered it a slight, or at the very least a reason to stop pursuing a conversation with this person... but the truth was that it was *not at all good* to be Oram Ludwickson...

Earlier this day, I had been someone else, and even though that life had its disadvantages, it was a lot safer and a lot more luxurious. And to my dismay, that life was feeling more and more distant and *unreal* by the hour.

When I recovered from my bout of laughter, she still had her icy blue eyes on me, betraying some fascination, one ginger eyebrow raised. "You think what I say is funny?"

"Hilarious," I said. "You're the funniest person in this whole mead hall. Which is probably why you were sitting here all by your lonesome."

She furrowed her brow. "Are you offering me insult?"

I smirked. "Only if you're buying."

She was up in a moment, swifter than I had expected, and her fist came flying at me. Still, I tried to jump up and back, but she got an 86 against my 52.

You receive 7 Physical damage (subdual)!

You have just received subdual damage. If you receive subdual damage while you have 0 Stamina, you will be knocked out.

In my clumsy attempt to dodge her punch, I had fallen off the stool, sprawling in the day-old, stinky straw. All around me, men and women burst out laughing. She sat back down, a satisfied grin on her face.

With a flick of my wrist and a quick word of power, I used Ghost Touch to lift her mug of ale from the table and chucked its contents in her face. It was a reflex—not thought through at all—but the roaring laughter continued as she sat there, mouth and eyes wide open, ale dripping down her face and under her cloak.

I laughed. "Now we're even," I said.

She blinked, brought up a slender hand to wipe her face clean.

What emerged from under that hand was a grin. "You are a trickster, Oram Ludwickson." She shouted for a girl to bring new ale, then fixed her icy stare on me as I rose, rubbing my sore backside.

"I like that," she added.

***

Her name was Roswitha Roholfsdottir Iron-Eye, and I was certain that she was indeed the most entertaining person in the whole mead hall. The world around us faded as we talked, drank ale from wooden mugs, and feasted on chewy sausage and salty bread.

At first, she did most of the talking. With some thinly veiled sarcasm, she referred to the Jarl as ruler of the 'great' nation of Histerborg, known for its pork and timber. Roswitha hailed from far to the north where the Snowlands lay. She had traveled here doing odd jobs, seeking to learn more of the world. Members of her family—her clan—traveled often, and only a few of them ever returned to the icy embrace of Watholme, their village built upon the slopes of a mountain whose peak was always buried among foreboding and dark clouds.

In my turn, I told her I had been an apprentice merchant, but that Fauns slew my master and left me masterless. Since I finished my story quickly, she pressed on. It was easy to trust her—and I wanted to—so I told her of my Awakening by the side of the creek.

"I don't remember a life from before that moment, except a life in another world..." I slowed down, thinking it over. "But even though I have only been here for a short time, that previous life is distant. I'm... not sure if I can return—if I want to return." I looked across at her and saw her beautiful icy eyes, large as she listened, and I smiled at her. "It probably sounds a little crazy."

"No," she said, reaching out and placing her hand over mine. She did it instinctively, because when she realized what she had done, she drew it back and gave a bashful smile. "I am Awakened too," she said. "But I *do* remember my life before. Many of my clan are Awakened; the Iron-Eyes are adventurers—some for better and some for worse. But of late, there has been talk of more Awakened like you—who have no knowledge of their lives before Awakening, and who say they lived in another world before this one. They seem to possess the body of another man or woman, pushing them out and taking their places."

"It feels that way," I said. *Interesting. There are more people from Earth here, it seems...*

"You had better not speak too loudly of it," Roswitha continued. Some here think it is a dark magic of the Masked One—an evil trick."

"Thank you," I said. "I'll keep my mouth shut. You don't believe that?"

With a broad grin, she fished into the collar of her ale-soaked cloak and brought up a rope necklace. Wooden amulets hung from it, each depicting a face, and she held one up: a carven, carnivalesque mask. "I serve the Tribunal," she said. "And that includes the Masked One. I am a Priestess of the Gods, and I do not fear the Masked One or his tricks."

"A Priestess?" I asked. "So, you heal?"

She laughed. She had thin red lips that contrasted with her perfect white teeth, and when she laughed her eyes squinted and little crow's feet formed that elicited a smile—

if not outright laughter—from me every time. "I suppose I can also heal, yes, although I prefer to fight."

I leaned in a little closer, and it made her blink with surprise. But she didn't shy away. Even though her presence was intoxicating, I could not forget about Anuina. In fact, the elfin qualities of Roswitha's face *reminded* me of the Elven Ranger and of how strongly I had felt about her. It was strange; I had been interested in multiple women before—what guy hasn't been?—but there was something more profound about my wish to connect with these women.

Does it have something to do with being a Phylomancer? A need to bind others to me...

"Are you all right?" Roswitha asked, a look of slight concern on her slender face.

I smiled at her. "I am," I said. "Well, not really. My experience in the forest was... bad. I, uh... I died."

"You died?" The confused frown on her face told me that the mileage on the death experience may vary.

"Yeah," I said. "I, uh, respawned at the creek where I Awakened."

She was silent for a moment, then shook her head. "So it is true..."

I looked around, suddenly very aware that we were in a public place. "What is true?"

"These new Awakened," she said, "the other ones like you; they can die and return." She looked at me with big eyes. "You are immortal..."

"Well, not *really*," I said. "Every time I die, I grow weaker, until I become too weak to return to life."

She laughed. "Well, that's still a lot better than what most of us face."

I grinned. "I suppose that's true."

We sat in silence for a while. Roswitha looked at me with great interest, and there was a familiar flutter in my stomach—it was a feeling I knew from bars and clubs; a sense of success at doing well with a girl. But now, it was amplified by a thousandfold, and warmth filled my veins, pushing away the images of death and blood that had haunted me on my journey through the forest.

"What will you do next?" she finally asked, her voice hoarse with the tension.

"I need to go back into the forest," I said. "I lost someone there. I believe the Fauns took her."

"The Fauns?"

"Yes, they're the minions of an Ogre named Athagort."

"Athagort Bone-Mangler?" she asked.

"I think so. Anuina—my friend was hunting him. I offered to help her, but the Fauns slew me and took her."

"Jarl Vitek has put out a bounty on Athagort," she said. "Some of the warriors here plan to form a band tomorrow and seek him out in the forest. But no one knows where he is."

But I do. I realized the knowledge of Athagort's location, unearthed by Anuina, was precious. Something in me made me want to tell Roswitha at once, but I decided to play it safe. "I will find him," I said.

She gave me a lopsided grin, icy eyes sparkling. "You are no tracker, Oram Ludwickson."

"Oh? And what makes you say that?"

"A hunch."

I chuckled. "Well, I'll find him either way."

She placed her hand on mine again, this time a conscious action, and warmth spread out from her touch, stirring deep within me. "We can do it together," she said.

"We will split Jarl Vitek's reward evenly among us… and your friend, if he still lives."

"She," I said. "If *she* still lives."

Her hand remained on mine, and her eyes took on a hazy quality. "Is she your lover?"

I licked my lips. "No… not yet."

She laughed, pure and with abandon. "You are a special man, Oram Ludwickson," she said. "That I declare. If you will have my help, we shall do this together."

I smiled and nodded, thankful for her offer. "I accept."

Liberating the Woods
Challenge level: 3 (difficult)

A Two-Headed Ogre by the name of Athagort Bone-Mangler and his band of Fauns have been terrorizing the Janneskog Woods, waylaying woodcutter and hunter alike. Jarl Vitek Warnerson Spear-Eater seeks bold adventurers willing and able to kill the ogre and his minions. Athagort and his minions make their lair somewhere in the Janneskog Woods. Roswitha Rolofsdottir Iron-Eye has offered to aid you in this quest.

Objective: Kill Athagort Bone-Mangler.
Bonus objectives: Slay at least ten Fauns; do not let Roswitha die or suffer grievous wounds.
Reward: 500 XP and 200 XP per bonus objective completed; 5 Golden Crowns; three items of Good quality or better.

***

We lay on the straw among the snoring warriors in Jarl Vitek's hall, covered in furs the serving girls had given us. There were a few revelers that did not sleep, and they continued their chatter until deep in the night. Normally, it would have bothered me, but the gentle drone of conversation and the occasional bout of good-natured laughter made me feel safer. That was a welcome sensation after my encounters in the forest.

Still, I lay awake for a long time. At first, I was processing what had happened to me, but as the day's events slowly fell into place in my mind, I found my eyes wandered more often to Roswitha's slender shape beside me, dwelling on how the fur hugged the hourglass contour of her limber body. By the rhythm of her breathing and the slight movements she made, I could tell she was awake too.

Does she feel what I feel? The attraction was a palpable thing, like a thread running between us. I remembered the description of my Phylomantic Bond ability.

> **Subjects must also be compatible; a strong, mutual attraction will signal such compatibility.**

What else can it be? But how do you ask someone to form a bond with you? Doesn't that just... happen? And what can I offer in return? She seemed a strong, independent spirit; would such an audacious offer not fill her with rage? After all, this was a woman who had punched me before I had even uttered four full sentences...

I closed my eyes, tried to direct my mind away. It was useless; for the greater part of the night, a hundred-and-one worries haunted me, from the most pedestrian concerns about a life I might never return to again, to the beautiful face of Anuina, now streaked with dirt and blood, her willowy body bound with cord as a horde of Fauns turned their lustful black eyes to her...

At length, uneasy sleep came.

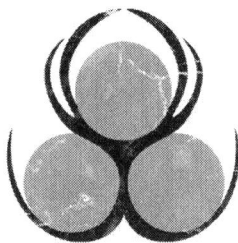

CHAPTER 5

When I awoke, Roswitha had somehow found her way into my arms. We lay huddled close together, pelts still separating our bodies, but I had draped my arm over her. She stirred and—as the haze of sleep slowly lifted from my eyes—looked at me over her shoulder. The sharp edge from last night had gone from her sleepy face, and she blinked wearily at me.

"Oram?" she muttered, voice still sleepy, blinking against the light.

I kept my arm on her a moment longer, and she hardly seemed to mind. Instead, she lay there and looked me in the eye. I felt an overwhelming need to pull her in and—

A rough prodding roused me from my fantasy. "Get up!"

I looked up to see an old crone push me with her foot. "Straw needs changing," she croaked. "Bugger off!" She gave me another spiteful prod, then headed over to the next sleeping form to wake it.

"Damn young'uns fucking all over the straw…" the old crone muttered as she hobbled off.

I exchanged a look with Roswitha. She looked confused for a moment, and then we both broke out laughing.

A short while later, after we had broken our fast with bread, cheese, and ale, we greeted the early morning. There was a springtime nip in the air, but the clear blue sky promised it would get warmer. It took me a moment to get used to the two suns and the earth-like moon that dominated the horizon. Still, I breathed in deeply, happy to fill my lungs with fresh air after the smoky and sour-smelling longhouse. I turned to Roswitha and focused on her; I had not gleaned her stats yesterday.

Roswitha Rolofsdottir Iron-Eye
Level 2 Priestess
Stamina: 18, Health: 6, Mana: 18, Sanity: 6

Impressive.

"Anything wrong?" she asked. The cold air brought out an enticing glow in her cheeks.

"Not at all," I said. "Let's go."

We passed through the gate unchallenged. I felt some apprehension at returning to what I now knew was called the Janneskog Woods. This time, however, I was not alone. Although I did wish we had a Ranger or a Rogue—a class that could spot any Faun trap well before they could spring it. I could have spent more time at the longhouse trying to find partners, but something told me that the warriors of Jarl Vitek may not have been so eager to share their loot.

When the trail brought us to the forest edge, I swallowed. I peered between the dark boles ahead.

Perhaps I shouldn't do this…

I felt Roswitha's hand on my arm. I looked at her over my shoulder and saw sympathy in her icy eyes. I gave her an appreciative nod and continued, the deep dark forest welcoming us.

***

"So, are you going to share your secret knowledge of where Athagort is holed up?" Roswitha asked.

The dark canopy had enclosed us—even during the day, my Light spell was more than a luxury to help us find our way.

"Yes," I said. "I only wanted to make sure we weren't within earshot of anyone else who might be interested, but the ogre and his minions are holed up at the Vaskhule Caves."

She nodded, jaw set. "Then that is where we must go."

"Only one problem, though," I said as I pushed a branch aside with my staff. "I have no idea where those caves are."

She chuckled. "Let me lead, then. I know the way."

I offered her a grin as she brushed past me. She shrugged her large round shield from her shoulder and loosened the loop around her axe in her belt.

I came up behind her, more attentive now to the shadows and hidden places of the forest than I had been the previous time... and *this* time, I saw them.

Shapes moved in the dark ahead—small, mischievous creatures. "Fauns," I hissed, "straight ahead."

Roswitha stopped, then peered into the dark. "By the Masked One, you are right."

When she halted, the Fauns knew their ambush had failed. Shrieking fury, four came out of the undergrowth, with two archers bringing up the rear.

Fuck… this is going to be tough.

Roswitha caught two arrows with her shield. She took a moment to brace herself and recover her Stamina as the four Fauns charged us. When the Fauns came within range, I extended my Pyromancer's Staff and focused flame through it. A gout of fire, thicker and brighter than before, came out.

My aim was off, but the Faun was not having a lucky day and stumbled into the flame, suffering 15 damage thanks to my staff. It fell down with a strange bark and lay there twitching as it burned up.

A moment later, the Fauns were upon Roswitha.

She braced herself to absorb the impact of their crude weapons. Not one of the tiny spears made it past her shield, but I saw splinters fly from the sturdy wood as they struck it. The Faun Archers shrieked and cursed, one chancing to hit its fellow as it fired at Roswitha. She caught the arrow with her shield, making it look easy to boot.

She's a perfect warrior!

Unfortunately, the other Faun Archer targeted me and sent his arrow arcing over the combatants.

Of course, fucking parrying was useless. Just my luck. I took the arrow.

You receive 4 Physical damage (piercing)!

The game mechanics were still so that the arrow didn't hit me, but my half-hearted brace for impact cost me some of my energy. I cursed the little Faun, but that was all I could do—the archers were outside my spell range.

Even as Roswitha dispatched one of the three remaining melee Fauns with her axe, I tried to set another one on fire with my enhanced Fire Sprout. Unfortunately, I missed and ended up burning a patch of shrubbery by the trailside at the rather high price of 3 Mana, bringing my total down to 7.

The one remaining melee Faun that had not wasted his Action dodging my Fire Sprout tried to stab at Roswitha under her shield. She sidestepped and swept his spear away with her axe and then spun on her feet to bury the blade almost a foot deep in the Faun's head.

God damn...

The archers fired, this time both at Roswitha, and even as she pulled her axe free of the Faun's skull, a swish of blood following in the weapon's wake, she caught both arrows with her shield. One bit through, the tip penetrating the shield and emerging from the other side, dangerously close to her hand.

Roswitha raised her axe and shouted, "I call upon the grace of the Crying One and the prowess of the Bladed One! Restore my vigor!" A white light shone around her, almost like a halo, and faded as soon as it had come. When it had gone, she had recovered her breath and looked ready for another bout.

A Stamina restoration spell, useful.

Not to be trumped, I projected another gout of flame at a Faun. This time, my jet of fiery death struck unerringly, despite the Faun's desperate attempt to evade it. The creature burned to a crisp with 12 damage, just enough to bring its Health down to 0. I gave an exalted cry of victory as the smell of burning fur reached my nostrils.

Despair was now plain to see in the Fauns' eyes. Still, the one surviving melee combatant pushed on, seeking to sting Roswitha with his spear. This time, she timed her parry just wrong, and his little spear shot over her axe. Luckily, her chain shirt turned the blow. It looked like she had two lines of defense: first was the shield, which she could use with her sword to parry or on itself to block; second was her chain shirt.

> **Like parrying, blocking with armor does not cost an Action, but it costs 1 Stamina per Encumbrance of the item used to block an attack. Regardless of whether a Block Check is successful, armor always absorbs damage equal to its Armor value. However, if not all damage is absorbed, the remainder is passed on through the wearer and the armor suffers a Breach. Armors also suffer a Breach on an unsuccessful Block check. After receiving a certain number of Breaches, an Armor is broken and rendered useless.**

That's pretty damn good. Maybe I should invest in some armor, provided mages can use it.

Both archers fired at Roswitha again, and she caught the arrows with her shield with some effort. She was sweating now, locks of ginger hair sticking to her forehead, and she raised her axe and called upon her gods again, causing her to glow for a moment. At once, she was restored and regained control over her shortened breath. She assumed a warrior's stance that was as impressive as it was sexy, ready for more fighting.

Now, it was my turn to move up. Burning through 3 more Mana, with only 1 left, I Fire Sprouted the remaining Faun. It dodged the jet of flame, but that left it with no Action to attack Roswitha.

After that, it was easy enough. Roswitha dispatched the defenseless Faun, took another volley on her shield, and charged the archers. They gave their best, but melee was not their strong suit, especially not against Roswitha and her healing capabilities. I assisted with a spear controlled by my Ghost Touch spell, and we brought the remaining two Fauns low together.

***

We stood there panting as we surveyed the carnage, and we exchanged a grin.

My eyes trailed over her—her cloak had slipped open to reveal the low-cut collar of her chain shirt. Beads of sweat had gathered there, and my body stirred as I watched them trail down her chest. There was a fire in her eyes as well.

You receive 600 XP.

Congratulations! You have reached level 2.

"Oh," I said. "Fuck yes, I—"

Still watching me with blazing eyes, Roswitha flung away her shield as if it was a Frisbee. It landed somewhere in the undergrowth. With four steps, she was with me, and I saw what she wanted.

I grabbed her as she came to me, and our lips found each other with a passion as fiery as the flames I conjured. I began pulling at her cloak, and she worked with me, straining—*fighting*—to get it off her. In my urgency to undress her, I pushed her over, almost tackled her. We landed with a heavy thud on the muddy trail, Roswitha below me, her muddy traveling cloak serving as a blanket of sorts.

Our lips separated for a moment and her icy eyes were clouded over with lust as she gazed deep into mine, her hands already seeking to undo my belt buckle, fidgeting and fumbling with an eagerness. "I want you," she hissed, her voice thick with lust. "*You*, Oram Ludwickson, and *only* you."

I replied by pushing my lips onto hers, hot with desire. She nipped at them as I stole her kisses, and her tongue found mine. I gripped her thigh, packed tight in leather, then began feverishly exploring her body for the straps and buckles of her armor. Her chain shirt was not that large—more a crop top, really—but it was impossible to get it off with my eyes shut and my mind swimming as I reveled in the sweet scent of her sweat. Laughing, she wrestled herself free from my embrace and rose to her feet to undress.

I sat on my ass, gazing up hungrily at her. She licked her lips, staring a bold challenge at me as she undid the many straps that kept her armor in place. With the cloak gone, I drank in the enticing hourglass shape of her body: her toned and slightly muscular midriff, the full swell of her breasts—visible even under her chain shirt, and the hypnotizing way her tight leather hose clung to her generous hips and thighs.

Fuck, she is one of the hottest women I've ever seen. And she wants to be mine...

I sat there, cock stirring in my wool hose, as the last of her buckles opened. The chain shirt clattered away, revealing linen wrappings that only covered her nipples and kept her breasts contained. My blood raced through me as she began unwrapping herself, one coil at a time. She smiled down at me, eyes blazing. "I don't know what you are," she said, almost to herself. "But I have never felt such a need for anyone."

I grinned and pulled my tunic over my head. She ceased unwrapping herself for a moment, just to take me in with hungry eyes. "Did you cast a spell on me, mage?" she asked.

"Maybe," I said, rising to my feet. I was half a foot taller than she was, and when she looked up at me, there was something so vulnerable in her eyes. "But if so, then I am under the same spell."

I reached out and wrapped her in my arms, oblivious of the dark woods and the surrounding battlefield. I placed a hand on each of her firm buttocks, kneading them through her leather breeches, and she bit her lip and gave a sigh as I pulled her in.

I helped her with the wrappings, and her naked skin burned against mine as I peeled the last coil away, revealing her pink puffy nipples. She had freckled shoulders, and some of her freckles reached down to the slopes of her full breasts; I wanted to kiss them all and could no longer fight my need.

Gripping her tightly, I kissed her neck; the salty taste of her fresh sweat prickled my tongue, and I took in her scent, wanting it to intoxicate me. She held me firm, whispering my name as my lips trailed down to the ridge of her collarbone and my hands came up to cup her full breasts. A slight moan escaped her as her hands peeled away my belt.

I left a trail of fiery kisses between her breasts, descending their slopes until I came to an erect nipple. I took it in my mouth and sucked on it. She inhaled with a hiss, and her hand shot down from my belt, squeezing my dick through my hose.

"Gods…" she muttered as I circled around her swollen nipple with my tongue.

As sudden as she had come at me, she pushed me away. She had an almost feral look in her icy eyes as she kneeled before me on her dirt-streaked cloak. Her feverish hands worked my hose, unwinding them and pulling them down at the same time. Her rough motions made me sway on my feet, and I reached for her, gathering up her long ginger braids, wrapping them around my fist.

With a rough jerk, she pulled away my hose. A moment later, she pulled down my braies, revealing my engorged cock. She licked her lips—so close to my thick tip—and wrapped her hand around my shaft. "You are no small man, Oram Ludwickson," she said, and a salacious grin appeared on her face even as she softly squeezed my throbbing length.

A moan escaped me, and I tightened my grip on her braids. "Think you can handle it, Roswitha Rolofsdottir?" I asked with a grin.

By way of answer, she gave me a rough tug that made my body tense, her eyes bold and challenging on me. Then, softer, she began stroking my shaft, bringing her free hand up to brace herself against my stomach.

I stood transfixed, watching her work my cock with eager and deft strokes, her breasts swaying with every move, the dim light in the forest dancing over the enticing ridges and soft curves of her luscious, youthful body. Power gathered in my veins, and I desired her—to be in her.

She brought her fine, elfin face closer to my cock, sticking out her long, red tongue to run it from the base of my shaft to the very tip. A shiver of anticipating pleasure mastered me, and for a moment I feared my knees would give in.

Eyes large and bold, she opened her beautiful, thin red lips and wrapped them around the tip of my cock. Warmth engulfed me, and I couldn't help but tug at her long braids, forcing her to take me deeper. A little yelp escaped her, but she took me nonetheless. The wet heat of her mouth overcame me, and I twitched inside her, some precum already leaking into her eager mouth.

God, I would never have expected a Priestess *to suck such a mean dick.*

Lips tightening, she began working on my cock, bringing one hand up to stroke me. The other slipped down the waistband of her leather breeches, and she let out a little moan as her hand found its mark.

It was too hot to watch her like that, crouching as she sucked me off, playing with herself—making herself ready. It was all I could to stop myself from unloading in her warm mouth. I moved with her, bucking my hips to her rhythm, and my pleasure built up from deep within, rising and rising.

Oh fuck, I'm going to—

I bit down, then gripped her hair tight to make her stop. Her eyes, tears already forming from gagging on my cock, looked up at me, questioning, pleading, and I pulled my rock-hard cock out of her mouth. "Let me fuck you," I said. "I want to make you mine." As I spoke, I lowered myself down to her.

Her eyes roved over me, contemplating, but I gave her no time. I grabbed her by her ankles and gave her a slight tug, making her fall on her pretty ass. She chuckled and gave me a seductive glance as she stuck her leather-clad, limber legs up in the air.

I needed no more invitation. I pushed her down onto her back, kissing her smooth stomach and heaving breasts as I tugged and pulled and jerked at her boots, finally getting them to come off. Before I knew it, I had my hands on the waistband of her leather breeches and pulled them down.

She looked at me, smiling, lying on her back, and wriggling as she helped me shimmy her mud-stained breeches off. With a great pull, they came away, revealing white linen underwear that was little more than a thong. My mouth watered as I studied her wide and beautiful hips, and she grinned up at me, kicking playfully at me with perfect, slender feet.

I laughed, then wrapped her legs under one arm, restraining her. She bucked and wriggled, laughing all the while in my grip. With my free hand, I roved over her body. Soft, warm skin yielded to my touch, and my desire burned all-consuming.

As if a sudden gust of wind had swept it up, our playfulness vanished, and Roswitha looked up at me with big, stern eyes, willing me on.

My hand shook a little when I grabbed hold of her undergarment and pulled it down her legs. She had a soft mound of ginger pubic hair, and the sweetest pussy I had seen in my life, with full lips glistening and ready, and an exalted sigh escaped me when I saw it. She spread her legs for me, and her scent—iron and sweat—released a burning hotter than the brightest forge. I loomed over her, my manhood erect and ready, and our eyes connected.

"Take me," she said. "I want to be with you, Oram Ludwickson."

The words came to me as if they were part of me—a mantra as natural as my very own limbs: "I forge my bond with you, Roswitha Rolofsdottir Iron-Eye. You are mine in heart and soul as I am yours, and we are bonded by our own free will, until we part as broken and unbonded or until we go to the next world or beyond. Will you honor this bond?"

"I will," she said.

No hesitation.

I lowered myself onto her, and we shared a shiver as our warm, naked bodies connected. She was so soft and yielding, yet her grip on me was firm and as eternal as the sky. She let out a soft moan as I pushed against her warmth, my member pulsing with life and passion, and her womanhood itching to take me in. "Take me," she said again, her voice a hoarse whisper.

Unable to keep us both waiting, I reached down to grab my cock and rubbed it through her wet slit, testing her, and she arched her back in pleasure. I pushed in with a deep sigh, allowing her to engulf me. The wet heat of her pussy burned me up, made me squirm in her hands, and my hips began to thrust of their own accord. "Gods…" she muttered, her nails clawing a trail across my bare back.

I plunged deeper, harder, and I picked up speed. It was unlike anything I had ever experienced before. Our souls became entwined, and the hands of the Gods reached down from their Mountain, picking us up and placing them in their midst as they marveled at the arcane divinity of our loving.

She squirmed in my grip, melded with me as I thrust inside her, consummating our bond. Her legs were wrapped around me, her heels pushing against my back to urge me on, and the slapping of our skin was like nature's oldest song. I felt her build up beneath me, as if her body was mine as well, and her whispers in my ear, pleading to take her harder, faster, deeper, were like kin to my own hoarsely mouthed desires.

I drove her on, my pleasure building up deep inside, until I knew she was there with me—at the zenith of our love, ready to plunge deep into ecstasy. She arched her back, and her body began trembling—quick, short jerks—as she begged, "Don't stop! I'm—oh, Gods, you're making me come."

I bit my lip as her pussy tightened around my cock, and our divine union transitioned into my primal need to fill her up. Unable to contain it, I roared my lust, braced myself against her squirming body.

I cried out as my first load of seed shot inside her.

She echoed my cry, wrapping her legs tighter around me and making me thrust deeper. I groaned, a guttural sound of pleasure, driven by her eagerness to take all I had to give her. Pure and ancient delight, toe-curling and mind-numbing, washed over me as I shared myself with her, filling her with more of myself.

Even as our pleasure mounted and our embrace tightened, my mouth found hers, and I kissed her deeply and full of fire. She answered with a blazing lust of her own as we rode the last waves of our pleasure.

As our euphoria receded, we drifted back down to the world, our sweaty bodies entwined as if we were a single, panting creature.

When I opened my eyes, we were on the dirt-streaked cloak again—or still?—clothes, armor, and weapons strewn about us.

I had trouble believing that I was anywhere else than just in Roswitha's arms. Turning to her, still lying on her warm body, still inside her, I saw her warm, generous smile as her ice-blue eyes studied me. I laughed—a kind of laugh I hadn't heard from myself in years—and she laughed with me.

"That was…" I shook my head, at a loss of words.

"It was indeed," she said, her voice small and just for me. "And it will be again, I hope."

I relaxed, resting my cheek on her shoulder. I wanted to lie like this forever and listen to her soft breathing, and I knew she wanted nothing else too as her hands softly caressed my back, causing a tingle where she had but moments ago dug her nails in.

It was bliss.

***

Unfortunately, the icy wind on my sweaty back—let alone on my exposed genitals—forced me out of my perfect dream with Roswitha. I gave her another deep kiss, then pushed myself up with a groan. A moment later, a text box appeared.

> **Congratulations! You have bonded someone to you using your Phylomantic Bond. Please review your character sheet for more details.**

It was true; I felt stronger, with a new power tingling in my fingertips. I looked at Roswitha, perfect in her nakedness, as she propped herself up on her elbows.

"Do you feel any different?" I asked her.

She chuckled. "I sure do…"

I grinned, then shook my head. "No, I mean more powerful?"

She stopped for a moment and considered it. "Hmm," she said. "Perhaps. I am unsure." She looked at me. "Why? Do you?"

"Yes," I said. "Let me see."

"Have you gained a level?" she asked.

I frowned. *That's a bit meta...* "Are you... do you know about *levels*?"

She smiled. "Of course. Am I not Awakened? All Awakened can mentally picture their abilities translated to simple values; we improve them as we gain knowledge and experience."

Wow... that's strange. "I had no idea you could do that too."

She chuckled, rising nimbly to her feet to scoop up her underwear and leather breeches. "You are special, Oram Ludwickson, but not *that* special. All Awakened see these things."

"Well, I did level up. But there is something else, too. Do me a favor and check your stats."

"Fine," she said as she put on her undergarment. "But do you mind if I dress first? It's quite cold."

I looked at her. "I do mind," I said, a dirty grin on my face, "but I'll let you get away with it."

She laughed and shook her head as she continued dressing herself.

I looked away and focused on the icon of the knight's helm—it was flashing to get my attention, and it prompted me to complete my level-up before I could do anything else.

You have advanced to level 2. As a reward, you may increase one of your attributes by 1. In addition, you receive 12 skill points to distribute among your skills as you see fit. Your Stamina and Mana also increase by a number equal to your Endurance and Power, respectively. Finally, the following randomly

selected attribute that was reduced due to a death will be restored by 1: Intellect.

Since you are a Phylomancer, you also gain the following abilities: Phylomantic Monitor, Phylomantic Link.

Please note that Phylomancers only gain new spells through their Phylomantic Bond; consult your character sheet for more information.

I got to work, happy to see some power increases. I stuck my attribute point in Intellect; together with my restored point, this upped the damage of my spells by 2—enough to let me kill those Fauns a lot quicker. I stuck 3 skill points in Elemental; 3 in Staff (I needed to get a bit better at parrying); 3 in Psionic; and 3 in one that had only recently unlocked: Summoning.

When I was done, my character sheet looked like this:

Oram Ludwickson (Human)
Level 2 Phylomancer

Attributes: Strength 2, Agility 5, Endurance 3, Intellect 8, Cunning 6, Power 5
Resources: Stamina 9, Health 3, Mana 15(18), Sanity 5
Skills: Dagger 2, Dodge 5, Elemental 8, Illusion 5, Intuition 2, Perception 2, Psionic 8, Staff 5, Summoning 3, Ward 5
Abilities: Phylomantic Bond (1/1), Phylomantic Monitor, Phylomantic Link
Spells: *Update through Phylomantic Bond*, Ghost Touch (0), Light (0), Fire Sprout (1)

Equipment: Pyromancer's Staff (Common)
XP/XP needed until next level: 1,000/2,000

Even though I was keen to see what my bond with Roswitha gave me, I decided to first check out my two new abilities. Phylomantic Monitor allowed me to always discern the location of anyone I had a Phylomantic Bond with. I tried it for a moment: the world around faded and became hazy. Roswitha, however, became a bright light at the center of it that drew my attention like a flashlight in the dark.

Okay, useful. If I'd had this with Anuina...

I shook my head and checked out the next ability.

Phylomantic Link (Phylomancer): Any spell you cast on yourself with a beneficial effect is automatically shared between you and anyone you share a Phylomantic Bond with, even if the spell normally only affects a single target.

I didn't have any buffs yet, but this would be useful in the future; I could just cast them on myself and affect my bonds automatically. No longer keeping myself in suspension, I opened the link to my Phylomantic Bond.

You have bonded with one or more subjects through your Phylomantic Bond ability.
Roswitha Rolofsdottir Iron-Eye (Human, Skanaaga culture, level 2 Priestess): Humans of the Skanaaga culture generally hail from the cold Snowlands to the north. Their rugged habitat supports only limited agriculture, but the northern forests are rife with game.

Skanaaga are known for their deep connection to the land, their ability to survive in the coldest climate, and their profound respect for the warrior. Bonding with a Human of the Skanaaga culture at your current level offers you access to the following spells: Frost Ward (0), Icy Hand (0), Fog (1), Freeze/Thaw (1), Ice Spikes (1), Trackless Step (1).

In addition, since your bond with this subject is intense, you and the subject gain the following advantages: +2 Stamina, +2 Mana.

Hot damn…

I checked out the spells. They were good, nearly all related to the Water element. There was also a Ritual: Trackless Step. Rituals cost no Mana but took longer to cast, making them unsuitable for combat or casting on the fly. Eager to find out the details, I perused my new spells.

The run-down was simple. Frost Ward was a level 0 spell that halved any water damage I received. Icy Hand was also a level 0 spell that dealt a meager amount of damage. It was cheap to cast, though—only 1 Mana—which made it a good fallback option. On the downside, it required me to get up close and touch my target.

Not the best idea for Captain Glass Cannon…

Fog created a thick cloud of fog, useful in a situation where I wanted to remain unnoticed, and Freeze/Thaw instantly either froze or thawed a body of water—good if I needed to cross a stream in a pinch. Trackless Step was a ritual. Simple enough in its effect, it allowed me to obscure the tracks of myself and any companions traveling with me so we'd be harder to track. I was going to use this one right away. It would ensure that none of the warriors Jarl Vitek had hired would track us and learn the location of the Vaskhule Caves to beat us there.

The spell that interested me the most, however, was Ice Spikes, another damage dealer. I focused on it to commit the stats to memory.

Ice Spikes
Spell level: 1
Mana: 3
Skill: Elemental
Element: Water
Description: Three icy spikes fly from your outstretched hand at up to 3 creatures that are no more than 5 meters apart from each other. You make only one Check to resolve the attack. Every creature that is successfully struck, receives 1-2 + Intellect Physical damage (water)

I had no spells that dealt damage in an area of effect yet, but Ice Spikes at least allowed multiple targets. I couldn't buff it as I could not cast level 2 spells yet, but my Intellect was high enough to assure a decent damage output. It probably wouldn't be an instakill, but it could wear a target down or finish a wounded one with ease.

This is looking good.

Finally, I surveyed my sheet one last time, noting my bond had increased my Stamina and Mana to 11 and 20, respectively. Satisfied, I nodded.

Time to get going!

***

"So," Roswitha said, ginger eyebrow arched, "you are a Phylomancer?"

I smiled, a little guiltily. Maybe I should have told her that before she made her vow. "I am," I said. "If you... regret what you did, we can end it just as easily. I only want—"

"No," she said. "I do not regret it."

I breathed in and nodded, keeping my eyes locked on hers. "Good," I said. "I want to keep you with me."

She chuckled as she shouldered her shield, then came up to me, placed her hand on my chest, and gave me a peck on the cheek. "In this life and the next, Phylomancer," she said. "Whatever it may hold." She gave me a playful nudge. "Come, let us see what these Fauns carried on them."

I nodded, shooting a glance at the trail behind us. "Good idea," I said. "But let's be quick about it. I have a way to keep any warriors of Jarl Vitek's off our trail, but we should not linger too long."

The four dead Fauns who had engaged us in melee had nothing on them except for their spears and loincloths. The archers, however, both wore scuffed leather armor.

"Think I can use that?" I asked Roswitha. The idea of putting on a lice-ridden hand-me-down worn by a dead Faun did not particularly appeal to me, but my squishiness was a source of some concern. Roswitha, however, looked at me like I had asked if cows shit gold. "You can," she said, "but it will interfere with your magic. Only certain classes, such as mine, can combine magic with spellcasting."

Kind of a relief, really. I nodded and ignored the armor. Somewhat reluctantly, I patted down the Faun Archers as Roswitha stood guard. Just to be sure, I took their flimsy shortbows and quivers with arrows; I could store them in my Vault, anyway. Apart from that, I found twelve copper coins, four silver ones, and a common dagger that looked like the one I owned earlier.

Frowning, I inspected the Faun who had carried the dagger. It was hard to tell with half his face slashed open, but he did seem to be the very same Faun that had ambushed Anuina and me and delivered the fatal arrow to my face.

"I know this one," I said.

Roswitha stepped closer and looked over my shoulder. "Strange company you keep, then."

A grim smiled formed as I studied the corpse. I was happy for the revenge. "No," I said. "This was one of the Fauns that ambushed me and my friend." I looked up at her. "We're on the right trail."

"Good," she said. "Now do your trick to keep Vitek's men off our back and let us make for the caves."

After giving my previous killer one final kick, I sat down by the trailside and took a handful of dirt. The complex words of the ritual came to me, and I slowly chanted them as I drew mystic symbols with my fingers, a slight shimmering remaining where I had cut the air, and finally throwing the handful of dirt to the wind.

Like with my other magical powers, the words of the ritual came naturally to me, as if I had known and practiced them all my life. It was an incantation that built layer upon layer of illusion to mask our passing. When I had finished, a prompt notified me my Check result was 41—*that should help keep them off our tails.*

"All right," I said, rising to my feet.

Roswitha stood close, a sardonic smile on her face. "Done making mud pies?" she asked.

I chuckled and gave her a slap on the bum. "Let's go," I said.

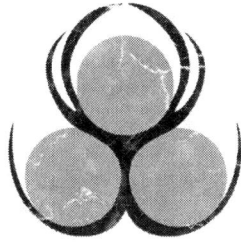

CHAPTER 6

The Vaskhule Caves began as a large opening in a rocky outcropping in the side of a large hill. The opening itself was in the shape of an inverted 'V' and was utterly dark.

Outside, however, there were a few stools made of stripped logs arranged around a campfire. Six Fauns either sat or hung around there—two of them archers. An elder, hunched-over Faun was with them. He wore a necklace with bone charms and stone tablets and leaned on a crooked staff, some distance away from the scurrying, arguing younger Fauns.

Faun Shaman
Level 2
Stamina: 12, Health: 4, Mana: 15, Sanity: 5

A spellcaster…
Roswitha and I sat hidden behind some low bushes. However, considering our skill at hiding, it was only a matter of time until they spotted us.

I looked at her, icy eyes fixed on our foes, a determined look on her face. "We need to get the spellcaster first," I said. "I don't know what he can do, but if it's healing magic, that's bad news."

She nodded. "They're healers, although few Fauns have the self-control and insight to practice that role with some skill."

I nodded. "I can hit the Fauns at the campfire with my Fog spell; that'll buy us some time to take out the spellcaster. After that, you tank and try to draw the Fauns close. My magic spells will do some serious damage; we'll finish them together."

She frowned at me sideways. "*Tank?*"

"Uh, face them in melee and keep them busy."

She chortled. "Be your little decoy, you mean?"

"You have a better idea?"

Her jaw moved as she watched the Fauns. A moment later, she shook her head. "We need a real warrior."

I squeezed her thigh and gave her a smile. "You *are* one. Ready?"

She gave a firm nod.

In a breath, I was up and casting my spell, spilling a splash of water from the jug we had acquired earlier. A moment later, just as the Fauns uttered their surprised cries, a thick cloud of impenetrable fog formed, centered on the campfire.

The only Faun that wasn't in the fog cloud was the shaman, and he glared at us, raising his staff and mouthing an incantation even as Roswitha charged at him. The distance was too great for her to get there in time, and a bright jet of flame leaped from the shaman's staff. She kept running as she raised her shield, ready to charge through the fire. With a rapid jerk of my arm, I cast Frost Ward as a level 1 spell, allowing me to call upon its effect instantaneous, and through my Phylomantic Link, Roswitha enjoyed the effect.

The fire struck her shield even as the shimmering icy layer manifested and dampened most of it. She held with ease, roaring a battle cry as she closed the last meters between her and the shaman.

The Faun's black eyes widened when he saw her coming, and he tried to step out of the way of Roswitha's expertly wielded battle axe. Anticipating the creature's move, she adjusted her strike somewhat and caused the Faun to make an awkward stumble in his dodge. A moment later, I saw his Stamina had been reduced to 0.

12 Damage on a single attack!

She was a powerhouse. I cheered her on and used my Action to close the distance between me and the shaman. At the same moment, the six other Fauns emerged from the fog cloud and spotted us. It was too late for the shaman, however; Roswitha swung her axe low, and even though the Faun stepped back, her brutal strike opened a huge red swath across his belly. Purple and red guts splattered to the floor as the shaman shrieked and fell.

Fuck yeah!

The other Fauns were not dissuaded, however, and because of our position, two charged me... I saw them coming and felt a deep, apprehensive churning in my gut, remembering well how I had fallen at their grubby little paws. To make matters worse, one of the archers fired at me, forcing me to use my Action to dodge. Lucky for me, I got a 94 against its 46. I stepped back, and the arrow landed in the dirt and stuck there, trembling.

A second later, the two screaming, snapping Fauns were upon me. Staff at the ready, I braced myself for melee combat.

Staff Check result: (69 + 5 Agility + 5 Staff =) 79 versus opponent's 34.

I tapped away the first spear with the butt of my staff, redirecting it at the forest floor. The Faun flew past me, shrieking what I expected to be a curse, and I resisted the urge to twirl my staff like a show pony. Instead, I focused on parrying the second attack.

Staff Check result: (19 + 5 Agility + 5 Staff =) 29 versus opponent's 104.

This one flew past my meager defense, and I had to skip back, almost stumbling to prevent the cruel tip from grazing my thigh, which the game translated to 6 damage. Together with the Stamina cost from parrying those attacks, I was already down to 3.

Up ahead, Roswitha was in her element and doing much better. She caught an arrow from the archer with her shield, then parried the other Fauns' melee attacks easily and with grace. She countered and struck a Faun from behind her shield with her axe, taking him in the collarbone. The creature barked as he pivoted on his feet from the force of the strike, then fell.

Since I had no Action to counter my Faun attackers, they both struck at me again. Lucky for me, the archer that had previously shot at me concluded Roswitha was a bigger threat and turned his attention to her.

This time, my attempts at parrying fared better: I blocked the first attack by feigning at the Faun, causing him to jerk back with a snarl, and the second spear I struck hard with the butt of my staff, sending the wielder staggering back. I followed up swiftly with an upgraded Icy Touch. White frost shot from my hand as I reached out to touch one of my Faun attackers. He tried to jump back with a fearful snarl, sensing the deathly cold from afar.

Elemental Check result: (67 + 6 Cunning + 8 Elemental =) 81 versus opponent's 62.

You deal 16 Physical damage (water)!

God damn! The Faun turned pale as I touched him, teeth chattering for a moment, and black patches of frostbite appeared on his body. I saw the film over his black eyes actually fucking freeze before they could full well turn up, and the Faun fell back, stiff as a board. I looked at the other with a grin. "You're next!" I hissed.

He stabbed at me again with his spear, but I butted it away with ease and did the same trick again, getting a 91 against a pathetic 15, dealing another 16 damage. My Faun adversary joined his fellow dead and frozen on the floor. Suppressing a desire to cry out victory, I looked at Roswitha just as she cut down the last of the Faun Archers.

I shook my head and chuckled. The calls were getting less close... We were quite the team.

I grinned at Roswitha from across a field strewn with dead Fauns, and she smiled back at me, showing me those crow's feet I loved, just as she brushed a ginger braid behind her ear. Desire for her stirred within, but I pushed it away. There would be time for that later.

Hopefully.

You receive 700 XP.

***

"You did well," Roswitha said as she cleaned the blood from her battle axe. Her sharp icy eyes were full of admiration.

I took a deep breath and got a noseful of forest air and the salt-and-iron hint of blood; it made me feel more alive than ever. I turned to smile at her. "So did you. It's a joy to watch you fight and an honor to fight beside you."

She laughed. "Not exactly *beside* me, Oram Ludwickson."

I chuckled and shook my head. We set to pilfering the corpses and found two Healing Potions—we each took one—and a Mana Potion: a small earthenware flask filled with a bluish, thick liquid.

> **Mana Potion**
> **Level 0**
> **Encumbrance: 0.1**
> **Description: Drink this Mana Potion as an Action to restore 1-12 Mana. This potion does not restore Sanity.**

I took the Mana Potion as magic was my primary damage-dealing ability. In addition, we found three silver coins and four copper ones. Most interesting, however, was the charm the shaman had been wearing. I studied it to see what it did.

> **Shaman Charm**
> **Level 1**
> **Encumbrance: 0.1**
> **Description: This set of carved bones and etched stone talismans protects the wearer. The wearer receives a +5 bonus to Ward Checks.**

"Ward Check?" I said, studying the crude object.

Roswitha sauntered over and studied the charm for a moment. "Warding works against mental attacks," she said, "much like a shield may turn a blade, a proper ward may halt an attack on your very sanity."

I turned the charm around in my hand, then handed the charm to Roswitha. "Here," I said. "I'm already insane, anyway."

She laughed, took my hand holding the charm and folded my fingers around it. "Keep it, Oram Ludwickson. And may it protect you well."

We exchanged a smile and—as if fate decreed it—turned our heads to the dark caves at the same time. Her touch comforted me, but the darkness was almost an evil of its own.

But if Anuina was in there, I wanted to find her.

I understood now that the compelling force that drew me to her was neither loyalty nor physical attraction—at least, not *only* those. Instead, it flowed from my newfound powers as a Phylomancer. She and I were compatible, and the force that drove me to her was as strong as the force that had driven Roswitha and I into each other's arms.

"You still wish to go on?" Roswitha asked.

I looked at her, determination settling in my mind. "Yes," I said.

She nodded. "Then let us go. If your friend is there, we will find her."

***

Even though it might lead to our untimely discovery by the Fauns, I cast Light on my staff to illuminate our path. Neither I nor Roswitha could see in the dark, and tumbling into a crevice or pit and breaking our necks would—for me—be anticlimactic or—for Roswitha—a very unfortunate end.

The caves seemed natural, and in the light of my spell we saw stalagmites, stalactites, and rock worn smooth by water that had long since seeped away. Here and there, dirt had gathered in patches and was now fertile soil for fungi, and a bright green moss crawled over the cave walls. Yet it was clear the place was inhabited; close to the entrance stood a handcart that the Fauns used to haul supplies into and out of their caves; it still contained several empty burlap sacks that smelled of dried meat.

I gestured for Roswitha to follow me as I held my staff high to illuminate our path. Even though we trod lightly, our footsteps carried far. The only other sound was the occasional drip of water or a whistling as a gust of wind passed over sharp rock.

Quiet… too much so.

With years of gaming experience, I aimed my staff a little lower to keep an eye on the floor—I didn't want to be

surprised by a pit trap or a tripwire. It seemed, however, that this world stuck to logical trap placement; this was the way in and out of the cave proper, and the Fauns had not trapped it.

We went deeper into the cave, and it grew narrower with every step, the walls literally closing in on us. After a few steps, a fetid stench came up and the walls rolled back. A moment later, an arrow flew at me.

I fucking knew it…

I suffered 8 damage, bringing me down to 3 Stamina, even as another arrow flew at me. This time I was aware, and I used my Action to dodge it. The shaft clattered against the rock wall behind me.

Roswitha was swift to step up. She healed me with a quick word and a glowing touch, reinvigorating energy blasting through my veins, then took position in front of me. She caught the next salvo of arrows on her shield.

She grimaced over her shoulder at me. "Time for a trick, Oram," she said. An arrow had breached her shield, and it was altogether looking battered.

With a quick spill of water from my jug, I called on a fog cloud just in front of us, between whoever had shot those arrows at us and ourselves. In the distance, I heard Faun chatter. It sounded furious and frustrated.

"Good call," Roswitha said.

I smiled. "Watch this." I retrieved one of the shoddy shortbows and quivers from my Vault, then cast Light on three arrows. I had the time; the fog cloud would not dissipate soon in these wind-still conditions. In the meantime, Roswitha healed me again and took an Action to restore her Mana.

When I was done, I had three arrows that gave off light in a 5-meter radius. I fired them from the shortbow, keeping

equal distances between them. When I dismissed the fog cloud, the second arrow I had fired revealed two Faun Archers in its light radius. They were about 20 meters away from us. An underground stream separated us from them; it was wide and deep, impossible to ford in a single Action.

"Gods curse it all," Roswitha said as she caught two more arrows with her round shield. "We need to find a way around."

"No need," I said. With a sigil of power and an incantation that came as naturally to me as my own breath, I cast my Freeze/Thaw spell and caused part of the stream to freeze over.

Roswitha laughed. "You have your uses," she said, brandishing her axe.

The Fauns shrieked in panic as Roswitha charged across the frozen stream, a broad grin on her face. She caught two more arrows before she reached them, then decapitated one with a masterful stroke of her battle axe. The other Faun fell from her next stroke, my Fire Sprout having brought his Stamina down. He hadn't even had the time to draw his crude dagger.

You receive 200 XP.

We took a moment to recover our strength, then explored the cavernous room. While largely natural, parts of it were hewn out and reinforced with logs black with age. Huddled away in a corner lay several piles of pelts and straw where—judging by the stench—the Fauns slept. A foul-looking pail nearby gave rise to the suspicion that the filthy beasts pissed and shat here too. We skimmed through their belongings, and it was only by chance that Roswitha found a small iron band.

Ring of Strength
Level 3
Encumbrance: n/a
Description: This simple iron band grants the wearer a +1 bonus to Strength.

"Wow," I said. "Shame about the level requirement."

She smirked. "I just became level 3," she said and slipped the band on.

I chuckled. "May it serve you well."

I was a measly 100 XP away from that threshold as well. There was no doubt in my mind that Athagort would be a bad-ass adversary, but if we could get me up to level 3 before we'd meet the fellow, I was pretty sure we'd stand a good chance against him. Hopefully, kicking his ass meant getting Anuina back.

There was only one way to go: a narrow cavern that snaked away to the right of where we had entered. Roswitha shouldered her battered shield, I took up my illuminated staff, and we continued on our way.

***

As we proceeded down the narrow passage, the smell of Faun dung made place for that of wet dog, and I exchanged a glance with Roswitha. We both had an inkling of what was coming. After we took a few more steps, we heard a furious bark and the excited snarl of a Faun.

One second later, two wolves flew out of the darkness ahead and into our light radius. I had a frozen moment in which I saw the whites of their eyes, bared fangs, and flattened ears. Drool flew from their slavering jaws as they came.

Feral Wolf
Level 2
Stamina: 18, Health: 6, Mana: 6, Sanity: 2

The corridor was narrow, and this time Roswitha was in the lead. I saw at once that she had dealt with beasts like this before. She braced herself behind her shield, limber body swift and smooth, and she made herself small before the coming onslaught.

They smashed into Roswitha with rabid barking. Claws scratched on wood, hind legs raked the metal rim, and snapping jaws tried to reach her. The creaking of her shield was audible even over the snarling and baying of the beasts. One of the creatures shot under her shield for a moment and snapped at her arm, but Roswitha pulled back swift enough.

Then, as the beasts withdrew, she brought her axe down. But these wolves were a lot faster and a lot stronger than Fauns. The beast jumped back, albeit at great effort, and Roswitha only just checked her blow; it was all she could do not to dull her axe on the cavern floor. "Damn beasts!" she grunted as she ducked back behind her shield.

I braced myself, now having a clear view of the two wolves, and made a mystic symbol of power. Two icy spikes flew out from my outstretched hand and shot at the wolves with a cold *swoosh*.

**Elemental Check result: (28 + 6 Cunning + 8
Elemental =) 40 versus opponent's 52.**

One wolf jumped out of the way, but the other had already used its Action to dodge and awkwardly stumbled back. My 9 damage—combined with the 8 damage it had suffered from Roswitha's axe—reduced it to 1 Stamina.

I smirked. The beasts were on the defensive now; Ice Spikes might not have the best damage output, but it forced unarmored enemies to use their Action to dodge, which was almost as good as actually hitting them. Forcing enemies to dodge was essentially crowd control.

The wolves could take no action, and Roswitha delivered a swift strike with her axe, striking her opponent even as it tried to dodge again. This time, her axe took the beast in the skull with a heavy thud. It gave a whimper and collapsed. I followed up with my Fire Sprout, getting a 105 against the wolf's 98. Close call, but the gust of flame hit home, delivering 11 damage. The wolf was out of Actions again, and Roswitha finished it with a stroke of her axe.

In the distance, the Faun handler yelped, and by the stomping of its hooved feet we knew he withdrew. He shrieked in his guttural native tongue, no doubt alerting the others.

Still, we took a brief moment to gather our strength.

You receive 300 XP.

Ding!
"I just became level 3," I told Roswitha.

She peered into the darkness ahead. From deeper down, a heavy roar resounded, echoing through the caves like the illest of omens. "Do it," she said. "We will need you at your full strength. But please make haste."

***

I focused on the icon of the plumed casque to open my character sheet and level up.

> **You have advanced to level 3. As a reward, you may increase one of your attributes by 1. In addition, you receive 12 skill points to distribute among your skills as you see fit. Your Stamina and Mana also increase by a number equal to your Endurance and Power, respectively. Finally, the following randomly selected attribute that was reduced due to a death will be restored by 1: Strength.**
>
> **Since you are a Phylomancer, you also gain the following abilities: Greater Phylomantic Link.**
>
> **Please note that Phylomancers only gain new spells through their Phylomantic Bond; consult your character sheet for more information.**

Good, I get my Strength back. Strength had been the bottleneck that made sure my third death would be permanent. Now, it would be my fourth. I consulted the sheet, added my attribute to Intellect, and invested 3 skill points in Elemental, since I was on my steady way to becoming an elementalist. I also put 3 points in Staff, Ward, and Dodge.

I opened the Phylomantic Bond screen and reviewed the new spells.

Your Phylomantic Bond with Roswitha Rolofsdottir Iron-Eye has offered you access to the following new spells: Frost Wave (1), Ice Vest (1), Summon Lesser Ice Imp (1).

In addition, since your bond with this subject is intense, you and this subject gain the following advantages: +3 Stamina, +3 Mana.

This is looking good: a summoning spell! I quickly opened each spell, perusing them with haste to get a sense of their use.

Frost Wave was a defensive spell that would cause a blast of icy air to erupt from my body to damage everyone around me. It dealt as much damage as Ice Spikes, but it could hit a lot more targets—provided I was surrounded, which was of course not the ideal situation... Ice Vest was a kind of mage armor that I could conjure up. I was happy to see it, but the correct use of the armor it conjured required the Medium Armor skill. I had no points in that skill, but the way I understood the armor mechanics, it wouldn't matter if I failed the check; the armor would still absorb damage equal to its Armor value. The only thing that would happen on a failed check was that the armor would breach—and in this case, be destroyed.

Still, a free damage soaker for 4 damage that lasts an hour...

I cast it immediately; I had an inkling it wouldn't take more than an hour before we saw some action, and my Mana would recharge before the next encounter, anyway.

The summoning spell, Summon Lesser Ice Imp, called a water elemental to my side for a minute. It got me excited; I loved playing summoners and necromancers—just hanging back and letting minions do the work. I had no idea how powerful an Ice Elemental was, but I was going to find out soon enough.

Finally, I checked my new ability:

> **Greater Phylomantic Link (Phylomancer):** Your Phylomantic Link now works both ways: if anyone with whom you share a Phylomantic Bond casts a spell with beneficial effects on themselves, you automatically share in the beneficial effect, even if the spell normally only affects a single target.

With a Priestess bonded to me, this was great; her heals and buffs would automatically affect me too.

All in all, a good haul. I gave my character sheet a once-over.

> **Oram Ludwickson (Human)**
> **Level 3 Phylomancer**
>
> **Attributes: Strength 3, Agility 5, Endurance 3, Intellect 9, Cunning 6, Power 5**
> **Resources: Stamina 12(15), Health 3, Mana 20(26), Sanity 5**
> **Skills: Dagger 2, Dodge 8, Elemental 11, Illusion 5, Intuition 2, Perception 2, Psionic 8, Staff 8, Summoning 3, Ward 8(13)**
> **Abilities: Phylomantic Bond (1/1), Phylomantic Monitor, Phylomantic Link, Greater Phylomantic Link**
> **Spells: Frost Ward (0), Ghost Touch (0), Icy Hand (0), Light (0), Fire Sprout (1), Fog (1), Freeze/Thaw (1), Frost Wave (1), Ice Spikes**

**(1), Ice Vest (1), Summon Lesser Ice Imp (1),
Trackless Step (1)
Equipment: Pyromancer's Staff (Common),
Shaman Charm, Dagger (Common), 2
Shortbows (Shoddy), 2 Quivers with Arrows
XP/XP needed until next level: 2,200/4,000**

Satisfied, I nodded at Roswitha. "All done," I said. "Let's go kick some ass."

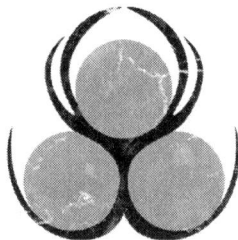

CHAPTER 7

A furious roar shook the cavernous hallway. The excited chirping and snarling of what sounded like a dozen Fauns followed in its wake. For a moment, I hesitated, and my hesitation resonated with my stalwart Roswitha through our deep link.

But then, the image of Anuina's perfect face dawned in my mind, and the thought of her being subjected to some brutish Ogre was too much.

I set my jaw and felt Roswitha's resolve strengthen with mine. She looked at me once over her shoulder, and then we were off.

I followed her closely, her beautiful and familiar form a beacon in the darkness, as the roaring ahead deepened. Lights flickered in the distance: the irregular orange and yellow glare of torches. We headed toward it at full speed even as silhouettes moved in the distance.

We came to clash in a large cavern. There were ten Fauns, each armed with a spear and a small shield—a miniature and poorly crafted replica of what Roswitha wielded.

Faun Warrior
Level 2
Stamina: 12, Health: 4, Mana: 9, Sanity: 3

Towering over them all, taking a position in the back, was a large and heavy humanoid built entirely of fat and muscle. From the folds of fat rose two heads, each with beady little eyes and mighty tusks that protruded from a broad mouth. However, one head seemed dumb, giving us a mean glare that told me it would charge at us as soon as it saw a chance. The other head seemed more malicious and intelligent; it studied the intruders in its lair with cruel interest. Its eyes lingered on Roswitha's fit physique, and I did not like the degenerate lust that clouded that glare.

Athagort Bone-Mangler (Two-Headed Ogre)
Level 5 (Boss)
Stamina: 48, Health: 8, Mana: 30(40), Sanity: 5

Hmmm… he's looking a bit strong.

With a bellow, Athagort sent his minions after us, and the horde of Fauns came cackling and chattering, brandishing their spears as the fires of hatred burned in their black eyes. As they came at us, Roswitha touched the talismans of her gods around her neck and muttered a brief prayer.

You are under the effect of a Shield of Faith spell. For 1 Round, Shield of Faith absorbs 10 Physical damage from any or multiple sources.

Awesome… my improved Phylomantic Link is in effect.

The Fauns clashed with us. Four ran past Roswitha toward me—even though I had halted my charge—and attacked me. I raised my staff and parried the first three attempts without too much trouble. However, the third one broke through, but the 6 damage it dealt left my Shield of Faith intact. Although the parrying had cost me 4 Stamina, I was pretty surprised to see that that was all.

I guess these Fauns are becoming small fry to us.

However, a quick glance at Roswitha showed me she had borne the brunt of the attack. She had deflected the Fauns' relentless attacks with her shield, and the thing was really coming apart. Although she wasn't wounded, she was already panting heavily from having to deal with six poking, murderous Fauns.

From the rear of the enemy line, Athagort bellowed a laugh, then drew some unholy symbol with his finger, and a ray of darkness came at me. I braced my sharpened mind, hoping to repel his attack.

Ward Check result: (67 + 5 Power + 13 Ward =) 85 versus opponent's 57.

Dark power tugged at my spiritual energy, as if it was trying to siphon it away from me. However, I used my considerable mental strength to keep those tendrils at bay and—although the effort cost me 1 Mana—I was strong enough to defend myself.

The confused and angry expression on Athagort's smarter face was more than worth it. I smirked at him, then drew a symbol of power in the air and spoke my words of power, and a mighty blast of icy air rolled forth as I cast my Frost Wave spell.

Elemental Check result: (70 + 6 Cunning + 11 Elemental =) 87 versus opponent's 21, 26, 71, and 24.

Fuck... I'm on a roll.

You deal 10 Physical damage (water) to all targets!

The Fauns shrieked as they ducked behind their shields. However, none of the flimsy things could withstand my arcane power, and the sound of those shields splintering under my terrible frost was like music to me. Ahead of me, Roswitha swung her axe, smashing a Faun through its shield and making it stagger, but he still stood and snarled viciously at her.

The counteroffensive was terrible. Roswitha cast another Shield of Faith before the Fauns began cruelly jabbing at her, forcing her to ball up behind her shield as she sought to parry them all. She was only partially successful; the last attack splintered her shield and pierced through her Shield of Faith. I saw her Stamina go all the way down to 4.

But before I could worry too much about her, the Fauns began attacking me.

I was breaking a sweat now as I brought up my staff to parry their vicious jabs. It began good as I butted one attack aside, then graciously spun my staff to feign at another Faun, forcing him to jump back and cease his attack. The next two were worse: one jab shot under my parry attempt and struck my Shield of Faith, dealing 6 damage. I had lost my balance, and the next attack connected just as easily, dealing another 6 damage. The Shield of Faith shattered, and the rest passed through to my Ice Vest.

> **Medium Armor Check result (untrained): (2 + 3 Endurance =) 5 versus opponent's 52.**

> **You have unlocked the Medium Armor skill! Congratulations, you may now invest in it upon gaining a level.**

Yeah...

The Ice Vest shattered, but luckily not before stopping the remaining 2 damage. I was now down to 7 Stamina, and things were looking bleak. Athagort rumbled a victory cry from the back, then muttered some foul words as he drew an unholy sigil in the air.

> **You have been targeted with a curse. You may defend against curses with either the Ward skill or the Dodge skill. Parrying and blocking is not effective against curses.**

I braced myself mentally, ready to fight the ripping and flaying energies that Athagort shot my way.

> **Ward Check result: (17 + 5 Power + 13 Ward =) 35 versus opponent's 82.**

This time, Athagort's dark powers made their way into my mind. A sudden pain wracked me, and from Roswitha's whimpering, I could tell she suffered the same effect.

You are under the effect of a Bane spell. For 1 Round, you suffer a -50 penalty to all Checks.

Damn, that is no minor effect. A moment later, Roswitha cast a healing spell.

You are under the effect of a Reinvigorate spell. You have restored 7 Stamina.

I was back up to 14. *Smart, you don't have to make a Check for those.* Following her example, I used my Summon Lesser Ice Imp, splashing some water in the air. I willed it into existence next to her, hoping it could give some succor—or distraction.

With Athagort's curse fading away, the Fauns renewed their attacks. Roswitha cast another Shield of Faith as the cruel torture of jabbing spears began anew. She parried as well as she could, but without her shield she was at a disadvantage. Three attacks got through, but her sturdy chain shirt turned those, even though she bruised underneath; a couple of iron rings flew from her armor and clattered away on the cave floor.

When the Fauns turned to me, I repeated my trick, trying—a little more desperate now—to butt the jabbing spears out of my way. However, I only succeeded once, and the first two cruel pokes did 5 damage each, shattering my Shield of faith. The third one did 6 damage, and I stumbled back from it, suffering my Stamina to wear down to 4. Almost immediately, Athagort's malicious energy focused on me, and I strengthened my mind to ward myself.

Ward Check result: (42 + 5 Power + 13 Ward =) 60 versus opponent's 71.

You receive 9 Mental damage (dark)!

Athagort's dark tendrils sapped at my mind, destroying my mental fortitude. It was akin to a sudden light depression—a sense of dread that came from no clear origin. A desire to turn tail stirred in me; I wanted to run somewhere to curl up in the dark and cry. *He is eating away at my precious Mana!* His attack had brought it down to 12. *We need to turn this around.*

I gave my Elemental the command to attack one of the Fauns that was harrying Roswitha, even as she cast another healing spell, healing us both for 6. Then, I said my words of power, hoping to rip the tide of Fauns gathered around me apart with another Frost Wave. This time, the scampering cowards were forced to dodge, wasting their Action and putting them on the defensive.

Elemental Check result: (69 + 6 Cunning + 11 Elemental =) 86 versus opponent's 80, 79, 41, and 81.

You deal 11 Physical damage (water) to all targets!

I felt like a god as the shrieking, clawing beasts paled before me, their corpses stiffening even as they fell, snot frozen as it dripped from their flat, broad noses.

Fuck yes.

But pride cometh before the fall. I did not allow myself to gloat, instead focusing on the battlefield as it unfolded before me. Athagort was none too pleased with my action. He roared, whipping his Fauns into a frenzy. Lucky for Roswitha, my Elemental distracted two of her four attackers, and together they pummeled the little beastie into submission, making it break into a hundred shards of melting ice.

Admittedly, the elemental was weak, but it had relieved Roswitha somewhat. The remaining four attacks she parried, although she was forced to turn one with her chain shirt.

Things are looking better. If I can position myself just right, I might get a couple of Fauns with my Ice Spikes spell, and that will relieve—

"Rooooarrrrgh!" Athagort rumbled as he stepped forward. "This ends here and now!" the smarter-looking head screamed.

"Uh-huh, yeah it does, yeah," the dumb head added, drool spilling from the corner of its mouth.

Brandishing a spiked club the size of a small tree, the Two-Headed Ogre charged forward…

***

Athagort came at us with a furious battle cry. I had reckoned him to be slow because of his size and fat, but he made amazing speed, much like a bull charging. He went straight for Roswitha, and I knew his charge came from some ability I was unfamiliar with when he broke through his own band of Fauns, knocking them aside, making their poorly wrought shields splinter as they sought to defend their frail bodies.

A flash later, he was upon Roswitha. With a swift motion, she cast her Shield of Faith, and her limber body readied itself as she sought to parry his strike. She sidestepped, and the dumb head uttered a confounded "huh?". Unfortunately, the smart head saw through her move, corrected the course of the cruel club, and struck her full in the abdomen.

Oh fuck...

She didn't make a sound as the club smashed into her, picked her up, and flung her five meters back. Her axe clattered to the floor beside her, and the dim torchlight gleamed on tiny rings from her chainshirt as they went flying. She landed in a heap, motionless.

Oh fuck, oh fuck, oh fuck.

A satisfied grin on his face, Athagort's smart head gave a nod, then turned to me.

Rage built up inside me, but I kept my head cool.

Focus on the minions or their combined attacks will drain all your Stamina.

With a curt thrust of my hand, I fired my Ice Spikes at the three Fauns who still had shields left. One dodged, but the others lost their shields and suffered some damage to boot. Roswitha had already wounded one of them, and that one went down with a shriek, body freezing even as it hit the cold stone floor.

Then, it was my turn to be pummeled; the three Fauns who had not used their Action to dodge came at me with fell shrieks, raising their spears to impale me. I readied my staff, took a deep breath, then began parrying their attacks. The first two Fauns were overzealous, and I easily butted their spears away, causing the crude iron tips to scrape the rock floor. The last, however, was a little cleverer and feigned, then struck low, and I had to hop back with little grace to avoid his attack.

You receive 5 Physical damage (piercing)!

With the Stamina cost from parrying, I was down to 2. Lucky for me, Athagort stood still, gloating over Roswitha. There was a mean and dirty glare in his eyes as they roved over her prostrate form.

Filthy fucker...

With a furious howl, I slammed down on the floor with the butt of my staff and spoke a word of power. Two of the Fauns jumped back from the effect of my Frost Wave, but a third one failed, and the 11 damage I dealt was enough to cause him to topple, blood freezing in his veins. However, this spell brought me down to 2 Mana. I would either need to drink my potion or begin casting my Sanity away. The latter wasn't really an option.

My spellcasting made Athagort look up from his dark contemplations with a disturbed frown. However, just as he stirred, so did Roswitha.

With a quick leap, she was on her feet. By the way she moved, I could tell she was hurt, and a quick look taught me she had only 2 Health left but had recovered 8 Stamina. With a shriek like a fury from hell, she attacked Athagort, striking him through his folds of fat. Athagort wore no armor, and he took 9 damage, adding the 2 Stamina from his parry attempt. The Ogre cried with bestial fury even as he raised his club for another attack.

At his master's bellowing, the only Faun with an Action left charged Roswitha. Straining through her injury, Roswitha turned the Ogre's club with a deft swing of her chipped axe and a quick duck, then turned the Faun's vicious little spear on the backswing. My heart went out to her as I saw her fight on like this, lips bloody, clutching what was no doubt a broken rib.

She is a goddess if I ever saw one.

My Action was less heroic. Hand trembling, I pulled a small earthenware flask from my belt, popped off the stopper, and drank the liquid within. It was salty with a faint hint of metal, and I had trouble gulping it all down.

You restore 12 Stamina.

Wow, the maximum. Sometimes you need a little luck.

Ahead, Roswitha opened her attack on Athagort again, swinging her axe with impressive effect. He was a meaty one, easy to hit, and his attempts at parrying were clumsy. Her strike made him stumble, and his fat chest already heaved with every breath. He was at 24 Stamina—halfway down.

With a roar, he raised himself and counterattacked Roswitha. Again, she parried his attack with a quick swing from her axe and an agile bound back. However, the Faun came up and stuck at her, and her response came too late to swat his spear away. Her chain shirt—already battered—suffered as it turned the attack.

I only had time to worry about her for a moment; the three Fauns that surrounded me opened their attacks, stabbing and jabbing as they shrieked and bounced. One of them bypassed my tired and ill-fated attempt at parrying, shoving me with the butt of his spear. I felt sore and numb where he'd struck, and for a moment I wanted to turn and run. They had brought me down to 6 Stamina again.

I gritted my teeth, drawing strength from Roswitha's bravery in her enduring struggle, and used my Icy Hand spell on one of the Fauns. It yelped and jumped back, using its Action but steering clear of harm.

Fuck... I am not going to last.

Roswitha was luckier. With a quick lash, she dispatched of the Faun that had been harrying her. Her axe took him square on the jaw, and the creature gave a muffled shriek as he collapsed, his brown face a red ruin. She could now focus on Athagort, who changed his approach and focused his foul magical energies on her. She braced herself, strengthening her mind, and for all I knew she resisted him. Then, at a bellow from his master, one of my Fauns headed over to attack Roswitha, and she only just turned his spear with her battered and bloody axe.

The only Faun that still had an Action left attacked me, but it was a poor and clumsy attempt that I easily butted away, swiftly using my last Mana to follow up with another Icy Hand. This time, my spell struck true, and I reduced the Faun to 1 Health with 15 damage—the maximum.

But that was my last… With 0 Mana, my mind was totally empty; I would have been unable to add one and one together if anyone in the cavern had been inclined to sit me down for some maths. In the shimmering torchlight ahead, Roswitha's axe gleamed red with blood. She focused her efforts on the Faun and with skill brought it down; he fell into a bloody heap at her feet as she stood there panting— near death: she was at 1 Stamina and 2 Health.

This is it…

However, there was hesitation in the eyes of the Ogre's smart head. He had only two minions left, and one was heavily wounded. He took a step back, raised his fat arms, and sang an incantation that came across as remarkably sophisticated for such a base creature.

Above Athagort's head, a rift opened, and through it I felt the sudden intrusion and heavy weight of a wholly black eye watching us. *"Tovatar ar-Run Khas Khal-Had!"* the Ogre sang, his voice pleading. The Fauns dropped their efforts at killing us, instead yelping and shrieking as if they were being whipped.

Something foul opened—something that did not only wish to kill us; it wished to *consume* us.

"Kill him!" I cried at Roswitha. "He is summoning something." My eyes feverish on the rift that widened over Athagort, I ripped my last flask from my belt and downed the vile, cloyingly sweet liquid.

You restore 6 Mana.

Roswitha struck hard, and the Ogre made no attempt to parry her attack, stumbling back before the onslaught of her fury, his Stamina reduced to 10. But the Fauns awakened at that and resumed their attacks on me. The wounded one barely lifted his spear, and I kicked him away with ease. The other one came swifter, but his panic made his action predictable, and I butted his spear away.

A strange humming began to emanate from the black rift that lowered itself over Athagort.

If it opens, we die.

I had no idea how I knew it, but I simply did. Ignoring the Fauns, I raised my hand, spoke a word of power, and let loose a mighty gust of fire at Athagort, even as Roswitha gritted her teeth, bloody foam issuing from her lips, and wielded her axe with two hands to bring the Ogre down. Athagort did not dodge or parry, and I struck him for 12 damage; Roswitha for 9.

It was enough.

Hairs on his body burning from my Fire Sprout, the Ogre reared and let loose a furious cry, curt short by Roswitha's mangled and chipped axe burying itself in the smart head, right between the eyes. There was a sputter of blood, then the great Two-Headed Ogre's eyes rolled up in his sockets and he sank to his knees, making the ground shake.

A raging hiss came from the black portal that was opening, and before it snapped shut, a dark tendril lashed out and tried to reach me. I saw madness and power in that tendril, and I knew the strength of the thing that commanded it was formidable and ancient. Then, the portal closed, cutting off the tendril, and it vanished like shadows in the light.

Roswitha sank to her knees with a sigh.

The two Fauns yipped and shrieked at their master's fall. A moment later, I froze them to death with a Frost Wave spell.

As their bodies hit the floor, I ran to Roswitha, crying her name out loud and wrapping her in my arms when I reached her.

***

When I had Roswitha in my arms, she gave me a bloody smile. "I'll live," she said, voice pained, but the spark of victory bright in her eyes.

I held her close, cradled her. "Fuck, you absolutely *rocked*," I muttered, forgetting that she probably had no idea what that meant. She held me, too—clung to me even—and for a moment the filthy, corpse-strewn cavern around us did not exist.

But our moment was fleeting.

The image of the black rift imposed itself on my mind, and I found my heart beating faster. I released myself from her embrace and looked her in her ice-blue eyes. "That rift," I said. "Do you know what it was?"

"No," she said, wincing and clutching her chest as she spoke. "I have never seen its like."

I thought for a moment, studying the corpses around us. *Anuina.*

I looked at Roswitha. Already, her Stamina and Mana were ticking back up. However, the Health loss remained. "Can you walk?" I asked.

She propped up on her elbows, wincing again. "I think so."

"I'll carry you if I have to," I said, trying hard to conjure a smile on my face.

She smiled back and shook her head. Slowly, steadily, I helped her to her feet, handing her my staff to support herself with. It took a few seconds, but she finally stood. Her breath was wheezy, and she clutched her ribs under the shattered chain shirt. She gave me a nod, and a grim, determined expression appeared on her face. "Let us find your friend," she said.

I took a deep breath. "Let's see what we can loot around here first. If we run into some kind of rear guard, I'd like to be equipped to the best of our ability."

I patted down the Faun corpses first, finding a lot of junk—bones, scraps of leather, teeth, pebbles, and other things Fauns likely held dear. However, I also found thirteen silver coins and forty-five copper ones divided among them, as well as three Healing Potions and one Mana Potion. I gave two of the Healing Potions to Roswitha and kept the other and the Mana Potion to myself. When I came upon the lifeless corpse of Athagort, I found a simple golden bracelet that he had worn as a thumb ring.

Bracelet of Mana
Level 3
Encumbrance: n/a
Description: This simple golden bracelet grants the wearer a +10 bonus to Mana.

Damn… battling Athagort might have been a bit easier if we'd had this one right away. With some reluctance, I continued my search of Athagort's body, but I found nothing of value. A few seconds later, a text box popped up.

You receive 2,100 XP.

Quest completed: Liberating the Woods. Bonus objectives (Slay at least ten Fauns; do not let Roswitha die or suffer grievous wounds) completed. Turn in your quest with Jarl Vitek Warnerson Spear-Eater for your material rewards!

You receive 900 XP.

Damn. That was a level increase for both of us… Still, I pushed the notification away and ignored the flashing icon of the knight's helmet and got up to support Roswitha. I showed her the bracelet, explained its attributes, and asked her if she needed it. She clutched her battered axe with one hand, her chest with the other, but she still managed a smile.

Gods, this woman…

"You keep it," she said. "Your magic is much more powerful than mine. We'll need to rely on it more in the future, I have no doubt." She then pointed in the direction from which Athagort and his minions had charged us. "Look," she said. "The caverns continue, and I see torchlight there."

I gave a firm nod. "Let's check it out."

***

We stalked down the cavern in file, Roswitha in the front and me in the back with my Light spell. As we neared the flickering torchlight, the fires reflect on shiny surfaces of what we guessed were metal, perhaps even gold. Despite her injury, Roswitha picked up the pace, eager to see what we might find.

As it turned out, Ogres hoarded much like Trolls did.

Athagort had made himself a throne room, decorated with tapestries he stole from traders and caravans. There was a throne carved of wood—of poor craftsmanship, but a throne nonetheless—and to its right was a pile of shimmering metal; the ill-gotten gains of the terror of the Janneskog Woods. To its left was a grislier pile of trophies: bones of all kinds, mostly human.

Or perhaps Elven...

The caves ended here, and my heart sunk despite the treasure. "She's not here," I said, my eyes fixed on the pile of bones.

Roswitha placed a hand on my shoulder and squeezed it. "I am sorry, Oram," she said. "We have done what we can."

"Fuck!" I cursed, then kicked at a rock lying on the floor. It flew through the air, then clattered to the floor, sound of its landing bouncing from wall to wall.

I have failed...

I had only known Anuina for perhaps an hour, yet the attraction I had felt to her—I understood its nature since I had bonded with Roswitha—had left an infallible impression. Her death was like a hole in my heart; an emptiness in a place that she had been supposed to fill. Somehow, Roswitha felt my loss, perhaps even shared it. She took me in a tight and loving embrace, and the sweet scent of her body and warmth of her arms gave me some comfort.

At length, I kissed her on her forehead and loosed myself from her embrace, resting my eyes on hers—big and full of sorrow for me. "Come," I said. "We shouldn't linger. Let's go through these items, see what we need, and leave. I'll guard the entrance."

Roswitha bent over the pile, rummaging through what seemed like coins, pieces of armor, and weaponry. "By the Masked One!" she exclaimed. "Look at this!"

I glanced over my shoulder to see her standing upright, holding what I could only describe as a plate bikini!

"Fuck," I muttered, studying the enticing leather bottom and imagining how it would hug Roswitha's shapely rump. A ribbon of cloth hung from it to cover her crotch, and the thought of her wearing something like that caused a stirring in my loins. The top would bring out the full round shape of her breasts by squeezing them together in their plate confinement. "That is... so very sexy," I said, although I hardly imagined it would be very protective...

"And look at its qualities..." Roswitha said, a wide grin on her face.

Light Plate of the Valkyrie (Good)
Level 4

Skill: Medium Armor
Armor: 12
Maximum Breaches: 8
Encumbrance: 2
Description: A tight-fitting set of plate-enforced garments suited for female warriors. Not only will this set of plate keep the body reasonably protected, but it will cause the jaws of friend and foe alike to drop.
Special qualities: The wearer receives a -5 penalty to the Sneak skill; +8 Stamina.

"Damn…" I muttered. "I guess you have no choice but to wear that, huh?"

She gave a wicked grin. "You would like me to?"

I shook my head. "*Like*? You would have trouble keeping me away from you!"

She gave a bold chuckle. "Good!" Then she turned around, teasing me with a wiggle of her luscious rump, and continued investigating the pile. She also found a good wooden shield to serve as a replacement for her own battered one, and a sword that made her eyes sparkle. When I studied the stats, I understood why.

Bastard Sword of Flame (Good)
Level 4
Skill: Sword
Damage (one-handed): 1-10 + Strength Physical damage (slashing) + 1-6 Physical damage (fire)
Damage (two-handed): 2-20 + Strength Physical damage (slashing) + 1-6 Physical damage (fire)

Encumbrance: 1
Description: This finely wrought sword is inlaid with golden patterns depicting flames. When swung, it radiates a heat to scald the wielder's enemies. This blade may be wielded in either one or two hands.
Special qualities: This weapon deals an additional 1-6 Physical damage (fire).

Using it would mean she'd have to invest some points in the Sword skill, but she didn't seem to care about that. She looked admiringly at the weapon, then cut the air with it. The flame carvings on the blade lit up, and heat devils followed in its wake. All in all, it looked fucking awesome, and I couldn't wait to see her in action with it.

In addition, there was a close-fitting suit of leather armor, obviously made for women as it had a split down the middle and was sculpted to fit a set of large, delicious breasts. Its stats were impressive too.

Huntress Skin (Good)
Level 4
Skill: Light Armor
Armor: 8
Maximum Breaches: 6
Encumbrance: 1
Description: A close-fitting set of leather armor that is often worn by Elven huntresses. It is as enticing as it is effective.
Special qualities: +8 Stamina; +2 Cunning

Neither of us wore leather armor, but I placed the set in my Vault. Other than that, we found two golden coins, twenty-one silver ones, and one hundred thirty-four copper ones. As I placed the coins in my Vault with the others, I gave Roswitha a nod. I had been excited about the loot—even though none of it was a good fit for me—but now my sense of loss for not finding Anuina mounted again.

As Roswitha made her way to the exit, I gave the cavern one last look, letting my doleful eyes rest on the pile of bones for a few seconds.

Farewell... I'm sorry that I failed you. I wish—

My ears perked when I heard a muffled sound. I raised a hand to halt Roswitha, then listened again.

Perception Check result: (44 + 6 Cunning + 2 Perception =) 52.

For a moment, all I heard was the soft drop of water somewhere, but then there was that muffled sound again. Definitely not a natural sound. "I hear something," I said.

Roswitha frowned at me. "Are you sure?"

I gave a firm nod. "Let's turn this place upside down."

***

It took us under half an hour to discover that one of the tapestries was fastened in place and hid a low passageway from view.

Heart beating in my chest, I cast my Light spell on my staff and—Roswitha right behind me—ventured in. Soon enough, I realized the sounds I had heard were muffled cries.

I crept faster and faster down the passageway, unable to contain my deepest, most sincere wish that I would find her.

And find her I did.

She lay curled up into a ball behind a fence, gagged and with hands and feet bound like she was cattle. Her dazzling body had been streaked with dirt, clothes torn where the Fauns had pawed and poked at her. One of her big, ivory breasts had spilled out of the scraps that remained of her black-dyed leather armor, but apart from a few scratches, that seemed to be the only damage she had suffered.

Her beautiful, piercing emerald eyes—with a touch of despair and fear to them—lit up when they found me, and a muffled cry rose from her throat. The tears in the corner of her eyes showed me she was as happy to see me as I was to see her.

"Anuina," I whispered, and I shot forward, kicking down the flimsy, Faun-made fence as I came. Roswitha regarded us warmly, then turned to guarding the passageway even as I slipped my knife from my belt and undid Anuina's bindings. When I removed her gag, she took a deep breath.

"Oram Ludwickson," she said, an edge of despair to her voice. "You came for me! I had thought you dead!"

"And I, you," I said in one breath as I cut the last of her bindings. "I—"

Finally loose, she was in my arms in a second, wrapping hers around my neck and hugging me close.

She began sobbing even as her smooth and supple body lay in my arms, safe under the protection of my arcane might and Roswitha's vicious blade. My body stirred as her soft, smooth curves pushed against me. I deeply needed to bind Anuina to my life as I had Roswitha, who stirred behind us, her breath coming faster as she shared my need to expand the bond.

But I lacked the power still to bind another. Also, I knew only one way to bind this woman to me, and even though her hot body pushed against me in a way that implied more than just consolation, it would be foolish to explore our mutual desires here. Who knew what still lived in these halls?

But I couldn't just stop. I placed my hand on the nape of her neck and drew her back. Her large, green eyes rested on me and her full, red lips parted slightly. Her breathing turned heavy, almost a soft moaning. I lost myself for a moment in the lusting emerald fields of her eyes, then I stooped to kiss her. With no hesitation, I placed my mouth on hers, my tongue pushing past her soft lips. A whimper of delight escaped her, and I learned the true bliss of kissing an Elf. It was like a drink of the clearest water, a whiff of the purest and cleanest field of flowers; I could lose myself forever in a woman like this. She pushed against me urgently, and it took every ounce of willpower to pull away.

I rested my eyes on hers—smoky and thick with lust. "We must go," I said, voice hoarse. "The danger has not yet passed; someone or something else may still come."

Her eyes cleared a little, and she gave a solemn nod. "You are right," she whispered.

I rose, but the moment lingered; I felt Roswitha's raw lust through our bond, and Anuina's was plain to see on her pretty Elven face.

To break the moment, I made swift introductions. "Roswitha, this is my friend, Anuina," I said to Roswitha, then I turned to Anuina. "Anuina, this is my friend and lover, Roswitha."

The beautiful Elf seemed disappointed. "Ah," she said. "Your lover."

Roswitha smiled. "Fear not, She-Elf," she said. "I am neither a jealous friend... nor a jealous lover."

Anuina's beautiful pale cheeks turned red, and she cast her eyes to the ground. I chuckled at this display of modesty, having always expected Elves to be comfortable with their sexuality—what other effect could living for hundreds of years as a deathly beautiful creature have? Still, I spared her a quip, even though Roswitha chuckled at Anuina's bashfulness, and helped the Elf to her feet. "Come," I said. "We will speak more once we are safe."

Her blush faded, and she gave a firm nod before following Roswitha and me out of the Vaskhule Caves and into the sunlight.

Quest completed: Athagort Bone-Mangler. Bonus objectives (Slay at least ten Fauns; do not let Anuina die or suffer grievous wounds) completed.

You receive 900 XP.

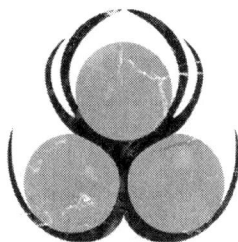

CHAPTER 8

You have advanced to level 4. As a reward, you may increase one of your attributes by 1. In addition, you receive 12 skill points to distribute among your skills as you see fit. Your Stamina and Mana also increase by a number equal to your Endurance and Power, respectively. Finally, the following randomly selected attribute that was reduced due to a death will be restored by 1: Power.

Since you are a Phylomancer, you also gain the following abilities: +1 Phylomantic Bond slot, Meta-Magic (Instant Spell; Overcharge Spell).

Please note that Phylomancers only gain new spells through their Phylomantic Bond; consult your character sheet for more information.

The smoky scent of the campfire put me at ease, and my appetite had been sated with hardtack and water—no luxurious fare, but it had tasted like a feast. It was time to do some much-needed upgrading.

I opened my character sheet and began working. I placed my attribute point in Intellect again, happy for having recovered my lost Power; its return netted me 5 Mana.

As for the skills, I invested 5 points in Medium Armor. If I was ever going to get some use out of protective spells like Ice Vest, I needed to get a lot better at it. Since it combined with Endurance—not one of my better attributes—I wanted to push quite a few points in. The remaining 7 points all went into Elemental; I was tired of my spells missing. I needed to increase my damage output, and that started by hitting my enemies more often.

When I saw that I had another Phylomantic Bond available, I felt a flutter of excitement. It meant there was a place now for Anuina. Still, I expected she had gone through a lot; I did not want to push her.

I focused on my level-up instead and reviewed my new abilities.

Meta-Magic (Instant Spell) (Phylomancer): By spending 4 additional Mana, you may reduce the casting time of a spell that normally costs 1 Action to cast to Instant. Please note that you can only affect one spell in such a way per Round and that the spell cannot be cast as an Interruption.

Oh, this is a great one! During all my previous battles, time had been the bottleneck. While the cost of this ability was substantial, it was extremely useful, especially in a bind.

> **Meta-Magic (Overcharge Spell) (Phylomancer): By spending 4 additional Mana, you maximize the damage output of a single spell.**

I already had visions of using both Meta-Magic abilities in the same Action. I could cast two overcharged spells at once. *God damn...* Culling my excitement, I opened my Phylomantic Bond with Roswitha to review any changes.

> **Your Phylomantic Bond with Roswitha Rolofsdottir Iron-Eye has offered you access to the following new spells: Create/Destroy Water (2), Frostbite (2), Iceplane (2), Windwalk (2), Windward (2).**
> **In addition, since your bond with this subject is intense, you and this subject gain the following advantages: +4 Stamina, +4 Mana.**

Oh yes, level 2 spells.

I was almost physically *hungering* for them. I focused on each, at the same time realizing I could now upgrade my level 1 spells to greater effect!

Create/Destroy Water allowed me to conjure about five gallons of water or destroy the same. Not riveting, but it could be useful in survival situations or when I needed water to freeze with my Freeze/Thaw spell. Frostbite was more interesting, however. At 2-12 + Intellect damage, it was a serious damage dealer. With my new Meta-Magic I could cast two of these bad boys and overcharge them to net 44 damage in one Action at the cost of 22 Mana... I had yet to see a sword to rival that.

Iceplane didn't seem like much at first, but I quickly realized it was area denial heaven! I decided to study its stats meticulously; I had an inkling I might be using it a lot...

Iceplane
Spell level: 2
Mana: 5
Skill: Elemental
Element: Water
Description: From a splash of water, an arcane sigil, and an ancient incantation, you create a slippery plane of ice with a 10-meter radius within a 50-meter range range. Creatures attempting to traverse the plane of ice must succeed at an Acrobatics Check that equals or defeats the result of your Elemental Check or be unable to move and waste their Action.

I grinned. Area denial was an important part of any battle, and this spell would certainly keep spear-poking Fauns away from me.

Windwalk was next; it was a simple teleportation spell that allowed me to teleport to any location within a short range, so long as I could see where I was teleporting. At 5, the Mana cost was a little high, but I expected I'd be using it a lot more in the future when my Mana pool increased. Windward, a defensive spell, was looking to be a lot more useful, so I studied it with care.

Windward
Spell level: 2
Mana: 5
Skill: Elemental
Element: Air
Description: You draw an arcane symbol in the air and speak the words that command the elements to envelop yourself in fierce gusts and gales of wind. Anyone attempting to target you with an effect that deals Physical damage suffers a penalty to their Check equal to your Elemental Check result. However, if you do not respond to an attack, it will still strike true.

This one was especially useful if you considered the Phylomantic Link. We'd still have to respond to the attack by parrying or dodging, but this spell would assure that the attempt at defense was most likely going to be successful. Feeling good about my latest acquisitions, I gave my character sheet a final review.

Oram Ludwickson (Human)
Level 4 Phylomancer

Attributes: Strength 3, Agility 5, Endurance 3, Intellect 10, Cunning 6, Power 6
Resources: Stamina 15(19), Health 3, Mana 30(47), Sanity 6
Skills: Dagger 2, Dodge 8, Elemental 18, Illusion 5, Intuition 2, Medium Armor 5, Perception 2, Psionic 8, Staff 8, Summoning 3, Ward 8(13)

Abilities: Phylomantic Bond (1/2), Phylomantic Monitor, Phylomantic Link, Greater Phylomantic Link, Meta-Magic (Instant Spell, Overcharge Spell)

Spells: Frost Ward (0), Ghost Touch (0), Icy Hand (0), Light (0), Fire Sprout (1), Fog (1), Freeze/Thaw (1), Frost Wave (1), Ice Spikes (1), Ice Vest (1), Summon Lesser Ice Imp (1), Trackless Step (1), Create/Destroy Water (2), Frostbite (2), Iceplane (2), Windwalk (2), Windward (2)

Equipment: Pyromancer's Staff, Dagger (Common), Shaman Charm, Bracelet of Mana, 2 Shortbows (Shoddy), 2 Quivers with Arrows

XP/XP needed until next level: 6,100/8,000

Okay, looking good...

***

With a nod, I shifted focus from the pop-ups and my sheet, and they faded away.

We sat around the campfire in a glade. Anuina was nursing Roswitha's wounds, and as she bent over to reach for a poultice she had made, I enjoyed the view of her perfect rump, wrapped tight in the Huntress Skin that Roswitha and I had gifted her.

I leaned back on my elbows and enjoyed the view, and it took me a few seconds before I realized Roswitha was watching me as I stared at the shapely Elf's round bum.

There was mischief in her icy eyes, and she tutted at me even as Anuina continued tending to her wounds.

I grinned back. *You lucky bastard...*

I had not thought much of my real life for the past two days in Aerda—there simply hadn't been much time. But now, as the warmth of the fire chased the night chill from my bones, I wondered if I would ever *want* to return, even if I could.

In this world, I had in two days become so much more than what I could ever have been outside of it. And I was on my way to nurture my arcane might and grow stronger still. And even a few failures along the way were tolerable. Of course, death was no cakewalk, but it wasn't the end either—at least, so long as I kept the numbers under firm control and made sure my stats wouldn't drop to 1.

The options in this world were just so much richer; the rules that much more clear.

I pushed away my musings and focused on the beautiful women in my company, how the soft light of the fire made its shadow-play on their soft and alluring curves. The fire crackled and popped, its smoky scent mingled with the crisp aroma of the pine forest, and I nibbled on my trail rations—hard tack and dry biscuits—missing a cold one.

After a while, Anuina fixed her work on Roswitha; she had wrapped my brave Priestess's beautiful chest in linen bandages and made her wear nothing but her cloak; plate armor would impede the healing. When Anuina gave us a soft smile and headed off to a nearby creek to wash her hands, I found Roswitha's eyes on me.

"She is quite a treasure," Roswitha said. "I understand what made you go after her."

I nodded. "Indeed, she is," I said.

The crackling fire lulled us into a brief silence, although our eyes remained locked. Finally, I broke it. "You approve of her then?"

"To join in the bond?"

"Yes," I said. "I feel that she matches me, just as I felt with you."

It was true: the Elf's presence was like the clarion call of fate; it was even as if she had always been with me. Apart from the bond of spirits, there was a deep visceral reaction as well, a yearning—a *craving*, even—that translated itself into a stirring in her presence that made my cock rise like a weapon in its own right.

A lustful smile played on Roswitha's red lips, and she raised an eyebrow. "Her joining us would delight me."

I smirked. "Good."

Anuina's return cut our conversation short. I drank in her sensual shape—the long and limber legs, the ivory strip of skin that her armor left open, from the rise of her collarbone to the enchanting region of her belly button. Her lips curled up in a knowing smile.

I committed the image of her perfect face and lustrous golden locks to memory, even as the desire to explore the most sinful of pleasures with her mastered me.

I took a deep breath, trying to focus my mind. "Come," I said, gesturing at the fire. "Sit and tell us what happened."

She sat cross-legged, close to Roswitha, and the flames reflected in her unearthly beautiful emerald eyes. "All I know is that I awoke bound in the Fauns' pen. They seemed amused by my presence and took to taunting and tormenting me, poking me with the butts of their spears. Some even seemed... lustful. But I was certain they were under orders not to truly hurt me, for an elder Faun with strange charms and a staff checked in on us regularly and would reprimand and berate the wardens."

I nodded and exchanged a look with Roswitha. "The Faun Shaman," I said. "We slew him first."

"Good," she said. "Although I am certain he stopped his filthy kin from doing worse to me, I do not rue his demise."

I could only imagine her ordeal... and the thought of Fauns and their black-lusted paws on her pure and immaculate delight of a body infuriated me.

"I do not know how long I lay there," Anuina continued, eyes still full of the horror of the Vaskhule Caves, "but they came to get me after some time. There were four of them, and they lifted me up like I was some swine or game they had hunted, pawing and pinching me as they carried me into the throne room where that vile two-headed beast sat, throne straining under his decadent, fat body."

She was silent for a moment as she reflected on that horrid moment, then looked up at me, her green eyes large and with an intelligent sparkle to them. "Of course, you slew him, so you too must have seen that one of its heads was cunning, if perhaps not smart, while the other might as well have belonged to a witless worm."

I chuckled. *She has a way with words.* "We had noticed," I said.

"Well," she said. "The cunning one's lips curled in a cruel smile as it studied me, and for a moment I feared that it would feast on me in depraved ways. It is known that these foul, misshapen offspring of Giants lust after the fairer sex of both Humans and Elves, and by my honor as a Willowsdaughter, I would have preferred death over being an Ogre's toy to be befouled and discarded. However, the

Ogre did no such thing. He gloated over me, then…" her voice trailed off, eyes again on the fire.

I stirred, looked at Roswitha, who had narrowed her eyes and was leaning forward. "Then what?" I asked.

She inhaled, fair chest rising, then blew out in a heavy sigh. "I suppose I owe you the truth. You have rescued me after all."

I sat back, reclining by the fire. "What you tell us is up to you," I said. "We saved you because we *wanted* to, because we would not leave you to whatever fate Athagort had planned for you, not to enforce our will on you or make you reveal your secrets against your own wishes."

Roswitha nodded. "You owe us nothing," she added. "All that we did, we did out of desire to lend aid. In the Snowlands we say that Men must either lend succor freely or bear the guilt of their omissions."

Anuina smiled. "Then your folk are wise," she said. "Unwarranted are the claims by many in the Southlands that the Northmen are barbarians."

Roswitha laughed—a cold and icy tinkle. "Unfortunately, *some* are."

Anuina's mouth quirked into a warm, dimpled smile. "Well, I will tell you of my own volition. It is clear to me you are good people, and I choose to trust you."

A happy stirring in my stomach told me this was proceeding as it should.

"Oram Ludwickson," Anuina said, turning to me. "When first we met, I told you of my sister, did I not?"

I nodded once. "I remember."

"Athagort did *not* kill her," she said. "He wanted me to tell him where she was."

I raised an eyebrow. "Something tells me she must be important."

She pressed her lips into a thin line, gazing at the fire once more, then nodded. "My sister and I, we are daughters of the Warden of the Willow of Liandrenn," she said.

Across from me, at the other side of the fire, Roswitha's pale eyes widened. *Well, she obviously knows what that means…*

"The Willow of Liandrenn?" I asked.

Anuina frowned at me, apparently incredulous that I did not know what she was talking about, but Roswitha swiftly intervened. "Oram Ludwickson is one of the new Awakened," she said. "Come to life with few memories; you must forgive him if he seems… *clueless*." She then smiled at me. "The Willows of Elvendom are ancient and powerful conduits that bind the magic of the Elves to the lands."

"I see," I said, not really seeing.

Anuina offered me a disarming smile. "I had an inkling something was unique about you when I first met you," she said. "You seemed hardly the merchant's apprentice…"

I smiled at the memory, as did she. It was only a few days ago, but they felt like a lifetime. And to be truthful, I had come fresh out of another life then.

"But Roswitha is right," she said. "Although it is altogether somewhat more complicated than that. The magic of our world is bound to certain elements—there are many: earth, life, death, fire, force, darkness, light: to name a few—and each element requires conduits to allow us to tap into them. The different folk and beasts use different conduits. My kin use the Willows, each of which is mastered by a great and powerful spirit."

"My kin tap into the ice mountains," Roswitha said. "The Glaciers of the Snowlands that span our home."

I nodded, wondering what *I* tapped into... magic sounded a little less appealing if it depended on an external source.

"The spirit that guards the Willow of Liandrenn is my and my sister's father," Anuina said. "Only rarely do such spirits sire children. And in such cases, they often care little for their offspring, leaving them to fend for themselves, for the spirits of Elven magic are fickle and quick to abandon what they begun.

"But our father is different from the others: wizened by years and of iron will, he is more akin to us Elves than to the Fae that he calls kindred since his ascension to spirithood. He loves us both dearly, and that is why we are his weakness." She looked wistfully at the fire. "And whoever can exploit such a weakness might gain control over the magic well he guards."

I understood now; control over the Fae spirit's daughters was leverage. "But what would an Ogre want from your father? And what would it do with control over a wellspring of magic?"

Anuina shook her head. "Not Athagort... he had a mind of small suffering and petty cruelties; he would never have had the presence of mind to come up with a plan to wrest control of the Willow of Liandrenn from our father."

"That means..."

She nodded. "I fear there is a more sinister power at work."

The tranquility of the fire was gone now, and the crisp scent of the pines seemed to no longer refresh my lungs as it had a mere moment ago. We sat in silence, all three of us brooding as we watched the flames struggle to keep the shadows at bay.

"The shadowy portal," I finally said.

Anuina looked up with a frown. "What do you mean?"

I looked at Roswitha. "You saw it too, right?"

She nodded, poking at the fire with a stick. "A black gateway," she said. "It sucked in the very light and left a terrible emptiness."

I looked at Anuina. "During his last moments, Athagort attempted to open a portal. We sensed a dark presence behind it, glaring at us. We were able to slay Athagort before the gate was fully open. On his death, it sealed again."

Anuina seemed terrified, her intriguing emerald eyes wide open. "A black portal, you say?"

"Yes. And what looked through it seemed to me to be a wholly black eye, full of hate and empty darkness."

She stared into the fire, her fear still leeching the color from her cheeks and the life from her eyes.

"Do *you* know what it was we saw?" I asked.

She shivered. "Did the Ogre offer any incantation? Did he speak words?"

I remembered them, clear as day despite their sounding alien to me, and nodded. "Athagort spoke something like the following words, *'Tovatar ar-Run Khas Khal-Had!'*"

Anuina's breath caught, as if the words were some spell to constrict her and cut the air from her lungs.

"Khal-Had..." she muttered.

***

"Khal-Had was once the Warden of the Willow, as my father is today," Anuina said.

It had taken her some time to process the information I had given her, and when she resumed her story, her voice had shrunk. "It was in a time long before the Elves came to Aerda—a time when the lands that my kin now rule belonged to savage Beastfolk."

"Beastfolk?" I asked.

"Yes," Anuina said. "The Children of the Antlered One, God of the Beastfolk. There are many of them, but the Fauns we have already encountered are most numerous, and they have always plagued these lands. The strong Hog-Men are among them, too, as are the Wargs of the Snowlands and the Gnolls of the Southlands. However, the most cunning, vile, and brutal race among them are the Satyrs." At the mention of the name, she sneered in a way I did not expect her to.

"Those black-hearted beasts seek the destruction and enslavement of all Humans, Elves, and Dwarves," she continued. "The men they would force into labor. The women they would use for their perverted pleasure or to breed, for these fertile beasts can make any woman birth a pure-blooded Satyr."

I had encountered Satyrs in several RPGs, and they were never pleasant…

"When the Elves came to these lands, we tried to live together with the Beastfolk, but they are primal and feral and would not share. We were made to fight, and through our unity and superior arms we defeated the more numerous Beastfolk and took the Willow of Liandrenn from them and claimed it as our own.

"We brought low Khal-Had, who ruled the Beastfolk as their king, and we elevated one of our wisest and greatest Sorcerers, my father, to become the new Warden of the Willow. By all accounts of those days, two centuries ago to the day, Khal-Had was slain, his blood, bones, and flesh returned to the earth." She swallowed, a muscle jerking under her smooth cheek. "Apparently, the accounts were wrong..." She looked at me. "The eye you saw is the Eye of Khal-Had, his manifestation as a spirit, and the Beastfolk must have found a way to call upon his spirit to return. Perhaps they have provided him with a vessel—a body to possess."

A momentary silence fell between us. Anuina seemed lost in thought, absently running her palm over her cheek as she stared at the flickering flames.

"You believe this Khal-Had would use you, the Warden's daughters, to extort control of the Willow of Liandrenn from your father?" I asked.

"I do," she said. "And if he succeeds, the Beastfolk will grow in power. They were complacent, divided, and decadent when we overthrew them, but they are a terrible force if united and with set will. They are strongly attuned to the elements of darkness and earth. With a proper conduit, their Sorcerers, Witches, and Warlocks will grow formidable...

"Perhaps the united might of my kin, once rallied, may still stop them. However, they will easily overrun the kingdoms of men that have settled the lands bordering Liandrenn, for they are weak from centuries of warfare and strife."

"Then he must be stopped," Roswitha said plainly. She had brought out her sword and set a whetstone to its edge, sharpening it with long, perfect strokes.

"Roswitha is right."

Anuina looked up at us both, hopeful. "You mean that?"

I gave a firm nod. "I was Awakened with arcane might," I said. "It is only right that I use it for the defense against a dark threat." The words came easily to me. I always played the good guy, never the mercenary or villain. I even had trouble playing evil protagonists in light-hearted and humorous dungeon keeper games, and I never went the evil route in RPGs. My gaming buddies always joked that I was lawful good at heart.

But Anuina made no jokes about my will to do good.

Her face flushed, and for the first time she seemed at a loss of words. She made do with actions instead, rising limberly to her feet and walking over to me. She kneeled beside me, wrapped her slender arms around my neck, and placed a passionate kiss against my cheek.

God, the feeling of her lips... They were so plump and warm, and I yearned at once to taste more of them. She looked up at me through thick lashes, emerald eyes sparking with a desire so unchecked it sent an electric jolt down to my loins.

I could not resist.

***

A deep sigh escaped Anuina's lips as I wrapped my arms around her and pulled her close.

From across the fire, I saw Roswitha look at us with a haze in her blue eyes. I waited for a moment until she gave me a curt nod as she bit her lower lip. With Roswitha's approval, I let my heart flow over with the molten heat I felt for this incredibly hot Elf. I took her chin in my hand and turned her to face me. Her eyes were closed, lashes

129

fluttering, and her plumps lips had parted slightly, swollen and red and ready to be kissed.

When we touched, a wildfire raged in my body, setting fire to my blood and causing my cock to stand to painful attention.

She answered my lust with a craving of her own, her body eager as we kissed. Her tongue was soft and warm, almost hesitant as I let the sweet wildberry sensation of her flood my senses. By the quickening of her heartbeat and the soft, encouraging moans she let out between my fiery kisses, I knew she wanted it as much as I did—that she was as drunk on me as I was on her.

She leaned into me, her tongue wrestling with mine for control, and her sighs of pleasure grew more urgent. My hold over myself was tenuous, slipping, and my burning hands already explored her smooth back—left bare by her skimpy armor—of their own volition.

With a heavy sigh, I drew back and kissed her neck.

She moaned, voice laden with lust. "What is this power... this power that you have?"

I said nothing, my kisses blazing a red-hot path along her neck to her jaw, and up from there to her beautiful pointy ear. The taste of her skin was like honey laced with the purest and most addicting of aphrodisiacs. I needed to savor all of her—I needed my tongue to acquaint itself with the most intimate parts of her.

"Your power," she muttered again, surrendering herself to my hungry embrace.

I opened my eyes as I kissed Anuina's neck, fixing them on Roswitha. She had settled back on her elbows, peeling away the bandages Anuina had applied with such loving care but a moment ago, revealing the firm globes of her freckled breasts. Her eyes shot pure flame of lust, and her desire resonated in me as my hand slipped down, finally grabbing hold of that luscious Elven ass I had been admiring all night.

"Oram," Anuina whispered, and the pleasure of hearing my name in her voice thick with desire stirred my blood into a raging tempest. I kissed her harder, sucking on her ivory skin as I placed my other hand on her yielding butt.

"Come," I whispered, and I pulled her onto my lap.

She rose for a moment to move with me, and her full breasts hung in front of me, jiggling under that slutty armor as she moved to settle where I had directed her to sit.

When she came down, the overwhelming heat of her body connected with mine, and the lust flared within me and threatened to burn down the very house of my soul. I ran my nose down along the elegant slope of her long neck, my hand peeling away the leather that covered her shoulder. I nipped at the soft ivory flesh that my eager, trembling fingers revealed. She moaned a gentle encouragement.

A moment later, her leather vest slipped off, revealing the sculpted beauty of her chest. Her breasts were hypnotizing to me, large and round, sitting high and pert on an otherwise toned and slim chest. She was as perfectly divine and elegant as only an Elf could be—as I had always imagined. She leaned back a little, biting her lower lip and watching from under long lashes as I admired her body.

"You are perfect," I said, voice breathy under the strain of self-control. I looked up at her, a commanding fire in my eyes. "I must have you."

The words made her stir on my lap as she folded her arms behind her back. With a grunt, I raised my hands and placed them on her firm breasts, kneading them. A moment later, I lowered my head, her skin like hot velvet beneath my searching lips, and sucked a perfect, pink nipple into my mouth. She quaked on my lap, fighting a losing battle against her wanton lust.

Gently, I lowered her onto her back in the naked grass of the forest floor. She lay there, an ivory goddess with a heaving chest, the light of the two moons dancing on her, casting shadowed regions on her body my lips would soon explore.

I pulled down the skimpy leather armor that had haunted me through the night. From the corner of my eye, I saw Roswitha crawl closer to us, she herself now naked except for the skimpy bottom of her armor. Our eyes connected for a moment, sharing the intense lust and wanton desire that raged inside both of us at the prospect of extending the bond.

With a hungry tug, I pulled away Anuina's armor. The moonlight shone on her bare breasts, her toned midriff, the enticing curves of her luscious hips, and on the cute tuft of blond hair on the forbidden swell of her mons pubis.

God, her pussy is perfect. Such a pleasing flower of pink heat and glistening folds.

Anuina looked up at me, hesitation on her face. Roswitha sidled up to her, stroking her beautiful blond hair. "Let him please you," she whispered, a lock of her red hair slipping free and mingling with the Elf's golden locks as she bent forward. It was a beautiful sight: my two breathtakingly gorgeous women together, one quivering with anticipation, the other comforting and sweet.

"But I have never..." Anuina swallowed. "I have not given my flower to any man before."

The thought alone sent a powerful jolt down to my already straining cock. Carefully, I stroked her thighs, the honey-sweet aroma of her skin already coming up to me. My mouth was watering at the thought of going down on her, of plucking that precious flower and devouring it, binding it to me with a magic that would reach deep into her soul.

"There is no man worthier," Roswitha whispered. Her slender fingers ran over Anuina's cheek, and she licked her lips, eyes blazing naughtily. No doubt she recalled the intense pleasure I had given her. "And there is no man *better*," she added.

Anuina softened under those words. Hesitation drifted from her emerald eyes, and the walls of her resolve crumbled.

As she relented, I lowered my head and kissed her thighs. Her heady scent invaded me, put me in a state of urgent need to taste all of her. I knew she felt the same way, for a needy shiver passed through her.

I kissed my way across the ivory sculpture that was her body, each sample of her building up my desire to have it all. My lips left a burning trail across her hips, her quavering stomach, up to her heaving breasts. I scraped my teeth against her nipple, and then bit gently, soliciting a deep moan of pleasure that rose from her curled toes. I came up, looking into those cloudy green eyes.

"I want you to ask me," I said, voice firm, even as my deft fingers brushed her silky thigh.

"Ask him," Roswitha echoed, stroking those locks of molten gold.

A whimper escaped Anuina's quaking lips, and then she spoke, voice laden with desire. "Will you take me, Oram?" she said. "I *want* you to."

Like a wolf on his meal, I shot down, eager to devour her. Stopping at the last, I grabbed her thighs and drew her long, slender legs over my shoulder to blow a hot breath over her swollen lips and clit. She squirmed, releasing another moan, and repeated her words with an urgency to her voice that brooked no discussion.

On a deep inhale, I buried my face between her thighs, licking and sucking, exploring every red-hot inch with my tongue. She rolled beneath me, her legs clamping down on my shoulders as she tried to coax me to give her the pleasure she pined for.

An airy sigh escaped her lips as my tongue stole a fleeting taste of those plump pussy lips, and by the Gods, it was like honey melting on my tongue; the womanhood of an Elf, I found, tasted of nature's finest bounty. I had to fight for control as her spell caught hold of me, for I was eager to forestall her pleasure a little for my own enjoyment.

She moaned. "Oram—" my name on her lips like those of the gods she prayed to "—do not tease me so! I beg!"

My heart banged in my chest, and I could hear hers do the same as we achieved the sync of lovers. I traced a final light trail along her inner thighs with my scalding tongue, and then even my resistance faltered. I pressed my face to the apex of her thighs and began lapping at her, tongue flicking in and out as I slaked my thirst.

She squirmed as I gave her the pleasure she needed, and my cock burned like iron in the fire as I tasted her. She was so soft and creamy, such a decadent and luxurious delight that I felt I must be a god for having been granted the joy of her.

Delighted ripples pulsed under her ivory skin as I pleasured her, and near-wordless moans came from her lips to plead and beg me for her release. She grew weaker under me, slipping away to that dream of undiluted ecstasy as her inevitable climax simmered deep within her. Suppressing a delighted grin at my control, I sucked her clit between my lips, then gently grazed it with my teeth, my reward an arching of the back and a tightening of the legs wrapped around me. "By the Misted One," she whispered. "You're making me—aaahh…"

I pulled back, breathing softly on her pulsing clit to tease her.

She moaned, squirmed, and struggled as she fought to make me continue and give her the release she so desired. "Don't stop," she pleaded. "I need it, Oram."

With a feral snarl, I dove back on her quaking pussy and ate her out. Her cry rang out in the forest, even as Roswitha's silky but dirty words goaded her into orgasm. And here in the forest, her legs draped over my shoulders, she could only submit and relinquish control to me as I licked the glistening, swollen nub of her clit. I plucked her sweetly scented flower and drove her over the edge and into the arms of her wanton orgasm. A cry of pleasure came out of her at last. Her hips bucked wildly against my face, her entire body humming in the throes of her orgasm. I did not relent, giving her the deepest and most forbidden of pleasure as she squirmed under me on the forest floor.

When I finally pulled back, licking my lips to savor her taste, she lay there writhing and panting. Then, the emerald fire of her eyes was on me, and she sat up with the graceful speed of an Elf, pressing up against my body, her voice thrumming against my chest. "Let me ride you," she whispered.

My cock pulsed at the thought. Even before I had lowered myself fully, eyes fixed on the colorful swath of galaxy overhead, she began tugging at my tunic. Roswitha helped her, and I lay in the grass, rich as a God of the Tribunal, as four slender and loving hands unclothed me.

When I was naked, the soft grass tickling me and the night breeze a crisp caress that carried the clean scent of the forest, Roswitha helped Anuina onto my lap. Her body quivering with anticipation, the Elf watched as the more experienced redhead lovingly palmed my infallible weapon. Roswitha gave me a bold look of her icy eyes, then lowered herself. Her smooth breasts brushed against Anuina's silky skin as she wrapped her red lips firmly around my cock.

Delight from out of this earth washed over me, caused a hot rush of blood to set fire to my veins. Anuina sat close, her itching pussy not one inch away from Roswitha's eager mouth making me ready. Absently, Anuina's hands gripped her firm breasts, pulling a little at the nipples, hard like pink gemstones in the moonlight.

I kept my eyes on Anuina as Roswitha's deft and expert mouth sucked on my cock and brought my ecstatic joy closer and closer until my balls were brimming with seed that needed to be nested deep within the warm cup that Anuina would offer me. "It is time," I said as force gathered in my core.

Roswitha drew back, pupils dilated from the pleasure. Her soft hands rested on Anuina's thighs. "Come," the redhead said to the Elf. "Rise and take him inside you."

Anuina gasped at Roswitha's soft touch and obeyed without hesitation. My cock twitched and pulsed in anticipation as Anuina's body hovered over me, white in the moonlight. Roswitha's hand was like silk on my cock, and her other hand rested on Anuina's ass as she guided the Elf down.

A feather-light warmth touched the tip of my eager cock, and a deep moan of pleasure escaped my lips. Then, the euphoric touch tightened around my shaft, and the cutest of whimpers escaped Anuina as I took her, plucked her flower, and entered her.

"That's it," Roswitha said, voice soothing. "Take him inside."

But by the Gods, is she tight!

Her pussy practically sucked on my cock as she lowered her entrancing and unearthly hot body onto mine. When I was fully inside her—her deliciously wanton ass settled on me, a despair of fiery desire in her emerald eyes—I rested my eyes on her beautiful body, commanding her with my gaze, as I placed my hands on her sweeping hips.

She bit her lower lip and brought up her delicious round ass, freeing my shaft to the cool forest air, and came down again to engulf me with her red-hot wetness. Beside her, Roswitha trailed a light hand over the Elf's apple-round ass, speaking soft whispers of encouragement as she watched us play.

Once again, Anuina rose, her beautiful breasts bouncing, her long Elven ears slightly bobbing with the movement. Her cheeks had reddened, and she let out another airy sigh of lust as she slapped back down on me. I began moving with her now, and she gasped, her legs quaking as I pumped into her with a slow, deliberate thrust.

A blaze lit up in her eyes as she took me deep. She placed her hands on my chest, rose, and came down hard. The symphony of our skin slapping together pulled at the strings of my body. A moment later, eyes still burning, she sat back and began grinding delicious circles on my rock-hard cock, her juices already dripping down.

With a salacious grin, she licked a slender finger and brought it down to her clit, still swollen from the pleasure I had granted her. I grinned as she began pleasuring herself, eager to learn that she was every bit as insatiable as I had hoped she would be.

As she moved faster, my pleasure rose. When Roswitha's deft fingers slipped under her round ass and found my swollen balls, the gentle prick of her touch drove me even closer. I watched Anuina, one hand rubbing the swollen nub of her clit, the other raised to her mouth, head thrown back in the reckless abandon of wanton pleasure, and I knew she was as close as I was.

"Gods," she muttered, opening her eyes to look down at me, her gaze hazy from the pleasure.

"Do it," Roswitha said, her fingers like gentle pinpricks on my balls—so close to bursting.

I gave a grunt, grabbed hold of Anuina to stop her from moving. Her breath rushed out as I postponed her pleasure, and the words came from my mouth in the commanding tone of a master of the arcane. "I forge my bond with you, Anuina Willowsdaughter," I said. "You are mine in heart and soul as I am yours, and we are bonded by our own free will, until we part as broken and unbonded or until we go to the next world or beyond. Will you honor this bond?"

Her fiery gaze rested on me, her body bucking and straining for release. "I will," she answered without hesitation.

And I released her.

She rode me like I was her stallion, rising and falling in the moonlight and driving me to the deepest of pleasure. The wet heat of her pussy engulfed me until it was my entire world, and I felt again as if the Tribunal elevated me to their Mountain and watched with awe at the power of our untamed and wild love under the open sky—the stars and moons as our witnesses.

She rose higher, and I thrust deeper, until finally she opened her mouth to moan, to scream, to let it all out. But I shot up, enveloping her in the urgent heat of my arms, and silenced her with a fiery a kiss as I coaxed a final and fiercely urgent orgasm from her body.

As she came on my cock, a spasm shot through me, and my own ecstasy mastered me. The most ancient and purest of delights overcame me as I spurted my warm seed deep within her. She trembled under the force of it, kissing me with a passionate fire that by far outshone the campfire beside which we made love. Roswitha's soft purring urged me on, and her deft hands kneaded my balls, milking several other hot loads from me as I held Anuina through the very last tremor of her pleasure.

Slowly, our divine delights faded, and we descended again from the Mountain.

We sat in a tight, naked embrace, Anuina's beautiful naked body quaking against mine. Roswitha sat beside us, her legs folded under her, as she stroked Anuina's smooth back and plucked at her long blond locks, in disarray after the intensity of our love-making. I held her tight, sharing my warmth with her, wishing for the moment to last.

Of course, it would not.

***

When the cold became intolerable, Anuina, Roswitha, and I released each other and got dressed, cheeks flushed and happy smiles plastered on our faces.

The three of us sat by the fire, covered in blankets and furs that Roswitha had brought. After the overwhelming pleasure of our love, even the water tasted like wine and the hardtack and biscuits were like mutton in honey with freshly baked bread.

We sat silently, basking in the afterglow of our pleasure and letting the flames keep us warm.

"We will do it together," I whispered. The words came unbidden, but Anuina and Roswitha nodded; their minds had been on the ordeal ahead of us as well. "We share this powerful bond," I continued. "I lend strength to you, and you to me. Together, we *shall* overcome."

The words brought comfort, and they snuggled up against me and each other. As I sat and enjoyed their presence in silence, my heart joyful over their presence in my new life, a text box appeared.

> **Congratulations! You have bonded someone to you using your Phylomantic Bond. Please review your character sheet for more details.**

Indeed, I felt strength gather within me. Eager to learn more, I opened my character sheet and reviewed the Phylomantic Bond.

> **You have bonded with a new subject through your Phylomantic Bond ability.**
> **Anuina Willowsdaughter (Elf, Sylvan culture, level 4 Ranger): Elves of the Sylvan culture are the predominant Elven race. They prefer to live in wooded areas, although many of them have mingled with Humans or even Dwarves. Others still are nomadic, traveling around the vast forests of Aerda to hunt and gather and trade, never staying too long in one**

place. Sylvan Elves are known for their deep connection to nature, life, and earth. Bonding with an Elf of the Sylvan culture at your current level offers you access to the following spells: Mold Earth (0), Boulder (1), Ensnare (1), Reinvigorate (1), Sustenance (1), Tremor (1), Barkskin (2), Spikes (2), Summon Beast (2), Word of Invigoration (2).

In addition, since your bond with these subjects is intense, you and these subjects gain the following advantages: +8 Stamina, +8 Mana.

Wow, the Stamina and Mana bonus doubled.

That was quite the boon. Still, I was even more curious about the spells. I decided to take my time by the campfire and study them all.

Mold Earth was utility: It allowed me to dig up earth or change it into difficult terrain that enemies could not charge across. Boulder was a spell that dealt a moderate amount of earth damage but also pinned the target under a big rock for a short while. Ensnare was a crowd control spell; it conjured up vines that went for a single enemy, kept them in place, and gave them a -50 penalty to any Checks they made.

So far, nothing too special...

Reinvigorate and Word of Invigoration, however, almost made me jump up. They were healing spells—the former with touch range, the latter long range.

No fucking way... My bond with Anuina unlocks healing magic?

This was something I hadn't even dared hope for. Most games were strict in not allowing arcane spellcasters—like I assumed the Phylomancer was—cast healing spells. The exception was more than welcome; this would alleviate Roswitha a little from healing detail and help keep me and my women alive longer. On top of that, casting it through the Phylomantic Link meant I would heal everyone at once.

This was something else.

I returned to the other spells, eager to see what other stuff there was. Sustenance was a spell that conjured food for a day for me and my companions from nothing but a nut or a few scraps of old food. Tremor was more interesting: it caused an earthquake in a small area, forcing enemies to succeed at an Acrobatics check or lose their Action. The best part, however, was that I could cast it as an Interruption, meaning I could force an enemy charging at me to make that Check first; if they failed, they lost the attack.

Barkskin was another mage armor. It provided less Armor than Ice Vest—only 6—but it was more durable and lighter, meaning it would cost me less Stamina to use, and I had little Stamina. I was likely moving to this one instead of Ice Vest.

Spikes was another area denial spell, but one that cause rocky spikes to rise from the floor, dealing substantial damage to anyone who crossed the affected area. And finally, Summon Beast allowed me to summon my 'Spirit Animal'. I was going to try that one, even it was only to see what my Spirit Animal was.

My bond with Anuina opened up a lot of druidic magic. The healing magic excited me as it made me into an all-round support king. The bottlenecks were Actions and Mana. However, my Mana was buffed by my items and the benefits from the Phylomantic Bonds, while my Meta-Magic abilities could mitigate the Action bottleneck.

I smirked, drawing my women closer as the campfire turned to ashes and cinders. They had both fallen into a peaceful sleep, but I remained awake for some time, staring at the wealth of stars and nebulae overhead and the slowly moving moons until I too fell into a happy and deep sleep.

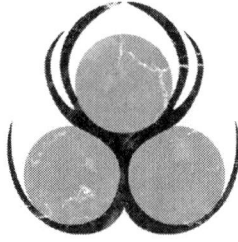

CHAPTER 9

I awoke to warm sunlight filtering down on me, and the soft murmur of conversation somewhere close by. For a moment, I thought I was back in my apartment—as if had all been some dream.

The flashing icons embedded in my view set me straight. I blinked against the sunlight, then became aware of an uncomfortable stiffness in my back—the benefits of sleeping outdoors.

I sat up.

Anuina and Roswitha sat side by side by the now-extinguished campfire, enjoying a breakfast of nuts and berries—they seem to have gathered a few while I still slept. They smiled at me; Roswitha in her own bold way, Anuina a little more abashed, cheeks reddening at the sight of me and—undoubtedly—at the memory of what had happened last night.

"Good morning," Roswitha said.

I yawned. "Indeed, it is." I looked over to their freshly gathered fare.

"Blackberries," Anuina said with a smile. "They grow by the handful near the creek."

"That sounds delicious."

Roswitha made a face. "I prefer breakfast with pork, bread, and ale," she said. "You will travel to the Snowlands with me some day, and when you feel the icy touch of the wind in my homeland, you'll know berries can sustain no man in the north."

Anuina gave a crooked grin, then snatched up the berries that Roswitha had been eating. "In that case, I'll take those."

I chuckled, shrugging the blankets off me as I rose. "I'm with Ros on this one," I said, taking in the glade around us as it glistened under a fresh layer of dew. "Bacon and bread will do for me just fine. Not sure about the ale, though…"

"Well, what do you drink?" Roswitha asked as she stole back a berry from Anuina with a swift move. Anuina covered the remainder with her hands, mock glaring at her bonded sister.

"OJ," I said, for a moment wistful as I recalled my previous—and rather satisfying—breakfast ritual. When both women looked at me with a puzzled expression, I clarified, "Orange juice."

"I was unaware that one could make colors into juice," Anuina said.

Great, no freaking oranges in this world… I chuckled. "Just take it from me: it goes well with bacon and eggs."

Anuina made a face, then ate another berry. "A man shall grow portly and become slow if he eats meat and eggs too often."

Roswitha grinned. "Portli*er* and slow*er*, you mean," she said as she threw a berry at me.

She was too fast, and I was indeed too slow, mind still clouded by my deep sleep. The berry took me on the cheek, and I gave her a mock stern look as I wiped the juice away. "You're on thin ice," I said.

"All my life," she replied, then rose and stretched. "But if we make for Jarl Vitek's hall, our shared dream of pork and bread may still become truth."

I nodded. "We can claim our reward for slaying Athagort. And perhaps we can seek his aid against this Khal-Had."

Roswitha sputtered a laugh. "I doubt it; the Jarls of these lands are no friends of one another, and I doubt Jarl Vitek will lend warriors to any cause that would draw them away from the defense of his own hold, especially to aid some Elf-King or other woodland sprite."

Anuina frowned for a moment but agreed: "We will find no aid among men for problems outside their borders."

I shrugged, kicking some life into my legs. "We'll never find out if we never try," I said. I realized I had no idea where the Willow of Liandrenn was. "Where does your father live?" I asked Anuina.

"Liandrenn lies several days to the southeast," she said. "My sister and I journeyed thence to here."

"Why?" I asked.

She smiled softly. "Father is… *protective*. He has given us much—given us all, in fact—and he is due our unconditional love, but he never permitted us to strike out on our own, preferring instead to keep us young and innocent, forever the Willow's daughters that bathe and laugh and sing in the clean waters that feed his tree.

"But my sister and I are too much like he once was; we have a heart for adventure—to travel and to see places, to taste the pleasures of life, however fleeting they may be when weighed against the long years of Elvenkind. We would even know the sorrow and dread of the common folk, for such things rarely touch the lives of my kin who dwell deep in the safe heart of the scented forests of Liandrenn."

I could listen to her all day.

"Unfortunately, we left father without a proper farewell, knowing he would try to dissuade us." She was silent for a moment. "He will be furious, for what he has feared has come to pass: I have lost my sister—she may well be dead—and I have been in the gravest of dangers myself."

"I doubt that would make him *furious*," Roswitha said. "A father's love may show itself as fury, but that is rarely its foundation."

Anuina smiled warmly at her bonded sister. "Perhaps you are right."

"Will your father welcome us?" I asked.

"Yes," Anuina said. "Although perhaps not warmly so... especially you, Oram Ludwickson. He will see what others may only guess at and know that you have possessed me and made a bond with me beyond those of mere mortals. The tether that binds us will be as plain for him to see as you and I see the branches of the trees around us."

"I have nothing to hide," I said. "I only want to help him repel Khal-Had—to help *you*."

Her emerald eyes warmed for me, and the smile that curled her lips brought some life to her face. "Thank you," she said. "If our fears are true, he will need the help."

"All right," Roswitha said, rolling her shoulders. "I will go gather up our gear. Best we be on our way."

"I will help," Anuina said, popping the last of the berries in her mouth and veering up.

With a simple gesture, I used my Mold Earth spell to bury the campfire, then retrieved my pack with Ghost Touch. Meanwhile, I focused on the flashing question mark. A quest notification popped up.

The Fate of the Willow Tree
Challenge Level: 4 (medium)

You have learned from Anuina Willowsdaughter that Athagort Bone-Mangler served Khal-Had, a vengeful spirit who was once the warden of the Willow of Liandrenn, and who now seeks to reclaim his former domain from Anuina's father, the Warden of the Willow. You have offered succor to Anuina and her family, and you must accompany her to Liandrenn to warn her father of the impending doom.

Objective: Speak to the Warden of the Willow at Liandrenn.
Bonus objectives: Do not let Anuina die or suffer grievous wounds; do not let Roswitha die or suffer grievous wounds.
Reward: 2,000 XP and 500 XP per bonus objective completed.

Well, it's time to turn in the old quests and begin with the new...

***

When the suns reached their zenith, we broke free of the tree line. The mead hall stood on its hillock in the distance, but the plume of smoke that rose from it was not that of a homey fire. It was thick, black, and much too wide.

We stood there in the suns' light under a cloudless sky, blinking against the light for a moment as our eyes adjusted after the gloom of the canopy.

Roswitha was first to draw the conclusion. "The hall burns," she said.

There was no need for discussion; Anuina took out her yew bow and strung it with the speed and skill of a trained archer. In the meantime, I picked some strips of bark, a handful of nuts, a few twigs, and several stones—material components for my new spells—as Roswitha watched the plume of smoke rise on the horizon.

Our preparations made, we set out at once, moving at double time even though the hillock on which Jarl Vitek's hall stood was still some distance away. The grassy plains shot by as we moved down the trail, and when we drew closer, we noticed the gates stood open.

We did not try to conceal ourselves, and an excited shrieking from inside the palisade told us we had been seen. A moment later, a dozen Fauns in leather scraps rushed out, spears at the ready. They were under the command of a large goat-like creature.

Like the Fauns, this creature had digitigrade legs, cloven hoofs, and a small puffy tail. Thick, black fur covered his legs and groin, rising to his belly button, but his arms and shoulders were likewise covered in fur, and he had pointed ears and long, coarse hair that he wore in a bun. Horns curled up from his head, and his skin was a purplish gray color. Slightly taller than a Human, the creature was altogether muscular yet lean and shared the elongated, goat-like features and the fully black eyes of the Fauns.

He roared with fury when he laid eyes on us. Crude iron plate covered parts of his body, and he wielded a battle staff with sinister, jagged blades at both ends.

I saw the hesitation in my women as this beast barked his fury, and the little Fauns gathered around him, eager to obey.

I focused on the beast for a moment.

Satyr
Level 5
Stamina: 36, Health: 6, Mana: 30, Sanity: 5

A quick glance at the Fauns revealed they were the same as the ones we had faced in the Vaskhule Caves when they strove side-by-side with their master, Athagort. Only these wore leather armor, not shields.

Faun Warrior
Level 2
Stamina: 12, Health: 4, Mana: 9, Sanity: 3

We got this… They're not as strong as Athagort was.
"Hold here!" I commanded, and Roswitha took position at the front, Anuina slightly behind her, her keen Elven eyes on the mass of enemies even as she drew her first arrow from its quiver.

I took a strip of bark from my sack, said the words of power, and called upon nature to cast my Barkskin spell. A moment later, a tight-fitting suit of bark closed around my chest.

The horde of foes charged, led on by the bellowing of the Satyr. They came howling and shrieking, trampling the earth as they came even as my Mana trickled back. Then, with an Elven curse as light as a breeze of wind, Anuina loosed her first arrow. Its tip gleamed in the sun as it arched high, then fell, finding one of the charging Fauns without error. The arrow struck its mark—the Faun did not try to dodge it—and tore into the leather scraps he wore.

Beside her, Roswitha raised the charms around her neck with one hand, her vicious bastard sword in the other. "I call upon the Bladed One! Lend us your blessing so we may smite our foes!"

You are under the effect of a Bless spell. You receive a + 50 bonus to your next Check, so long as you make it within an hour.

Roswitha's blessing sharpened my mind, and I raised my staff high. I spoke an ancient incantation to call upon the elements and drew a sigil of might in the air. With my free hand, I retrieved a stone from the spell component pouch at my belt. Even though I only generated a 16, Roswitha's blessing raised the total result of my Check to 90, and the small stone I held in my hand vanished as jagged spikes rose from the ground the Fauns were about to charge over.

The Fauns roared and shrieked as they entered my field of spikes. Only two of them made it through unscathed; the rest had the spikes turn their scrappy armors to nothing, and three of them even crashed into the spikes in such an unfortunate way that the jagged rock drew deep wounds on their legs and feet. They emerged wounded and bleeding, only to be greeted by a hail of arrows from Anuina.

It was amazing to see: her hands moved faster than my eyes could trace as she nocked five arrows in what seemed but a moment. Of the arrows she fired, four struck true, bringing down the three wounded Fauns without difficulty. I almost felt pity for the creatures as they lay there, riddled with arrows and torn open by cruel rock.

The others panted and looked at us wide-eyed, hesitation obvious in their black eyes. But the Satyr roared and raged, urging them on as he navigated the spiked field with great strides, iron armor keeping most of his body safe from grievous wounds.

On came the Fauns. Doubt was clear in their eyes, and they still had some distance to cover. Seeing no need to change a winning formula—and blessed again by Roswitha—I cast Spikes again. This time, I used my Instant Spell ability and followed up with Iceplane, splashing water from the jug hanging from my belt. The two spells combined beautifully, creating an almost alien landscape of jagged, frost-covered stone spikes that rose from an icy sheet as treacherous as the sea.

The Fauns blundered into it, and none came out. I saw them struggle and fall, slipping on the ice and impaling themselves on the rock. Anuina's bright eyes scoured the treacherous landscape, her face the very image of deadly focus, and she loosed three shafts at the desperately moving patches of bloodied brown skin or fur that she could still see.

Then all fell silent.

Only the Satyr remained. With a furious bellow, he waded into the field of ice and jagged rock.

Like the Fauns that served him, he was never to emerge. Several of Anuina's arrows and two of my overcharged Frostbites, guided by Roswitha's blessing, ended its life.

With a sound much like bleating, he collapsed, clutching at his frostbitten skin and the cruel shafts sticking out from his body.

Fuck, I feel like a god!

Of course, the rampant spellcasting had reduced my Mana to 10, and I knew this would not work for an engagement that we would expect to last longer—or one where we could not rain hellfire down on our foes from afar, but god, was this good!

I grinned at the warrior women standing before me. Roswitha responded with a smug grin of her own, while Anuina raised an eyebrow and made a little mock, at-your-service curtsy.

Absolute champions.

***

You receive 1,100 XP.

I blinked the pop-up away as I dismissed the fields of spikes and ice I had conjured. When the rock had returned to the earth, the corpses of the Fauns and the Satyr lay there. We gave them a quick once-over, discovering a smattering of coins—five silver ones and thirteen copper ones.

Weapons at the ready, we made our way into the palisade-enclosed courtyard.

"No corpses," Roswitha said.

Indeed, the hillock was pristine. Only Anuina spotted two dead men in chainmail. They had been dragged away from where they fell, and both had a red ribbon that ran from ear to ear.

Slit throats... We exchanged glances.

Anuina kneeled beside one of the corpses to touch its sallow skin. "The corpses are cold," she said. "These men died last night."

"They attacked under the cover of night," Roswitha said. "Sneaking up on these men like cowards to slit their throats."

I gazed up at the hillock and the smoldering remains of the hall. A section of it had already collapsed. "Is it normal for Fauns to attack Human settlements so openly?" I asked.

"Not at all," Roswitha said, frowning down at the dead Human.

"If only for practical reasons," Anuina added. "Fauns are too fickle and chaotic to form bands large enough to pose a threat to anything other than a lone caravan. The numbers we have seen united so far—first in Athagort's vile company and now here—are most unusual."

"But I suppose Khal-Had's will could bind them," I suggested.

Anuina nodded. "They respect strength. If Khal-Had is mighty, I suppose he could unite the clans of Satyrs and their Faun servants."

Roswitha turned her icy gaze to Anuina. "And is he? Mighty?"

"He certainly was a force to be reckoned with when he was still the Warden of the Willow," Anuina replied. "He may have lost some of his power, but I doubt he shall have lost all. But why would he attack the hall of some insignificant Human king?"

Roswitha furrowed her brow. "Jarl Vitek Warnerson Spear-Eater is hardly insignificant," she said. "He may be a glutton and a drunk, but he has fielded warriors in dozens of raids and half as many pitched battles. He is a warrior-king and deserves some respect."

I raised a hand. "Let's not get into the particulars of which king does or does not deserve respect. I'd be more interested to find an answer to Anuina's question, even if she worded it unfortunately."

Anuina's lips pressed into a line, but she said nothing more.

"Let us go look," Roswitha said. "We may yet find a trace of them."

Our guards up, weapons at the ready, we went up the hillock. As we made our way, we found more corpses: men and women cut down in little but their undergarments. Some of them had a blade or axe nearby, but none of them were armored.

It all painted the picture of an honorless slaughter; the Beastfolk came down from the Janneskog Woods under the cover of night, slit the guards' throats, and crept into the hall for a red slaughter, and only a few of Vitek's men and women had died on their feet.

"Cowards," Roswitha muttered, visibly upset about the slaughter.

"They are cruel," Anuina said. "Little more than animals and driven by a base desire to do wrong."

At the top of the hillock, we got a better view of the devastation of Jarl Vitek's hall. We approached it from the south so that the steady wind blew the acrid smoke away from us.

Here, among the rubble and charred rafters, I found that my guess was right: most of the dead lay where they slept, pelts and blankets drenched in blood even as they still covered their bodies.

As my eyes scoured the hall, I saw the Fauns had—in some cruel mockery—placed Jarl Vitek in his throne and pinned him to it with daggers driven through his hands.

Then they had set fire to him.

The smell of burned flesh and hair was blood-curdling and nauseating, even with the wind whipping it away from us.

Quest failed: Liberating the Woods. Since Jarl Vitek Warnerson Spear-Eater is dead, you can no longer claim your reward from him.

Yeah, no shit.

I looked away. Roswitha and Anuina had already begun a cursory investigation of the charred ruin, but the raiders had taken everything of value, even the ample supply of food that Jarl Vitek kept in his hall. I had no idea how far away the next settlement was, but I was thankful for my Sustenance and Create/Destroy Water spells; those would make sure we could meet the basic needs of survival.

Instead of joining my women in going through the ruins, I made a lap around the burning building, descending the hillock somewhat on the north side to stay under the thick smoke. From here, the view was splendid: to the west unfolded the Janneskog Woods. It was a vast forest, thick and old, and ran from northwest to southwest as far as my eye reached. In the far distance, the trees hugged a mountain range, mist and clouds rendering its high slopes nearly the same color as the sky itself.

To the north, forested hills rose and dipped, their colors transitioning from green to blue as the distance increased, until crisp white mountain tops broke them. East and south of here were grassy plains, and now for the first time I noticed a road ran through them. It followed the course of a river—a silvery ribbon that broke the sea of green. When I squinted my eyes, I saw travelers on that road—smaller than ants. The road came from the south and veered away toward the east.

Now that I had a sense of the lay of the land, I returned to the women.

To my surprise, I found Anuina in tears with Roswitha's arms wrapped around her. The tall Priestess of the Skanaaga spoke words of consolation that did not seem to come naturally to her. I rushed toward them, and when Roswitha saw me coming, she loosened the embrace.

When Anuina rested her emerald eyes on me, she fell in my arms, sobbing.

"Wh—what happened?" I asked.

Roswitha had a doleful look on her face and something helpless about her; she was as ill at ease with crying women as most men were.

I, unfortunately, had offered my shoulder to many—even when the grief was of my making. I held her tight, deciding to be silent until she was ready to speak. We stood like that for a while, and it was hard not to be overcome by her grief; the death around us, the destruction—charred corpses littered the floor, men and women in their prime slain in their sleep like cattle.

I clenched my jaw. This had been a game to me, but in this moment I realized that was untrue.

At length, Anuina's sobbing grew softer. Eventually, she drew back from my shoulder. An Elf even in grief, her tears brought a dolorous elegance to her face that was breathtaking—as if she were some primal goddess on the Mountain, crying over the wrongs the children of the earth wrought on one another.

"My sister…" she finally said. She raised a trembling, clenched hand and opened it, revealing a brooch of delicate gold in the image of a leaf. "This is hers," Anuina said, biting back a sob. "She was here, and they came for her." The words broke her, and she rested her cheek against my chest and broke out crying.

I held her and looked at Roswitha.

I did not need to ask the question; Roswitha knew what I wanted to ask and shook her head in reply.

They had not found Anuina's sister among the slain.

"We'll find her," I whispered softly to the Elf trembling in my arms. "We'll find her and make it right."

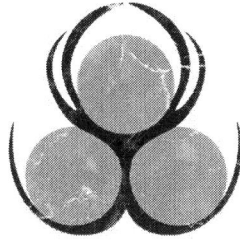

Chapter 10

Whe left the burned-out husk of Jarl Vitek's hall behind us as the two suns of Aerda began to dip behind the hazy mountains in the west.

It was strange to leave this place a burning ruin. I had memories here—of my first nervous encounter with the Humans of Aerda. They had been 'NPCs' in my mind then, and I stifled a chuckle at the thought of now referring to Roswitha or Anuina as an 'NPC'; they were more alive to me than many I had met in my previous life…

But foremost, it was the place where I met Roswitha. I rubbed my jaw—where she had punched me within a minute of our meeting.

A painful but fond memory.

We turned to the plains ahead of us.

"Let us make for the road east of here," Anuina said, her voice still hoarse from tears shed earlier. "We may follow it for two days until we reach Wealdhaven.

"From there, a road leads into Liandrenn that the locals call the 'Elvenway'. That will take us to Thalumir, a small trade station where my kin make a sparse trade with the Humans of these lands."

I nodded, looking over my shoulders at the sky as it turned a fiery orange.

"And from there?" Roswitha asked.

"Beyond Thalumir there are no roads," Anuina said. "The woodland folk need no such thing to travel our ancestral woods. We may find the Willow of Liandrenn if it wishes to be found; but I know father will wish to see me and thus allow us to make our way to his Willow."

I frowned. "So, we just wander around the forest until your father decides to let us find him?"

"Yes, that is the long and short of it," Anuina said.

"Sounds a bit... *unprepared.*"

Roswitha, walking a few meters behind us, chuckled.

But Anuina smiled warmly at me. "Such a Human concern," she said. "Fear not, the forest itself will guide us."

"Well, since I *am* Human, I am no stranger to Human concerns... But I trust you; if you say it works, I won't doubt it."

She placed a slender hand on my arm. "Thank you, Oram Ludwickson."

We navigated the grassy plains mainly by ear, following the mounting wash of the river. The plains were a lot less even and a lot more difficult to navigate than they had seemed from atop Jarl Vitek's hillock, but we finally broke free from the waist-high grass when we crested a hill and found the dirt road waiting.

The road was little more than a muddy rut drawn by passing wagon wheels, although an effort had been made to keep it free from encroaching shrubbery.

Happy to reach even ground, we stretched our legs and rested while the suns dipped behind the mountains in the west. Finally, guided by my Light spell, we continued for some time until the stars broke out above us, shining bright and multi-colored among purple, green, and pink nebulae.

We made camp, ate the last of our provisions, and drank from the clear river.

Unlike last time, we agreed on a rotation for a night watch.

***

During my watch, I sat in the dim, enchanting light of the moons and stars. A crisp wind blew over the plain and cleared my mind. With my companions lying nearby, I felt a lot less lonely than I had been before I... *arrived* in Aerda.

The strangest thing was that I had never realized what *true* company was. I lived a life that consisted of working hard and earning a royal amount of money. In my free time, I partied with colleagues or played video games with strangers I had labeled 'buddies'. There was the occasional woman in my life, but it rarely ended well. They either tried to tame me and got rebuffed, or they saw it was no use and turned away not to look back again.

And I stayed behind.

Work hard, party hard, hang out with colleagues or shallow acquaintances. Rinse, repeat.

I inhaled, tasting the grass and the trees.

Perhaps Aerda Online was the best thing that could have happened to me, even though I still had no idea what actually *had* happened.

"Are you all right?"

I looked behind me to see Roswitha propped up on her elbows, fur blanket covering her up to her chest. The icy glow of her eyes was even more enchanting in the light of the stars and the moons.

I gave her a quick and easy smile. "Just thinking of days gone by."

Her lips quirked into a smile. "Ah, regrets, hm?"

"Maybe."

She rose, blanket wrapped around her. "And what ghost out of your past haunts you?" she asked as she sat down beside me.

"One of loneliness," I said.

She placed a soft hand on my shoulder. "I find it hard to imagine you were ever lonely."

I laughed. "I don't think I ever realized I was," I said. "Lonely, but not *alone*... if that makes sense."

"It does."

I wrapped my arm around her. "And what keeps you up?"

She looked up at the stars. "I have never been so far south as we will go once we pass Wealdhaven."

An eyebrow shot up. "Really? I thought you were well traveled."

She shot me a glare. "I *am*. This is just very far from home."

"So, you're homesick?"

She sighed. "Perhaps." She flicked away a pebble with her fingers. "It is unfitting of an Iron-Eye," she said. "We are all travelers and adventurers, but I sometimes wish for something altogether… less itinerant."

"Oh yeah? Like what?"

She shrugged. "Ah, it does not matter," she said.

I gave a curt chortle. "You can't do that!"

"Do what?"

"Tell me you want something and then not say what it is."

"I suppose that *is* unfair…"

I smirked at her. "Spill it."

She chuckled and nudged me with her shoulder. "Very well. I have always dreamed of building a house for the gods, the Masked One especially, for he has always favored me. It would be a place of prayer and sanctuary for those who seek the guidance of the gods; a place for them to stay and learn—to train perhaps, in the arts of the mind and body."

I perked an eyebrow. "Really? You never gave me the impression that you were *that* pious."

"I am a Priestess!" she said, outrage half real and half mocking.

"Yeah, but you don't talk a lot about it and—"

"So, what you are saying is that all priests are *gabby*?"

I laughed. "Well, I might be prejudiced. Where I'm from, religion is a thing that people tend to push in your face—if they do not outright kill you over it."

"Do they worship a god of slaughter?"

"It sure seems that way sometimes."

She shook her head. "Well, the Tribunal has the Blooded One; he is perhaps somewhat like your god."

I raised my hands. "Not *my* god."

She narrowed her eyes at me. "Who is your god then?"

"*You* are my goddess," I said, voice smooth.

I was rewarded with a flat palm smacking against the back of my head. "You are a fool, Oram Ludwickson," Roswitha said, although the mirth was clear in her eyes.

"So, what do you say to this," I began. "When we finish this business with Khal-Had and live to tell the tale, we will see about finding a place to build your place of prayer?"

Her eyes narrowed, almost mistrustful. "Why would *you* want that?"

I shrugged. "I enjoy being around you," I said, adding in a whisper, "I must like getting my ass kicked."

A laugh escaped her, and her eyes warmed up. "Very well," she said. "I would like to do something like that… with you."

"Good," I said, pulling her closer. "In the meantime, you can teach me more about the Tribunal."

She nodded. "I can do that."

We fell silent after that, each of us occupied by our own thoughts. After a while, Roswitha's soft breathing told me she had fallen asleep. Gently, I lowered her and covered her with her blanket.

When Roswitha's time came to take over from me, I let her sleep, sitting out her watch as well.

***

Our journey took us south for two days. By the time the walls of Wealdhaven dawned before us, we were all very thankful for my Sustenance spell. There had not been a single roadside tavern; not even a merchant or local farmer willing to sell us some victuals. According to Anuina, that had been different in the past, but the road from Alonsby to

Wealdhaven had grown dangerous of late. With the burning of Jarl Vitek's hall, whose men often patrolled the road, it would get a lot worse before it would get any better.

Although Wealdhaven was a city by the standards of Aerda, it looked like a hamlet to me. A wall of loose-fitting stones enclosed it—little more than boulders stacked on top of one another with the gaps between them filled up with crumbling mortar. The parapet and walkway were made of crude planks, and the walls jutted out in the shape of a half circle at regular intervals. There, wooden scaffolding supported a pointed roof of planks, offering shelter to the guards that patrolled it.

And many did patrol it. As we approached the city, situated on a slight rise, the sunlight gleamed on helmets and spears. The lands to the south of Wealdhaven were farmland, and rows of green crops coming to life in the springtime broke the wildness of this world.

There were farmsteads too, but they were hardly the spitting image of a beautiful land in peacetime; every one of them had some sort of palisade with alarm bells or stacks of wood for signal fires to call for aid.

As it looked, Wealdhaven was not safe.

I glanced over at Anuina and Roswitha. "Looks like a land at war," I said.

Roswitha furrowed her brow. "I came here a Bloodmoon past," she said. "It was not like this then."

"A Bloodmoon?"

She frowned at me, then remembered I knew little of this world. "We measure time by the red moon at night, the Bloodmoon," she said. "It waxes and wanes over three fortnights."

Forty-two-day months. I nodded.

Roswitha pointed at the enclosed steads in the surrounding farmland. "Most of these were not fortified back then," she continued. "The people of Wealdhaven have worked hard to defend their homes, it seems."

"It was not like this when I was last here, either," Anuina said. "I do not understand it; the Humans of Wealdhaven have little to fear, for my woodland kin keep the forest of Liandrenn and the Elvenway safe. I know no better than that their only worries are brigands and highwaymen, perhaps the occasional Troll, Ogre, or Hog-Man that comes stumbling out of the swamps east of here. A century ago, when I was but a youngling, Orcs and Goblins still raided out of the Loewngarda Mountains to the southeast, but their clans dispersed when the Dwarves of the Covenant of Smiths built the city of Jerna Hallar to extract the riches of the mountains."

I nodded slowly as my eyes roved over the bowl-shaped depression in the land that Wealdhaven commanded from its raised ground. Men on horseback rode hither and thither, patrolling the narrow roads that meandered the land and connected farms and outlying hamlets to the city. I saw several burned-out husks as well; steads or even clusters of four or five houses that had been put to the torch.

Something is definitely wrong here…

"We should go down and see," I said. "And while we're there, we might as well sleep in a proper bed and purchase some supplies other than conjured food…"

The women nodded, and we headed down at a brusque pace.

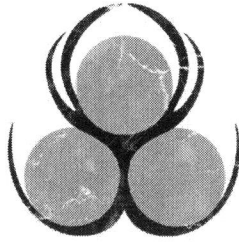

CHAPTER 11

The stink of Wealdhaven reached us before its sounds did. It was a sour stench—a mix of smoke, livestock, shit, piss, sweat, and something raw underneath that was probably the smell of some workshop, perhaps a tannery or a blacksmith.

Roswitha did not flinch when the smell hit us, but Anuina wrinkled her nose and made a face. "I cannot understand how Humans can live in such filth," she said.

"And Humans cannot understand how you Elves all keep so clean," Roswitha said and barked a laugh.

Anuina thought for a moment. "We bathe?"

I chuckled as I led them on.

Riders passed us by—men in long chainmail hauberks, nasal helmets with gold-plated browbands and engraved noseguards, and round shields with a golden rune painted on them that looked like a tree. They gave us suspicious looks as they rode past, and although we were eager for news, I was not inclined to ask these men for any.

The awful stink waxed as we neared the wooden gates in the walls of Wealdhaven. There was a short line to get in—farmers with hand-drawn carts mainly. Spearmen in padded armor and nasal helmets stood guard, holding shields with the same golden rune we had seen before. A bearded man in a rich tunic and an utterly ridiculous wide-brimmed head sat behind a desk and took coins from each entrant, giving them a carved stone tablet in return for some coins.

When we got to the front of the line, the official eyed us suspiciously from under the tasseled brim of his hat. "Greetings, travelers," he said, his words insincere as coffee-machine chatter. "You have come to Wealdhaven, grand capital of Jarl Strumma Hardenkson Life-Tree's hold." He narrowed his eyes. "May I ask what brings you hither?"

I stepped forward. "We have come to purchase supplies and rest before we continue south."

"South?" the man asked.

I nodded.

"Down the Elvenway," Anuina added.

The man turned his eyes to my fair companions, first Anuina, then Roswitha. He made no effort to hide his shameless looks at their half-naked bodies. "The Elvenway, hm?" he said, eyes finally resting on Anuina's emerald eyes. "Visiting your woodland kin, I wager? Well, the Elvenway is dangerous these days."

"How so?" I asked.

He looked back to me. "Elves are fickle friends," he said, and I felt Anuina stiffen beside me. "The Sylvan Folk have not kept the road safe; Beastfolk roam there. Of late, they have become bold enough to even reach for the holdings of Wealdhaven, burning and pillaging with the blessings of the Antlered One, it seems. As such, we no longer send traders and diplomats south." He spat on the floor before eying me again. "Only spearmen walk the Elvenway these days."

"We can hold our own," I said.

"Is that so?" He chortled. "You look like a body-hawker with his pair of street waifs."

A growl from Roswitha made him turn his eye to her.

"One of them a Skaanaga, nonetheless," the official continued, and a smile of vitriol appeared on his lips. "Of course, it is none of my business." He reached into a leather pouch at his side and took out a small stone token with a rune carved into its surface. "I shall give you passage for one day. Come sunset tomorrow, you must leave Wealdhaven. The price is two copper coins per head." He counted us with his fingers. "One, two, three... is six copper."

I took six coins from my Vault and placed them before him on the desk. He studied them warily for a moment, as if they might turn to ashes before him, then handed me the token. "By order of Jarl Strumma Hardenkson Life-Tree, you have leave to enter Wealdhaven until sunset tomorrow."

I took the token, gave the ill-mannered official not another look, and strode into the city with Anuina and Roswitha following close behind.

***

Wealdhaven's main street was a rutty, muddy road that led to a small keep at the city's center. The keep had a modest wooden palisade of its own, and its first two floors were built of the same loose-fitting rock and mortar as the city walls. Smaller streets branched off from the main road, leading to houses made of wood or wattle and daub. Thatch and straw roofs finished it all off. Some areas were obviously poorer; the housing there consisted of tents and improvised shelters.

The road ended at a small square in front of the gate in the keep's palisade. Since the square was unpaved, ruts and constant treading had rendered it muddy, but there was a large inn, a few stalls, and several stores. Voices drifted our way from that direction, and small groups of people littered the square, drinking, eating, making purchases, talking...

All in all, it was quite the shithole.

We made our way to the inn, earning ourselves some mistrustful looks from the unkempt locals. Anuina especially seemed to bear the brunt of the stink eye, which made me believe the locals had no particular fondness of Elves.

The smells that came from the inn were a little more inviting: roast meat—probably pork, ale, and fresh bread. A small crowd stood outside under linen awnings that the years and the suns had turned a brownish yellow. They flanked the doorway, from beyond which a merry orange-and-yellow glow greeted us. We made our way past the revelers and into the inn.

The ground floor was high and long, somewhat reminiscent of Jarl Vitek's hall, with wooden beams and rafters supporting the ceiling. Straw covered the floor, and a rickety stairway led up to what I assumed were the guest quarters. Several crude tables made of unrefined wood stood in the common room, squeezed together with benches to sit on. In the back stood a hearth—the only stonework in the hall—with an enormous kettle hanging over it.

About a third of the tables were occupied, and most of the folk were farmers who had sold out for the day or locals who came to enjoy a mug of ale as evening drew closer. There was a small company of Dwarves, too—the first I saw in Aerda. They dressed and appeared similar to the locals, except short, squat, and bearded. There were also three men who looked like mercenaries or warriors, scarred and muscular, with armaments arranged around and leaning against their table.

Across from the entrance stood a long bar. There, a slender, vulpine man stood drawing ale. Three buxom maidens in skirts cut off at the thighs and small linen tops that revealed toned midriffs distributed the orders to the various tables. The man's eyes fell on us and a warm smile spread on his lips—it was sincere enough, even if a bit cunning.

I walked over to the bar. Roswitha followed with an easy step, and most of the men gathered gawked at her. Anuina had become a little more self-conscious from the townies' glaring; she moved more carefully, not at all eager to receive lustful stares from the revelers.

"Greetings and welcome," the innkeeper said. "Blessings of the Walking One upon you."

I was unsure if there was an appropriate ceremonial reply, so I just said, "Good evening." A bit underwhelming, but then again, I had a pouch full of gold, so I assumed he'd forgive me any cultural slights.

"My name is Adalrik Kettilson, and this—" he made a sweeping gesture at his inn "—this is Rodrik's Head's Inn. How may I serve?"

I leaned on the bar. "We'd like to stay the night," I said. "There's three of us. We'd also like your best food and drink."

"Have you a token?" he asked.

I showed him the engraved stone the official had given us. Satisfied, Adalrik gave a nod. "You can stay here in the common room if you wish. The straw is fresh; my girls will give you blankets. We also have a private room for rent. I can move some beds in."

"The private room, please," I said.

He grinned, eyes sparkling with the light of a man who enjoys making money—*a lot*. "That'll be seven silver coins," he said. "Board and food."

I took ten out of my pouch and placed them on the bar. His eyes rested on the three extra coins a moment before he looked back up at me, an unspoken question in his eyes.

"We'd also like information," I said. "Wealdhaven is in a different state from what it was a Bloodmoon ago. We're keen to hear what has happened. and we're paying because we want reliable and truthful information, not gossip and speculation."

He reached out, sweeping all the coins off the bar and into his apron with a single motion, then smiled at me. "Eat and drink," he said. "Once you've had your fill and I find some time, we'll burn half an hour's candle together, and you may ask me whatever you please. I shall answer truthfully. I'm afraid that's all I can spare; it's promising to be full tonight."

"That sounds fair," I said, realizing that it probably wasn't.

"Please," Adalrik said. "Seat yourselves. We will bring you stew, bread, pork sausages, and a few pitchers of ale."

My stomach growled when Adalrik told me what was on the menu, and we quickly found our table for the night.

***

By the time we had eaten our fill, the inn was getting crowded. When Anuina and Roswitha excused themselves to inspect our chamber, I sat alone at our table, enjoying a mug of ale as I let my meal settle.

A group of four loud and somewhat drunken merchants disturbed my silent contemplations as they made their way to a table close to me.

"War is what it's going to be, I tell you!" one of them said, obviously not caring who would hear him.

I sat up and perked my ears.

"War, you think?" another merchant asked. He was lean and had a shrewd look about him; by his movements, I could tell he was the soberest among them.

"Aye," the first speaker said. He was lanky, drunk, and walked with a limp. "What with all the soldiers and such."

"War with whom?" another, elder merchant asked.

The limping one spat on the straw, then beckoned over a serving girl. "Who can tell with these accursed northern jarls?" he said. "One day they're the closest of friends—and the next? Mortal enemies."

"You don't make a very strong case," the sober one said.

"Ah, but he does!" said the fourth merchant in the most pedantic of tones. This one was fat and seemed to be the richest among them, with golden rings adorning his sausage fingers.

"It is not just the barbarian jarls who are uneasy," he continued. "I have been farther south, and in Skegaraugh and Eaisach spears are gathering: the lords of the Losrain are uneasy. From even farther south comes word of arms mustering among the Caerolian dukes under their Child-King. And does it not strike you as odd that the woodland folk of Liandrenn have turned even more inward than they are normally wont to do? And what's to say of the Covenant of Smiths? Or the Elves of Firnuin or Llathangal? Their borders are all sealed more tightly than a miser's purse; men-at-arms patrol them, and they are wary and ask many questions of visitors."

The sober one narrowed his eyes, obviously not the type to speak his mind too quickly.

The elder merchant spoke more lightly. "Nonsense," he said. "The Fair Folk have always been fickle. And Dwarves are as mistrustful as they are greedy. As for the ways of the Losrain and Caerolians... well, who can say? Fools do what fools must, by the Wizened One, and I never saw a method to their madness."

The fat merchant chuckled, exchanging a glance with the limping one. "Perhaps, perhaps," he said. "Suffice to say I have made my preparations. War is not good for all trade, but it is for some."

The sober one sat up. "Ah," he said, "but here comes a well-traveled man who may yet shed some light on the musters of lords unknown to us."

All of their heads turned, and my gaze followed theirs. Through the front door a man came in, tall and dark of skin, dressed in a mud-spattered black cloak, his eyes a piercing blue under long black dreadlocks, bound at the nape. There was something odd about this man, and it was not merely that his skin was dark in a place where I had seen only fair-skinned Humans. His eyes rested on me too; I drew his attention as much as he drew mine.

I focused on him, even as he focused on me.

Rahandi the Seven-Paw
Level 9 Captain
Stamina: 50(87), Health: 5, Mana: 20, Sanity: 2

Damn... level 9.

But there was something else, too. With an easy step, he strode past my table, greeting the merchants in a deep voice.

"Captain Rahandi," the fat one said. "Sit with us! We were just discussing current affairs."

The man sat down among the group of merchants. They quickly pushed a mug of ale his way, but he declined it. The limping merchant frowned. "You don't drink ale?"

Rahandi was silent for a second, then glanced at me over his shoulder. "Only if it's Budweiser," he said.

My heart nearly stopped.

***

The merchants exchanged confused looks, then broke out laughing.

"Rahandi," the fat one said. "You are a peculiar one! Come, if you won't drink, let us talk at least!"

I sat watching them, my heart pounding away in my chest.

Budweiser...

The merchants tried to get Rahandi's opinion on the affairs of war, but the man parried their questions and spoke with them instead of their journey south. It soon became plain that he would serve as their escort. They were headed to the city of Gotansby, southeast of here, and they meant to follow the road out of the east gate of Wealdhaven that led past the swamps. There were Fauns abound—and worse, or so Rahandi said—and by the simple fact that these four merchants were hiring a level 9 adventurer to guard them, I knew the road must be dangerous indeed.

Fucking Budweiser.

I picked up other telltale signs—the way he spoke was not as... well, *medieval* as that of the others, and at one point he said they should assemble 'at 8am', which led to confusion with the merchants.

However, after some time, their plans had been made and there was a lull in their conversation. Rahandi used the opportunity to excuse himself. He rose from the bench, gave me a meaningful nod, and headed outside.

I took my mug of ale and followed.

***

The air outside had grown colder, and fewer men now stood under the awnings. Rahandi was waiting for me a few paces ahead, and when he knew for certain I had seen him, he turned into a shadowed alley. The suns had already set, and it was very dark in there.

I hesitated for a moment. *This guy can kill me without even trying. But then again, he's the only one I've seen so far who's... well, not from here.*

If I wanted to know more, there wasn't a choice. I set my jaw and followed.

He was waiting in the alley in the glow of the moons, leaning against the wall of the inn.

"Yo," he said, a big grin on his face.

I laughed—I really couldn't respond in any other way except by breaking out in tears. The greeting sounded unreal but, at the same time, so much like *home*. I hadn't even taken the time to ask myself if I missed home, and now that it finally showed itself in the casual gamer's greeting of a stranger, I found that I did.

"Weird fucking shit, huh?" he said.

I took a few more steps toward him, the threat totally faded. "Do you have any fucking clue—any at all—about what the fuck is going on?"

"I was gonna ask you the same, dude," he said. "You're the third one I met, and they all had the same story: waiting for our preloaded copy of Aerda Online to unlock."

"Fuck," I muttered. "And no one has any idea what happened?"

"Nah, man." He looked past me and frowned. "Where you from?"

"Seattle. You?"

"Burlington, Vermont." He grinned. "Guess I got here a few hours before you did."

I chuckled. "It shows, man, you got five levels on me."

"Yeah, and three deaths probably. I spawned in a bunch of ruins in the swamps east of here; they were crawling with Undead. Getting ganked three times over by a horde of Ghouls got one of my stats all the way down to one... I almost didn't make it out."

"Damn," I said.

"Yeah," he said. "I'll be level nineteen before I fully recover from that shit and get all my stats back."

"I feel you, man, I'm still recovering from my death at level one."

He smiled, then looked me over. "Phylomancer, huh? You an early supporter?"

"Yeah," I said.

"How's it play?"

I chuckled and shook my head. "It doesn't feel like playing to me," I said. "I guess the bonding is pretty powerful stuff; I just unlocked healing spells through one of my companions."

He nodded. "Sounds OP."

"I know, right?"

"So, listen, man," he said. "I'm meeting up with the two others I met: some English dude and a girl from Oklahoma. We figure we stand a better chance together. We're headed to Gotansby; I got a quest to escort a couple of merchants there. From Gotansby runs a pretty good road farther south. Once you pass through the kingdom of the Caerolians, there's supposed to be a big old sea with a lot of small independent city states. Life's good there, I heard, and with powers like ours, we could take control of one of those places."

I perked an eyebrow. "Control?"

"Yeah," he said. "We want to establish something like a base of operations, you know? So we can have the peace of mind and the resources to try to figure out what happened to us, and how we can get back."

Get back...

"Besides," Rahandi continued. "This place—" he gestured around him "—these lands aren't exactly safe or stable."

I frowned. "How so?"

"Well, as far as the lands of Humans on this continent go, you have the Losrain to the south, the Caerolians farther south, and the Skaanaga to the far north... and then you have these lands—the lands ruled by the Askil jarls. Of all the Human realms, they are the most divided and vulnerable." He leaned a little closer. "Something is brewing here, man. The way I hear things, the roads have gotten a lot less safe over the past few Bloodmoons."

"Yeah," I said. "I've been hearing a lot of that."

He smiled. "Now if this was a game—like an *actual* game—then fuck... trouble is where you'd find me. But those ghouls brought me way too close to death—*real* death—and for some reason, I'm pretty damn sure I won't respawn back home in Burlington once that happens. Either way, I'm not taking the chance until I know for sure."

He makes sense... I nodded.

"Join us, man," he said. "Get the hell out of Dodge before whatever is brewing here hits you in the face and won't let you get up."

"Do you have any idea what exactly this threat is?"

He sighed and shook his head. "I don't really know," he said. "But word is that there's a lot of Beastfolk abound. And the jarls aren't uniting against them, while the Elves seem... well, *unresponsive*."

"I'm headed to the Elves," I said. "At least, I picked up a quest to go there."

"What? Down the Elvenway?"

I nodded. "Yeah."

He made a face. "I wouldn't, man: sticking around here is a recipe for trouble. Everyone who can is leaving."

It made perfect sense. Why hang around when things seemed to be going south? If this was a game with endless respawns or maybe an XP or gold penalty if I died, I'd be the first in line to start punching, but Rahandi was right about death; we had no idea what would happen. Would we return home? Roll a new character? Simply get a timeout before we could respawn?

Or would we utterly and irrevocably die?

But the heart had something to say too; I had promised Anuina I'd stick around to help, and she had joined my Phylomantic Bond. She was more than a friend—more than a lover. And even if she wasn't, what kind of man would come back on his word? I promised I'd help.

So I will fucking help.

I smiled at Rahandi. "I'll take my chances," I said. "Thanks for the heads-up, but I'm not one to abort a quest."

He looked at me for a full second. "It's not horseplay, man," he said. "It's not a game."

"Yeah," I replied. "I think that's exactly the reason why I can't come."

Promises to NPCs were easily broken; promises to living, breathing people I loved not so much.

He sighed and veered up. "All right, man. You do what you gotta do. Just remember: if you need to turn tail or just need a few friends who literally know where you're coming from, come find us."

I gave him a warm smile. "Thanks, man."

He reached into his pocket, then handed me a ring. "Here," he said.

I studied it; it was a band of silver with intricate patterns that resembled Celtic knots.

"I was saving it for the chick from Oklahoma; she's a spellcaster. But it might serve you better where you're going."

I focused on the item.

Ring of Shielding
Level 4

Encumbrance: n/a
Description: This intricately patterned silver band increases the Armor of any armors conjured through the Projection skill by 6.

"Wow, dude," I said. "Thanks! Are you sure? I mean, this is some seriously epic shit."

He chuckled. "I think it'd be 'meh' for her; she was level 7 when I last saw her." He extended his hand, and I shook it. "I hope it serves you well, man. Come look for us when you're done here."

I nodded. "Thanks."

With that, we headed back into the inn. Rahandi returned to his merchant clients, and I sat back down at our table. My women were still gone, but that was all right; I had a lot to think about.

***

About an hour after my talk with Rahandi, Adalrik the innkeeper came to pick us up and led us to a small back room. He let out a deep sigh—obviously tired from a long day's work—and sat down after pouring all three of us some ale.

"So," Adalrik said, eying us all with his shrewd gaze. "You want information?"

"Yeah," I said. "Things are piecing together already, but it seems there are rumors of war?"

He pressed his lips together as if the word tasted sour. "War... Well, I cannot say if it's going to be any *more* war than we normally have. The jarls are always bickering, and not a Bloodmoon passes without one raiding into the lands of another."

"But there is more than that, isn't there?" Roswitha asked. "Were the steads and farms around Wealdhaven burned in a raid led by a hostile jarl?"

"No," Adalrik admitted. "The survivors told tales of Beastfolk raiding in the night, stealing kith, kin, and belongings. They set fire to the houses before dawn and retreated."

"Retreated to where?" Anuina asked, her eyes betraying a fear that she could guess the answer.

"Liandrenn," Adalrik said, eyes fixed firmly on her. "The home of your woodland kin."

Anuina grew pale at his words. "But that is not possible. My people would never allow Beastfolk to make their home in Liandrenn; we are sworn to guard the forest."

He shrugged. "As the old rhyme goes: 'Be it flying hen or hairless mare, only the truthful word of an Elf is more rare.'"

Anuina threw him a glare, but his face remained stoically expressionless.

I sat back, ignoring his jab at Anuina for now. "So, Beastfolk are raiding out of the forest?"

Adalrik shrugged. "Those are the rumors, but there has not been an official confirmation from Jarl Strumma's mouth; he is silent about the threat. I do know that Jarl Strumma has sent men down the Elvenway and to the edges of the forest to guard it, and I spoke to a captain who returned from there. He told me the Beastfolk are testing the defenses in a manner most shrewd and tactical—as if they were organized and commanded by an experienced warlord. The Beastfolk have never before tested us so, let alone been able to muster the numbers and the unity needed to stage an attack."

"We've seen it firsthand," I said. "We come from Jarl Vitek's hall, Histerborg. Beastfolk burned it down three nights ago, Jarl Vitek with it."

"I've heard the news," Adalrik said. "The Janneskog Woods were always dangerous; the Beastfolk have made it their home since before Humans came hither. Still, an attack on a hall is unprecedented. We of Wealdhaven hold no love for Vitek—he tolled traders bound for Alonsby and farther north excessively—but his passing will mean the road to Alonsby will be even more dangerous."

Adalrik sighed. "I admit, these are dangerous times, and many of those with the means to leave Wealdhaven have either already left or are considering leaving. It feels as if a storm is brewing."

Anuina leaned forward. "And there has been no contact with my kin? Surely, they must be able to tell you more?"

Adalrik looked up at her. "You are the first of the Sylvan Folk that has come to Wealdhaven in almost a Bloodmoon. I do not know what counsel my Jarl Strumma keeps, but we common folk have received no word from your kin... and their promise remains unfulfilled."

I placed my hand over Anuina's when I saw she was about to retort. She glared at me but was silent. I turned my eye to Adalrik. "Thank you," I said. "We would like to purchase supplies for the road. Food that keeps and ale if you can spare some. Perhaps enough for two fortnights."

He nodded. "I can arrange that, but trail rations are sparse. It will cost you."

"How much?"

"Five golden coins and six silver ones."

"By the Masked One!" Roswitha exclaimed. "That's extortion."

Adalrik shrugged. "As I said, many are leaving Wealdhaven. As such, supplies for travel are dwindling."

"It's fine," I said, and I began counting out the coins. "We'll offload some of our excess gear in the morning before we set out."

He counted them under the glare of Roswitha and Anuina, then gave me a nod. "I will have your things ready in the morning."

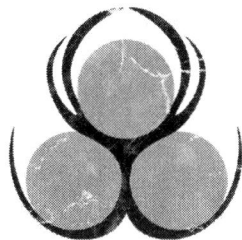

CHAPTER 12

We broke our fast at Rodrik's Head Inn on bread and cheese, downing a mug of ale each, except for Anuina—she drank boiled water.

I had hoped to see Rahandi again—if only to bid him farewell, but I could not find him. His merchant clients were still here, dealing with hangovers of varying intensity, but the man himself was nowhere in sight.

After breakfast, we paid a visit to the market stalls and stores of Wealdhaven. We offloaded the excess equipment we had taken from the Fauns, but it netted us only twelve coppers; apparently, flimsy gear was not much in demand.

We left Wealdhaven through the south gate, handing over the stone token that allowed us passage to the guards. They gave us a last warning about the Elvenway, saying that it was dangerous to venture down that road.

We thanked them for their concern before moving on.

South of Wealdhaven, we walked through farmlands— fields of crops demarcated with low stone walls. However, they soon grew sparse and made way for more rugged terrain until the only trace of civilization was the road itself.

Every five hundred steps or so, we found a stone with an Elven symbol carved in it; Anuina told us they were markers, so that travelers knew how long until they would reach the next settlement.

As evening drew in, the surrounding land rose. Copses of trees sprang up around us, and it became hard to see too far ahead past them. The road began meandering too, riding between the rising ground or slinking around knots of trees. We camped on high ground and decided not to make a fire to avoid drawing attention to ourselves. When it began raining, the mood in our camp became gloomy. We dined on the simple fare Adalrik had provided, set out a watch, and rested.

Morning came gray and somber. We went on our way and by midday reached a crossroads. Smaller trails ran east and west from here, but the Elvenway continued south. A wooden watchtower oversaw the waypoint. It was garrisoned by ten men, and they bore on their shields the same rune that we had seen in Wealdhaven.

The eldest of the bunch, a grizzled and scarred veteran in well-oiled chainmail, came forward to stop us.

"Halt," he said. "In the name of Jarl Strumma Hardenkson Life-Tree, whose hold you are about to leave. Who are you?"

I stepped forward. "I am Oram Ludwickson. These are my companions: Rodwitha Rolofsdottir Iron-Eye and Anuina Willowsdaughter of the Sylvan Folk."

He eyed us suspiciously, especially Anuina. "What business have you in Liandrenn?"

I nodded at Anuina. "It is her home. We are escorting her there."

The guard nodded. "They will have told you already at Wealdhaven, but the forest is dangerous. We have not had word for some time out of Thalumir, and the last trader to return has told us it was abandoned."

"Abandoned?" Anuina asked.

"Aye," the guard replied. "Not a soul to be found. They have all disappeared."

"And no word has come from my kin?"

He snorted, then shook his head. "Fickle as storms," he said. "We've heard nothing."

Anuina looked at me, her eyes large and desperate. "Something is terribly wrong."

I nodded. "Maybe we need to reconsider going in like this. I think—"

From out of the forest ahead, a flat horn sounded. First it was just one, then another followed, and then several more.

"They are coming!" a man in the watchtower cried out as he and his companion reached for their swords.

The grizzled veteran turned toward his men. "Shield wall!" he bellowed as he drew his swords with a ring.

The familiar cries of Fauns sounded in the distance. Among their excited shrieking was a heavy, guttural grunting I had not heard before. I exchanged a quick look with my companions, but the determination in their eyes was unmistakable.

I gave them a nod as I began casting Barkskin. "Let's get ready."

***

Out of the edge of the forest, a horde of Beastfolk came howling. As I prepared my spells, I counted at least thirty

Fauns and five Satyrs. Worse, among them loped humanoid creatures that stood over two-and-a-half meters tall. They were fat, bloated and pink, and their heads resembled those of hogs—tusks and all—but their beady eyes had a maliciously intelligent glow to them.

"Hog-Men," Anuina whispered.

I cast a quick look at the guardsmen; they were all level 3 Warriors with 20 Stamina each. The veteran was level 4. I shifted my gaze to the enemy even as I cast Windward on myself and—through my Phylomantic Bond—on my women, giving any opponents seeking to attack us a -51 penalty for 10 rounds.

Faun Warrior
Level 2
Stamina: 12, Health: 4, Mana: 9, Sanity: 3

We knew these; they were nothing special. But thirty of them... that was something else.

Satyr
Level 5
Stamina: 36, Health: 6, Mana: 30, Sanity: 5

We had taken the previous Satyr we had encountered down with ease, but we had the advantage of range then. This time, there were five of them, and they would be with us within a breath...

Hog-Man
Level 7
Stamina: 56, Health: 8, Mana: 32, Sanity: 4

Damn... There were only two of them, but they looked tough.

I braced myself as the horde came shrieking and howling. Roswitha had time to join the shield wall and to get a Bless spell in, invoking the Bladed One for succor. Anuina fired a volley of four arrows, downing two Fauns. A moment later, the enemy struck the shield wall. Raging and bellowing hate, they tore into the warriors, Fauns clustered around the Satyrs, who bore long axes, while the Hog-Men raged independently with huge clubs.

Two of the warriors went down as bodies clashed in a tempest of iron and blood; one was brought low by five stabbing spears to have his heart impaled by a bellowing Satyr, while the other had his skull caved in with a single strike from one of the Hog-Men.

The shield wall suffered the brunt of the attack and—to the credit of Jarl Strumma's men—did not break rank. With a furious cry from the veteran, they set to their grim work and gave the Beastfolk answer in kind to their charge. Axe and sword hacked away at the Fauns as they tried to scamper out of the way or attempted to deflect well-wrought iron with weathered fur and leather. Here, a Faun went down shrieking, clawing at his innards even as they gushed from his opened belly; there, a Satyr howled in pain as two warriors hacked on his spear arm. The snap of his bone was sickening, and the Satyr gave a pitiful cry as he fell back clutching his hand, now hanging from his wrist by but a few tendons.

Roswitha stood with the men of Wealdhaven. Like a beautiful fury of battle, she held braced behind her shield, every muscle in her body tense as she took the violent assault of a Satyr on her own. She fought like a beast, her powerful voice a clarion call across the battlefield, bringing down the blessing of the Bladed One on those who strove for the defense of Wealdhaven.

Inspired by her strength and determination, I cried out and let loose my arcane power. I targeted the three remaining Satyrs with the full fury of two overcharged Ice Spikes, the first Check still profiting from Roswitha's Bless spell.

> **Elemental Check result: (47 + 6 Cunning + 18 Elemental + 50 Bonus =) 121 versus opponents' 112, 25, and 31.**

All hits!

You deal 12 Physical damage (water)!

The second wave went straight after it, and since they had no Action left, they could do nothing against it except roll their Armor Checks, and the mechanics never showed me those.

You deal 12 Physical damage (water)!

Although none of them suffered grievous wounds, the damage output was high enough to freeze the iron armor they wore to the point that it shattered, leaving their bodies unprotected. The Mana cost was enormous—18—but it was worth it; if we were going to survive, we needed to thin the Satyr ranks *and* keep them occupied.

Anuina followed up quickly with a volley of arrows, striking each of the Satyrs. The first one she hit in the eyes, and the beast let out something like a goat's bleating and collapsed. The others took serious Stamina damage.

But the enemy did not relent before our counter. The pushing and shoving at the shield wall continued. Although all but one of the Satyrs had used their Action, the Hog-Men still towered over the melee, slamming left and right with their fearsome clubs, spattered with blood and brains. They were supported by the Fauns, twenty-three still, who scurried between their larger allies to get their vicious little jabs in.

Four more warriors of Wealdhaven went down under this violence, one shrieking as he fell over, clawing to retrieve his severed leg that lay a meter from his prostrate form. Another stumbled back, cradling his belly, and his face turned white, eyes watery when he peeked down to see his bowels snake out from between his fingers.

Seeing that they were unable to break the shield wall, one of the Satyrs barked an order at a group of Fauns to flank us. Four Fauns broke free from the melee and charged at Anuina. She held no weapon with which she could parry, and she chose not to dodge. Luckily, her armor—though scanty—blocked the weak jabs of the Faun spears, even though the leather chipped away in places.

I think she can deal with those little fuckers on her own...

I focused on the melee again; the biggest threat lay there. The men of Jarl Strumma were brave warriors, all. Despite the slaughter among their numbers, their eyes blazed below iron-rimmed caps as they set to the defense of their native lands. The veteran bellowed for his men to fight, and the counterattack came swiftly. A Hog-Man, skin rent open and lacerated by axe and sword, perished with a last furious grunt, while one of the Satyrs fell bleating, a sword of Wealdhaven buried deep in its hairy chest. Under the tide of slaughter that washed shield and axe blood-red, six more Fauns fell, trampled underfoot, decapitated, or skulls bashed in by iron-rimmed shields. Roswitha supported the troops; she reinvigorated one of the warriors who stood panting heavily and was close to being overcome.

It was inspiring.

I slammed the butt of my staff on the ground, splashed water from my jug, and spoke an arcane incantation. It took great accuracy, but I cast an instant Iceplane spell right under the cloven hooves of the Beastfolk, sparing the warriors of Wealdhaven of its effect. As the Beastfolk stumbled or fought to retain balance, I followed up with an upgraded Ice Spikes spell to target the two remaining Satyrs and the Hog-Man. Unfortunately, the results were abysmal: a 26 and a 34. Only one of my attacks struck true; the Hog-Man did not dodge.

You deal 10 Physical damage (earth)!

The Hog-Man gave me a furious, pig-eyed look as the jagged spike of ice wore away the last scraps of armor on his body.

Close to me, Anuina discarded her bow and drew an arming sword. With an Elven cry of war—beautiful as it was terrible—she set herself to sword-work, slashing at the Fauns that had sought to overwhelm her. Although there was grace in her fencing, she wasn't as effective with a sword as with her bow. Still, it seemed to me she would hold her own.

Ahead, the melee continued mercilessly. Only four guardsmen, including the veteran, still stood to meet the third push of our foes. However, the attack was weaker than before; many of our foes had already spent their Action dodging or slipping on the ice and were unable to weigh in. The men of Wealdhaven stood their ground against this violence, easily parrying or blocking their foes' furious attacks.

In this chaotic clash of arms, the last Hog-Man singled out the veteran. He waded toward the elder man with a rabid grunting, pushing friend and foe aside. A furious battering of the Hog-Man's blood-splattered club left the veteran panting, but he held his own without suffering grievous wounds. No warrior of Wealdhaven fell during this push, and hesitation dawned in the black eyes of our Beastfolk foes. Meanwhile, Anuina had no trouble parrying the attacks of the Fauns, especially with the aid of my Windward spell.

"They waver!" the veteran shouted over the din of battle. "Push now! For Wealdhaven!"

"For Wealdhaven!" the remaining soldiers echoed, and even one wounded man climbed to his feet, clutching his bleeding flank as he raised his axe and ran back into the fray.

Furious was the onslaught. The din of iron hammering on armor and flesh was deafening, as were the snarls of Beastfolk and the howling of the warriors of Wealdhaven. Four more Fauns perished in a storm of swords and axes, their dark blood spilling on the trampled ground, bodies falling to join those of their kin, trampled in the mud. Roswitha's voice rose clear above the noise as she used her magic to heal the veteran, who faced his Hog-Man foe with energy renewed.

I focused on the Hog-Man now. With a cry that bade the elements to bend to my will, I drew an arcane sigil of might with my staff, then projected from its tip an upgraded Fire Sprout, aimed at the Hog-Man that towered over the melee. Having no armor, the creature snarled and tried to step out of the way of my vindicating fire.

Elemental Check result: (29 + 6 Cunning + 18 Elemental =) 53 versus opponent's 114.

Damn it...

The Hog-Man ducked, and the jet of flame found only a patch of grass to burn up.

Only 5 Mana left...

Anuina was still in her melee with the Fauns, dancing around them, aided by the winds of my spell. With a swift cut that severed a Faun's jaw from its face, she made her first melee kill.

The Beastfolk wavered. Many lost their footing on the ice I had conjured, and the Hog-Man had already spent his Action dodging my Fire Sprout. The attack that followed was half-hearted, but a jab from a Faun spear brought low the wounded warrior who had rejoined the fray. He sank to his knees, cruel iron tip lodged between his ribs, spat blood, then slumped to the side to die on the blood-soaked soil.

"Kill!" the veteran howled in the midst of battle. "Avenge!"

The men's faces were grim, locks of hair stuck to their sweaty faces framed in blood-spattered iron. They hacked and hewed, slaughtering three more Fauns, and I now clearly saw that some had an ability that allowed them to renew a failed attack. Roswitha supported them again with healing magic, renewing the vigor of the man who looked most hounded.

I hesitated; my Mana was coming to its end, and I learned now the lesson of spending too much early on in battle. It was a lesson I thought I had already learned through the many games I had played, but it was somehow different if you were in the middle of it. I raised my staff, spoke the familiar words that called upon fire, and blasted the Hog-Man with my Fire Sprout. This time, he could not dodge my attack, and my gout of flame hit him. The squeal was that of a pig; the smell that of pork.

I grinned.

You deal 16 Physical damage (fire)!

Close to me, Anuina kept up her sword-work, hacking away at the Fauns. But by her movements, I could see she was getting tired, and a quick focus revealed she was down to 16 Stamina. She would need succor soon.

Again, the Fauns gave a half-hearted push. There were but seven of them left to face the four sturdy men of Wealdhaven, supported by Roswitha, and over half had already lost their Action on the ice I had conjured. Those who hadn't, stayed close to the Hog-Man, jabbing with their spears at the veteran warrior who parried them with shield and sword. Then, the veteran raised his blade, and his tired but determined men pushed again. Three Fauns fell, and Roswitha spent more of her dwindling Mana on healing the veteran who was positively tanking for us right now.

My magic all but spent, I cast Ghost Touch on a battle axe dropped by a warrior and attacked the Hog-Man with it.

Psionics Check result: (88 + 6 Cunning + 8 Psionic =) 102 versus opponent's 35.

You deal 20 Physical damage (slashing)!

Damn... I had forgotten how good this spell was when used on an effective weapon. My attack brought the Hog-Man to exactly 0 Stamina. He staggered and swayed. A moment later, he received a quick hack across his face from the veteran's sword, and he was brought low with a whimper, dying on the soil he had tried to conquer.

After that, it was but clean-up duty. The remaining Fauns fought weakly, and some even tried to flee. Luckily, Anuina's arrows made sure none returned to whatever haunt they occupied in Liandrenn to tell of their defeat.

We were victorious...

You receive 1,400 XP.

***

"Thank you for your aid," the veteran said.

He had a fresh gash across his arm, and his chainmail hauberk looked like it needed repairs.

Of all his men, he was best off.

My stomach churned at the sight of the battlefield. Close to me, a lightly wounded warrior tended to a man who lay pale and wide-eyed, muttering something unintelligible as he clutched the stump that had been his leg and tried to rise to feet he no longer had. Elsewhere, another warrior held the hand of his brother-in-arms, calmly listening as the other spoke words to convey to his wife and child even as he struggled to keep his innards inside, fighting to buy himself the time he needed to speak his final words.

This is no game…

The blood drew from my face as I turned back to the veteran.

"It would have been worse had you not been here," the man continued. "I doubt we would be standing here. Jarl Strumma will learn of what you did today."

I gave a nod, feeling guilty because I survived—unharmed. "I… I wish we could have done more," I said.

The veteran patted me on the shoulder. "Good man," he said. "But you did all that was within your power." He nodded at Roswitha and Anuina. "You and your companions. It has been long since the woodland folk fought with us; we will not forget it."

"What will you do now?" I asked.

He looked to the battlefield. "Send to Jarl Strumma for aid," he said. "The Beastfolk grow bolder, and we'll need more men here. The wounded will need care; the dead their burial rites." He turned his stern eyes to me. "And you?" he asked. "Will you continue into the forest? After what you have seen here today?"

I exchanged a glance with Anuina. If anything, she seemed more determined, and she stepped forward, elegant and gracious as only she could be. "I *must* go," she said. But I will bear neither you nor Roswitha ill will if you turn around now, for it seems Liandrenn is in a much worse state than any of us had dared to dream."

I shook my head. "I am no fair-weather friend," I said. "You are my companion, and companions stand together. If this is the scourge of the land that needs dealing with, *I* shall not avoid the confrontation and slink away."

Anuina's expression warmed. Wordless, she gave me a thankful nod.

Roswitha came up and placed her hand on Anuina's shoulder. "Well said," she added. "I will not take flight either… if that even needs saying at all."

The veteran gave an appreciative grunt. "The bravery I see here is often lacking in the youth of today. Go with the blessings of the Bladed One, may his will guide your hand. I wish I had something to give you, but our supplies are stretched thin as it is."

"We'll do fine," I said.

"But I *will* say this," the veteran said: "return to Jarl Strumma if you make it through the forest, knowing that his Captain Ydbrad Ydbradson will speak on your behalf, so that any tidings you bring or deeds you have done he will reward as honor demands." He struck his chest with his fist. "That I promise."

I gave a firm nod. "Thank you."

"Now," he said. "I must tend to my men. If you enter the forest, heed this advice: stick to the path until you see Thalumir. Then, veer left a little until you come upon an old oak tree with a split trunk. Head straight south from there and you will come to a spot where you can enter the outpost under the cover of some ancient trees; you will not be seen until you move to the center or make yourself known… it may help, should Thalumir not be in the hands of friends or allies."

Anuina frowned. "I did not know about that…"

Ydbrad gave her a gap-toothed grin. "It is not only Elves who are secretive. Us men of Wealdhaven have a few tricks of our own…"

I grinned and shook his hand, gripping his wrist as was the custom of warriors, and with that we parted, finally leaving the hold of Jarl Strumma behind us.

We had entered Liandrenn proper.

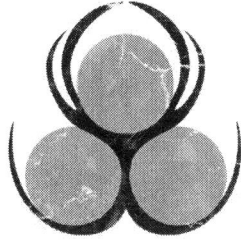

CHAPTER 13

When we were an hour into the forest, we took a short break. My character sheet icon had been flashing, and it was the same for Anuina and Roswitha; we had all leveled up on the previous battle's XP.

Level 5...

Once we sat, I focused on the icon.

> **You have advanced to level 5. As a reward, you may increase one of your attributes by 1. In addition, you receive 12 skill points to distribute among your skills as you see fit. Your Stamina and Mana also increase by a number equal to your Endurance and Power, respectively. Finally, the following randomly selected attribute that was reduced due to a death will be restored by 1: Endurance.**
>
> **Since you are a Phylomancer, you also gain the following abilities: Mana Surge.**

Please note that Phylomancers only gain new spells through their Phylomantic Bond; consult your character sheet for more information.

I put my attribute point in Intellect once again. It seemed a bit broken; increasing damage was much better than increasing the other stats, except maybe Power to get more Mana. The skill points I invested in Druidcraft, Teleportation, Medium Armor, and Elemental—3 to each.

Having done that, I checked out Mana Surge.

Mana Surge (Phylomancer): By spending 3 Stamina and spending an Action, you may regenerate 3-18 Mana.

That could be very useful, especially if I rolled higher numbers. It was better than the potions I had anyway.

Eager to learn about any new spells, I checked out my Phylomantic Bonds.

Your Phylomantic Bond with Roswitha Rolofsdottir Iron-Eye has offered you access to the following new spells: Ice Shield (2).
Your Phylomantic Bond with Anuina Willowsdaughter has offered you access to the following new spells: Ground (2).
In addition, since your bond with these subjects is intense, you and these subjects gain the following advantages: +10 Stamina, +10 Mana.

I frowned. This was meager: only two new spells. I gave them a quick check. Ice Shield gave immunity against water or fire damage for 1 round—useful if we faced wizards, or if we had an unfortunate encounter with something that could breathe fire... or ice. The Ground spell allowed me to bring a flying creature down to the floor. The idea of a flying foe worried me. I hadn't even considered they existed yet. But this spell was going to help were we to run into any.

Well, only two spells, but at least we're ready for fire- or ice-breathing dragons.

Finishing up, I gave my sheet a last inspection.

Oram Ludwickson (Human)
Level 5 Phylomancer

Attributes: Strength 3, Agility 5, Endurance 4, Intellect 11, Cunning 6, Power 6
Resources: Stamina 24(34), Health 3, Mana 36(59), Sanity 6
Skills: Dagger 2, Dodge 8, Druidcraft 3, Elemental 21, Illusion 5, Intuition 2, Medium Armor 8, Perception 2, Psionic 8, Staff 8, Summoning 3, Teleportation 3, Ward 8(13)
Abilities: Phylomantic Bond (2/2), Phylomantic Monitor, Phylomantic Link, Greater Phylomantic Link, Mana Surge, Meta-Magic (Instant Spell, Overcharge Spell)
Spells: Frost Ward (0), Ghost Touch (0), Icy Hand (0), Light (0), Mold Earth (0), Boulder (1), Ensnare (1), Fire Sprout (1), Fog (1), Freeze/Thaw (1), Frost Wave (1), Ice Spikes (1), Ice Vest (1), Reinvigorate (1), Summon

Lesser Ice Imp (1), Sustenance (1), Trackless Step (1), Tremor (1), Barkskin (2), Create/Destroy Water (2), Frostbite (2), Ground (2), Ice Shield (2), Iceplane (2), Spikes (2), Summon Beast (2), Windwalk (2), Windward (2), Word of Invigoration (2).
Equipment: Pyromancer's Staff, Dagger (Common), Shaman Charm, Bracelet of Mana, Ring of Shielding, 2 Shortbows (Shoddy), 2 Quivers with Arrows
XP/XP needed until next level: 9,600/16,000

Getting my Endurance point back and the ever-increasing bonus from the Phylomantic Bonds gave my Stamina a much-needed boost. That would help if I needed to call on my Mana Surge ability, since Stamina powered it.

I dismissed the sheet. It was not the most powerful of level-ups, but I had a feeling level 3 spells might soon come my way, and I was very keen to see what they had in store for me.

I sat back and waited while Roswitha and Anuina finished up. After that, we ate a bite, then set out deeper into the forest.

***

"It's quiet," Anuina said.

I hadn't noticed, although I did have a somewhat ominous feeling that something was amiss. Now that Anuina had given it a name, I heard it too. Or rather, did *not* hear it too.

Roswitha said nothing; she was on her guard and did not seem comfortable at all.

"Something terribly ill is afoot," Anuina said. "The forest is watchful, *hostile* even."

I had to trust my Elf companion on that; detecting the dispositions of shrubs and trees was not my forte. "What do you suppose is going on?" I asked her.

She shook her head, emerald eyes drifting from tree to tree. "I can't say, but Liandrenn feels almost as hostile and foul as the parts of the Janneskog Woods where the Beastfolk still dwell."

"Well, that's no good," I muttered.

"Hardly," she said, sarcasm plain in her voice.

We moved cautiously down the edge of the path, sticking to the trees as much as possible. By some premonition, my companions had drawn their weapons, Roswitha wielding her sword and shield, a few steps behind Anuina, who had her bow in hand, arrow loose on the shelf.

As we went on, the canopy grew denser, and less light filtered down to the path. It took only a short while before we imagined snarling Beastfolk hiding behind every tree. I wanted to use my Light spell, but Anuina advised against it.

"It will only serve to make *us* more visible."

Unfortunately, that made sense.

When a gloom settled on the forest, we knew sunset was nearing. Soon, we would trade the sparse light of the two suns of Aerda for total darkness; the light of the two moons and the nebulae would not be able to pierce the roof of leaves and branches.

"It is best to make camp while we have some light to find a defensible location," Roswitha said. "I would not want to continue down this road in the dark and find us forced to camp in a place where we are easy marks for Fauns… or worse."

I looked to Anuina, and she gave a nod. "I had hoped the forest would feel friendlier so early on, but I agree: continuing is more perilous than waiting."

We found a small glade by the roadside that offered us at least a limited view of the surroundings so that there would be time to rouse the others in the event of a threat. We pitched no tents, and we kept wood for a campfire handy, should we need flame to protect us, but we did not light it yet.

Roswitha took first watch, and I lay down beside Anuina, huddling close to her soft body for warmth; the forest had been cool during the day with so little sunlight coming down, but it was downright cold now. She gave a satisfied mewl when we pushed our bodies close, and I was pleased that even in circumstances like these, my body still responded to hers.

However, it was near impossible to catch sleep. Midges flew in by the thousands to feast on us. And if it wasn't the midges, then it was a branch poking my back, a curious beetle or spider crawling over my face, a disturbing hoot from an owl, or another, less easily identified forest sound.

I lay with open eyes, holding Anuina, and by her steady breathing I knew she had less trouble than I did falling asleep.

Then came the first growl.

It was soft—some distance away perhaps, but it was no wise owl, friendly fox, or curious squirrel.

"Did you hear that?" I softly asked the huddled shape by the unlit campfire.

"Aye," Roswitha said. "And I wager it was no friendly critter," she added, echoing my thoughts.

I let go of Anuina and sat up, any thought of sleep banished. "What should we do?"

"We wait," Roswitha said. "And keep you handy to light the fire if necessary."

"I can dig a trench around us," I said.

She barked a short laugh. "You have your uses, Oram Ludwickson, but shoveling is not one of them."

I gave her a crooked grin. "Nothing so pedestrian, my dear," I said. With a quick arcane symbol, I used my Mold Earth spell to dig a trench around us that would be difficult to charge across.

Roswitha watched with wide eyes, obviously caught by surprise as I turned the dirt without even touching it, then chuckled and shook her head. "At times like these, I could push you down and ride you for an hour."

"I am unlikely to object to that, my dear warrior woman," I said.

She stood there smiling, arms folded, an image of beauty and strength, as I worked my magic and made us a trench. When I had finished, we heard another growl.

"It's closer," I said.

"Aye."

It came again, louder… furious.

Trees snapped in the distance, and the very ground shook.

Goosebumps pricked my skin. I took a step back. Out of the black forest, I felt hate coming in waves; something watched us with murderous intent.

"Wake the Elf," Roswitha hissed. "We are hunted…"

***

The thing that came crashing out into the glade was monstrous, a mixture between a bear and a man, with the wholly black eyes of the Beastfolk that glared at us with evil intelligence. It was easily three meters tall, dwarfing us and even some trees around the glade. The beast reared up on its hind legs, sniffing the air as if savoring our scents.

Corrupted Bear-Shifter
Level 10 (Elite)
Stamina: 121, Health: 11, Mana: 66(86), Sanity: 6

"By the Misted One," Anuina muttered. "This is one of my druid kin… but corrupted."

"Let's save the analysis for later," I muttered.

The Bear-Shifter gave a furious bellow and brandished its claws. A moment later, it charged us. Luckily, my trench prevented it from attacking right away.

"Behind me!" Roswitha called out, and she braced sword and shield, waiting for the horror to come.

She didn't need to say that twice. I raised my staff, spoke a few words of power, and cast my Windward spell.

Elemental Check result: (78 + 6 Cunning + 21 Elemental =) 105.

There… try to hit us now.

Anuina focused on the beast, then nocked three arrows in rapid succession and fired them. We all stood perplexed as the beast shrugged them off with little effort, its Stamina only lowering by 4.

"This is going to be tough," I muttered.

The Bear-Shifter now clambered out of the trench, furious gaze resting on us. But instead of the animal charge I had expected, it rose to its hindquarters and howled.

Your Windward spell has been dispelled.

Then the beast charged.
Great, it has the same Meta-Magic as I do.

But even without the protection of my spells, Roswitha was an excellent bladeswoman; using shield and fiery brand to effect, she caught and parried the massive claw as the Bear-Shifter came for her, even though she trembled under the strength of the blow. Just as she tried to regain herself and counter, the beast swung twice more.

Both blows landed, slamming through her defenses. Her shield creaked, splinters flying, and her plate caught the remainder of the vigorous might behind the beast's claws.

Her parrying and defending had brought her Stamina down from 60 to 43.

Fuck... This thing is not joking around.

Quickly, Roswitha rose to her feet. She screamed the fury of the Snowlands as she swung her fiery brand at the creature. As the sword came down, passing the defenses of the beast, the markings on the blade ignited in flame. It was one of the most bad-ass things I had ever seen.

And yet, the beast didn't so much as flinch, losing only 1 Stamina from its parry attempt, and then 1 more from whatever check it made to mitigate the damage Roswitha dealt.

Natural armor... it probably has a hide thicker than leather.

It was time to try out my healing magic. I drew an exalted symbol in the air and called upon the Salved One as

I cast Word of Invigoration, using my Meta-Magic to make it an instant spell.

You healed Roswitha for 15 Stamina.

Then, I rumbled another incantation and threw an overcharged, upgraded Fire Sprout at the beast. It did not dodge my attack, and I dealt 23 damage to it. When I saw its Stamina lower from 112 to 99, I knew.

10 Armor.

I relayed this information to my companions. "We can do this!" I added.

Anuina gave a nod, then began firing her arrows again. She kept her emerald eyes fixed on the beast in total focus as she stood straight like a young sapling, firing arrows faster than my eyes could trace. As she launched her shafts at the beast, I saw her Stamina drop by 13.

It seems Rangers pay for their abilities with Stamina...

The first arrow dropped the beast's Stamina by 17, and the two that followed by an additional 29 each, bringing the beast down all the way to 24!

Fuck... I gawked at her. She was a total badass... *And here I stood thinking I was the major damage dealer. Her level 5 must have been a shitload better than mine...*

The beast roared fury, but its matted fur told of how tired it was from dealing with Anuina's mighty barrage. Still, it had another trick up its sleeve. Again, it reared itself and rumbled something that sounded arcane to my trained ear, and its Stamina shot up by 61. Then, the Bear-Shifter turned its eye to me and charged.

Oh fuck.

I slammed my staff on the ground and cast Tremor under the Bear-Shifter.

Elemental Check result: (96 + 6 Cunning + 21 Elemental =) 123 versus opponents' 97 and 101.

The earth under the Bear-Shifter shook. It tried to maintain balance as it glared at me in confusion, but the tremors I had created were too intense. To prevent itself from losing its footing, it had to halt its charge. Unfortunately, in my eagerness not to get attacked, I had targeted Roswitha too. She stared daggers at me as she wobbled on her feet and tried to keep her footing.

Still, had that thing reached me, I would have been dead.

I followed up by raising my staff and calling upon the element of Life, summoning a Spirit Animal right in front of me to defend me from any attacks.

My level 4 spirit animal, I learned with appropriate disappointment, was *a shark*.

I sighed as it lay there flopping on the forest floor.

After a moment, my useless spirit animal died and despawned.

The look Anuina shot me was one of utter bewilderment. Luckily, she persisted with her volleys, firing another hail of arrows at the beast, lowering its Stamina by 32, 17, and 23, leaving the damn thing at 11.

The beast roared, its attention now definitely shifted to Anuina, and charged at her, but not after healing itself for 70 Stamina. Anuina yelped as it lay into her, and she had no means to defend herself. The first attack she dodged, wasting her Action, but her armor had to take the two that followed, and the enticing leather garment suffered scratches that bared one of her full, ivory breasts. She stumbled back, uttering a cry that cut me to the bone as the beast brought her down to 9 Stamina.

Roswitha was quick to utter a prayer to the Tribunal, beseeching them for aid and restoring 12 Stamina to Anuina, but that was not going to cut it.

I expected the beast would dispel Windward again if I cast it, so I stuck to Tremor, casting it instantly. This time, I took care not to target my ally.

Elemental Check result: (31 + 6 Cunning + 21 Elemental =) 58 versus opponent's 81.

Well, fuck! One more try.

You can only cast one Interruption per round.

Fuuuck. Slightly panicking, I threw a splash of water from my jug and cast Iceplane.

Elemental Check result: (95 + 6 Cunning + 21 Elemental =) 122 versus opponent's 105.

I sighed with relief as the beast slipped while attempting to retain its footing. A moment later, Anuina had her sword out; she could parry now, at least. Still, the beast dispelled the icy plane with an instant. It cost him 11 Mana though; he was not going to keep that up forever.

"Keep the beast occupied!" Roswitha called out as she healed Anuina for another 12 Stamina. "Don't let it act!"

That was a *very* good idea. I hit the Bear-Shifter with another Tremor.

Elemental Check result: (82 + 6 Cunning + 21 Elemental =) 107 versus opponent's 77.

The beast roared with fury as it lost its footing and its Action again. The earth trembled all around it, and Anuina did a nimble somersault away from him, leaving her sword and drawing her bow. It sang as she loosed her arrows, lowering the beast's Stamina by 62 to 18.

The Bear-Shifter stood on the trembling ground, desperately seeking balance, as it tired itself out deflecting arrows. Still, it had its instant spell left, and it healed itself back to 69 Stamina. But it was fighting a losing battle now.

If we could keep it under control.

Roswitha's Bless spell was indeed a blessing when it came; she invoked the Bladed One, and I felt divine strength rage inside me.

Now, to lay down a lasting effect. I raised my staff, spoke words of power as I splashed some water from my jug, and cast Iceplane.

Elemental Check result: (33 + 6 Cunning + 21 Elemental + 50 Bonus =) 110 versus opponent's 51.

Again, the beast lost its footing as it bellowed its frustration. I saw the smile curl Anuina's lips; she knew it—if she could deal enough damage, the beast would be forced to heal himself and my effect stayed in place so it would likely lose another Action. And that would win the day.

She fired, sharpness of her kin in her eyes, hands moving fast and skillful as if she were thrumming the harp. She took 56 Stamina from the beast. Reduced to 13, the beast roared and healed itself for 60, but it knew its end was near. Roswitha charged at it, bringing her sword down and lowering its Stamina by 10 as it stumbled and wobbled.

On my turn, it rolled a 33 for its Acrobatics Check, failing and losing its Action. I raised my staff, a victorious smirk curling my lips as I let loose my arcane might. I cast two upgraded Fire Sprouts, shooting gusts of flame at the beast. I didn't have the Mana to overcharge them, but I hoped it would be enough.

You deal 17 Physical damage (fire)!

You deal 15 Physical damage (fire)!

The Bear-Shifter was at 51, and the glare it gave me was death.

Anuina's bow sang. The first two arrows the beast managed to awkwardly dodge. The third one, however, landed in its chest, piercing that thick armor so that it was embedded down to the feather.

She had dealt 93 damage, of which 63 went through. Combined with the cost of 3 Stamina for using its armor, that was enough to completely eat away its 51 Stamina and 12 Health.

The beast reared one last time, slipping on the ice as it clawed at the arrow that had mortally wounded it. Then, a surprisingly human cry came from its throat as it fell, shedding fur and shrinking. As it went down, its facial features became less bestial and changed into those of an Elf with grizzled black hair.

"No!" Anuina cried out as a look of recognition shot across her face.

Her bow clattered to the ground, and she ran toward the fallen Elf.

***

You receive 1,200 XP.

I quickly willed away the popped-up text as I ran after Anuina.

She stopped beside the Elf as he gave a hacking cough. He was an elder Elf, clad in a robe of deep gray with ornate patterns on it in golden thread that resembled Celtic knots. Now that he had shifted back from his bear shape, he also wore a necklace with a silver amulet in the shape of a face laced in mist and a bracelet of silver.

Anuina slumped beside him, her trembling hands reaching for his. "Alfuinar," she called out, her voice wracked with pain and guilt. "I did not know! Misted One, help me! I did not know."

I stood behind her, unsure what to do. The Elf was dying, and my spells would not bring him back; I did not yet have the power to do that.

"Misted One," Anuina wept, "please, please, please."

The Elf smiled, a blooded grin, and he reached out with a pale hand and folded it over Anuina's. She looked at him, tears clinging to her long lashes, and he spoke softly, as if he bought his words with great pain. "Child," he said. "Have no regrets… You did not… kill me. You *freed* me."

"Alfuinar!" she said as she looked him up and down.

The way her heart shattered as she saw her own arrow deep in his chest brought tears to my eyes. I kneeled down behind her, my hand on her shoulder.

"Alfuinar," she said again. "What happened?"

The Elf shook his head and coughed. "Khal-Had has come, child. We were fools to not see through his... his ruse. He bound many of us to him through a fell magic we have not foreseen, blinded by his honeyed words and calm wisdom." His eyes turned, then shot back and forth erratically as he fought to hold on to life. "He is... he is the druid that came from the south... Ylavurin. He deceived us, Anuina Willowsdaughter, and he—" the Elf broke out coughing, then fell silent.

For a moment, it seemed he had died. Anuina clutched his hand, panic rising in her terse body. But the Elf spoke again. "He deceived all us who claim to be wise... he deceived your father."

"No," she whispered.

"Go to the Willow," the Elf said. "Stop it. Stop Khal-Had... Free your father." His blooded, trembling hand reached into the pocket of his robe and reappeared holding a small, clear jewel—perhaps a diamond—encased in a silver star. "Take this Lodestone," he said. "It will show you the way to the Willow's roots where... where Khal-Had works his evil, even if his magic will seek to thwart you finding the way... Do it now, while the magic of... our kin may still... help you... find... him."

With that, the Elf's eyes turned up in their sockets, and he breathed his last, still clutching the jewel.

Anuina broke. She draped herself over the body and sobbed uncontrollably.

As Roswitha stood guard, I picked her up and held her against me, felt her shaking and quaking in my arms—now a frail and broken thing, while moments ago she had seemed unbreakable in battle. Crying, she buried her face in my neck, and the sweet wildberry scent of her overwhelmed me.

"He was my uncle," she finally said, when she had regained her breath. "Brother to my father, and one of the ruling druids of Liandrenn."

"I am so sorry, Anuina," I said.

Another sob escaped her. "How could we have been so blind?" she said. "I remember Yluvarin's coming… to think he was Khal-Had all along! And that he has been planning this for years!"

"We will get him," I said. "We came this far, and we will get him."

Roswitha's slender hand found Anuina's shoulder, and the fiery warrior woman looked down at the Elf with resolve in her icy eyes. "Come, sister," she said. "As my people say: 'the time for tears is after the time for swords'. First, we must carry out your uncle's dying wish, lest it be too late."

Anuina looked at her, then at me, and the silent and hidden strength I loved so about her returned.

"We are bonded," I said, holding her and pulling Roswitha closer. "One body, one mind. We will be victorious together… or we will burn together."

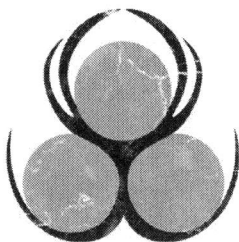

CHAPTER 14

W e lay Alfuinar to rest by the roadside, covered in his cloak. If we were to survive this ordeal, Anuina would retrieve him and give him the burial rites that he deserved. And if we didn't… well, then it mattered little.

We took no more time to rest, knowing that every moment was of the essence if we still wished to stop Khal-Had. Anuina took the jewel entrusted to her by her uncle and, speaking a few soft words in Elven, the precious stone contained in the silver star lit up. It resembled a flashlight, only its beam shone in a fixed direction—the way we needed to go.

We had to leave the road to follow it, and I felt the slightest hesitation when we gave up this last vestige of civilization, the breadcrumb trail that could lead us back to it, and entrusted ourselves to the forest and the magic of the Sylvan Folk that was still supposed to control it. But Anuina showed no such hesitation. Neither did Roswitha, who was more of this world and more used to its wonders than I.

I followed suit. My words had been true; I was willing to die with these two women.

And I meant *really* die.

We moved together, weapons at the ready, as the forest grew thicker and thicker. After a while, boles of magnificent size sprang up around us and soon enough, they were all we could see. It was the first actual view in Aerda—apart from the sky—that seemed alien to me. The only trees I could imagine that grew to a similar size were redwoods, but I had never seen those in real life. And these trees had trunks and branches that were almost white, topped with leaves of gold and silver; they seemed to shine with a light of their own, and the forest here was brighter that it had been along the road.

However, as we made our way, we noticed an increasing amount of those trees withering away as we passed them. They shed their splendorous leaves, which lost their colors and turned brittle even as they fell, and black rot ate away at their majestic trunks. Even as we passed through this decay, the light of the jewel grew weaker.

Anuina beheld the death of those trees with a set jaw and a dolorous glow in her emerald eyes, but she led us on. "We are getting closer to the roots," she said. "Khal-Had is there. But the magic of my kin is faltering, and the Lodestone is growing weaker." She looked at us over her shoulder, a determined fire in her gaze. "We must make haste!"

Deeper into the forest we went, and the rot got worse with every step. The woods had been silent when we first entered them, but they came alive now with sounds. Unfortunately, the cries, the snarling, and the howling that resounded among the diseased and dying trees were a far cry from the regular sounds of a forest.

Through the growing darkness, the Lodestone showed us the way until, at long last, we came to a mighty tree that dwarfed all others.

"The Willow," Anuina whispered, her voice reverent and humble before this avatar of her kin's magic.

It was a tree of vast girth and great height. Along its length ran carved symbols of elegance, adorned with detailed woodwork and depictions of animals and humanoid beings that were all connected by long braids of symbols that resembled Celtic knots. Among the lamenting leaves shone delicate but bright lights, as if the very stars had descended from the night sky to settle among the branches of the Willow.

At the bottom of the tree sprawled a network of tangled roots intertwining, rising and falling as they dug into and around the massive rock upon which the Willow stood perched. Black veins with an oily shimmer ran up from those roots, staining the otherwise clear and spotless wood. They tapered and finally faded higher up the Willow, but we saw them expand slowly even as we stood there.

"The Willow is *changing*," Anuina said, her voice fear-laden and weak. "Khal-Had has it in its grip." She held her bow tightly, her fingers turning white.

"Are we too late?" I asked, finding that my voice sounded weak and humble in this dark moment, as if I were subconsciously afraid that speaking too loudly might rouse the tree itself.

She stood there, shoulders slumped, as she watched the Willow change. "I'm not sure," she said.

"Only one way to find out," Roswitha said, her voice as clear as it always was.

"She's right," I said.

I took a step forward, placed a hand on Anuina's sharp shoulder. "Let's go."

We circled the mighty trunk until we found a shadowed fissure in the rock. Here, the roots had parted, and one would only have to stoop slightly to prevent the reaching tendrils from touching one's head when going in. But the fissure itself was foreboding: a cloying smell wafted out from it—as if there was delight and beauty in such excess that it had become decadent and corrupt. And as the three of us stood there, a delighted but insane cackle echoed in the darkness within.

My heart sunk, but the strength of my bonded women coursed in my veins: the raw courage and fiery lust of my Roswitha and the purity of heart and quiet passion of my Anuina, and I knew that it mattered little what we would find within.

We would face it together.

To my surprise, I was the first to step forward. I drew an arcane sigil and cast Light on my staff. Its glow chased away the shadows lurking around the entrance, and as I took another step, the shadows deeper within suffered a similar fate.

The next moment, my women were with me, and we ventured into the cave together.

***

Our footsteps echoed down the silent, narrow passageway. The rocky surface underfoot was cold and slick, and we heard the faint trickle of water around us; puddles had gathered in the seams and cracks of the rock. The smell here was cloyingly sweet but also earthy—as if something pure struggled underneath it all, fighting to stay alive.

The cavern itself was a passage through the natural rock that had been worn out over the years. Thick roots crawled along the ceiling, some dripping with water. Many of these roots had the same oily black, rotted glow that we had seen outside. Intricate carvings ran along the rock wall, but they were more primitive than those we had seen on the tree itself. They depicted large and small humanoids with horns or antlers as they hunted or fought. It reminded me most of the drawings of cavemen.

This is not Elven art.

"Is this place old?" I asked, unable to suppress my curiosity.

Anuina looked at me over her shoulder, eyes wide and with a feverish glow to them. "Yes," she said. "This place was already ancient when my kin wrested it from Khal-Had two centuries ago. We believe it predates Human and Elf alike in these lands."

It dawned on me then that the Beastfolk were the original inhabitants of Liandrenn. Had they always wielded dark magic? Or had the defense of their land forced them to embrace wicked power? The drawings here did not hint at forbidden and nefarious practices; the Beastfolk depicted were hunters and gatherers...

I pushed the questions away. Whatever their past, they now threatened Humans and Elves with their plundering and foul magic.

They needed to be stopped.

As we went on, a deep chanting drifted toward us from the darkness ahead. I did not recognize the tongue—it was certainly not Elven—but Anuina's grip on her bow tightened. "A Beastfolk spell," she muttered.

I exchanged a look with Roswitha, and the warrior woman stepped up to walk but a pace behind Anuina.

A moment later, the chanting stopped, and an evil snarl resounded in the dark. Anuina stopped, her chest heaving, and the warrior woman Roswitha stepped past her, battered shield and flaming brand in hand.

The fell snarling grew louder as we stood there, gripping sword, staff, and bow until it crescendoed into a high-pitched shriek.

"Khal-Had knows we are here..." Anuina whispered.

A voice rang out that shook the very rocky floor we stood on. "Who comes?" it demanded. The voice sounded as cloyingly sweet as the foul stench that stuck to my nose and permeated even my worn tunic.

"Who interrupts the rightful reclamation of the Willow?"

The voice went through my skin and seeped into my bones. A powerful urge to turn tail and run rose from the pit of my stomach. The others were equally affected: Anuina stood frozen, shaking like a leaf, and even the resilient and willful Roswitha faltered, doubt visible in her combat stance.

"Well?" the voice demanded, making the rock walls shake.

"Oram Ludwickson," I said, surprised at the clarity of my voice. "I have come to the aid of the Woodland Folk and the Humans of Wealdhaven and beyond."

A slow, poisonous chuckle seeped down the passageway; it turned my bones to jelly and made me wish to lie down. "So," it finally said, when its mirth had trailed off. "An Awakened... and a denizen of a world beyond ours, no less."

I swallowed and sensed Roswitha's and Anuina's eyes on me. "I—"

The voice cut me off, sharp and hateful. "What business have you here, *Oram Ludwickson*?" it said, voice mocking the name, as if it was aware it was not my own. "Why come and meddle in affairs you do not understand?"

My courage faltered, and my two women looked at me as if I were alien to them. I opened my mouth to speak, but no sound came.

"What do *you* know of the history of this land? What do *you* know of our rights to this tree, and what do *you* know of lawfulness at all? You, who have lived your entire life on stolen land and grown fat on meat you did not kill? You have no place here, *Oram Ludwickson*, and you have no idea what your foolish meddling may bring about. Our world has sparse need for the weak-minded, jelly-spined fools of yours. We are no *game*, Awakened, and we are not for you to *play* with."

I took a step back, feeling like an idiot as I clutched my staff and wore my charms, ring, and bracelet. I stared at the items. *Do they even work? Do I even command the arcane? Or* am *I just playing?*

"Fool," the voice hissed. "You wish to leave? Then by the power of this Willow, I shall let you. You need but will away! Simply focus that soft, weak mind of yours on the land of milk and honey that birthed you. Return to your entitled life of pampering and decadence—Aerda has no need for the likes of you."

Is it that simple?

I looked at Anuina, at Roswitha.

NPCs...

Perhaps I should.

I began it, and true enough: I sensed it in my bones. It was like the power of the Willow flowed through me, and in my mind's eye I saw a light shining some distance away—a light that would get closer if I kept walking this mental road. It would take me away, back to Seattle, where life made sense and where the biggest risk to my health lay in crossing the street or having the poor luck to become ill with some disease the brilliant minds of my world could not yet cure.

No more battle, no more monsters and fiends, no more claws and teeth reaching for my neck, and no more sleeping on louse-ridden straw or in the rain. Instead, I would have showers, clean clothes, job security, *McDonald's*—my mouth watered at the thought.

"He is fading," Anuina said, her eyes widening.

"Go!" the voice said. "Begone, spirit, and return to your living grave."

My living grave...

Power flowed from me. Part of me felt pain at it seeping away; never had I known such strength, and never would I wield it again. But the voice was right: I was making a fool of myself here. I did not belong, and I had gotten myself into a situation I couldn't possibly comprehend.

This world is not for me, I—

Roswitha stepped forward, resolve in her icy eyes, and the blank 'NPC-ness' that had possessed her a moment ago, faded. She placed a hand on my shoulder, locked her gaze onto mine. "Stay, Oram Ludwickson," she said. "Don't let the poison on his tongue sway you or make you believe you are less than you truly are. You belong as much as I do, as much as Anuina does."

My jaw clenched. The light in the distance beckoned.

"If you stay now," the voice hissed, "the window will shut."

The choice… I knew it would come, but now that it was upon me, it was difficult beyond relief. Home had many comforts, many knowns, and even though my life there had slowly become a routine, there were ways out. I could live that life with renewed vigor and try to squeeze every drop from it.

Roswitha's hand gripped my shoulder, and in her icy blue eyes I saw the hope and the strength she had tethered to me. "We need you," she said. "*I* need you."

My gaze shot past her, found the enchanting green of Anuina's eyes, set now in a pale and worried face. No sound issued from her full lips, but she mouthed the same thing.

I need you.

And I needed them.

I pushed away, and the light faded. With strength renewed, I returned to this body, returned to the here and now, my fingers strong around my staff. I felt the life pulse from Roswitha as that beautiful, lopsided grin appeared on her face, and the bond that connected me to my two women radiated power.

"I stay," I said.

With a desperate shriek, the voice cried out its hatred. "Kill them!" it shouted. "Kill them all!"

From down the tunnel, furious howls rang out.

"Here they come," Anuina whispered.

This time, I felt no fear. "Come," I said to my women, voice steady. "We will meet them together."

***

We ran toward the howling, our weapons at the ready. We heard the patter of bare feet on the rock grow louder until finally we spotted movement ahead.

"Brace yourselves!" I called out, and Roswitha took the front, shield at the ready. Anuina took position behind her left shoulder and I behind her right.

With a horrid wail, three hideous figures jumped into the radius of my Light spell. They were Elves… or rather, *had been* Elves. Their faces were contorted into a furious snarl of hatred, and the otherwise radiant and beautiful eyes of their kin replaced with the pure black of the Beastfolk. They had grown fangs and their hands had been warped into nails; skin rent and opened to allow for the cancerous growth of talons. They still wore tunics and robes in the fashion of their kind, but they were stained with dirt and blood.

Corrupted Elf
Level 6
Stamina: 49, Health: 7, Mana: 21, Sanity: 3

A moment after they came into the light, they were upon Roswitha. A mighty battle cry came from her throat as she stood fast with shield and sword. There was enough room for the three misshapen creatures to converge on her, and all was lost to me in a flurry of claws and snarling faces.

With skill beyond compare, Roswitha parried attack after attack. Her every movement was part of a graceful but efficient dance to deflect claw and tooth with shield and fiery blade. Then, instead of countering, she held the line for us, keeping the snapping, snarling creatures at bay, and cast a spell to restore her own Stamina.

I cast my Windward spell, and blazing gusts of air formed around all three of us to tug at and hinder the attacks of these warped creatures. Anuina began her relentless salvos of arrows, and as Roswitha held her own against the vile beasts, Anuina and I dealt death to them. It amazed me to see how efficient we had become, each falling into their own role. Within a minute, three Corrupted Elves lay dead at Roswitha's feet, and our Stamina and Mana trickled back.

You receive 2,100 XP.

Burning with pride, I placed a hand on Roswitha's shoulder and pulled her in as Anuina sidled up close to me, some color having returned to her cheeks.

"We can do this," I said. "We are perfect together."

Roswitha smirked, then planted a kiss on my cheek. "When this is over and we still live…" she shook her head, a dirty promise in her eyes.

Anuina smiled up at me, love plain to see in her pretty eyes as they echoed Roswitha's promise.

Oh yes.

"Come on," I said. "Let's not make Khal-Had wait."

***

In the distance, a light shimmered. The feverish chanting intensified as we drew closer, and I recognized the voice now as the one that had spoken to me earlier.

Finally, we arrived in a monstrous underground cave with a pool at its center that was fed by dozens of icy underground streams. A knot of thick roots rose from that pool of water, and at their apex, the roots bundled into a massive trunk that grew up and away, burrowing into the living rock.

The roots of the Willow... its heart.

Before it, hovering almost a meter over the surface of the pool, was a Corrupted Elf. He had once been tall and lithe, but coarse and matted fur now grew on his hunched back, and his hands and feet had mutated into thick and dangerous claws, rending his own skin. Cancerous growths dotted his back, leaking a strange green ooze into the pool that gave the water a toxic yellow glow.

When we entered, the Corrupted Elf turned, still flying on wings unseen, and grinned at us.

Anuina shot forward, and I only just raised my hand in time to stop her from rushing to the Corrupted Elf.

"Father!" she cried as I stopped her short.

I realized that the leering face, pale and laced with black veins, teeth deformed into fangs that had cracked the lips even as they grew, had once been that of her father.

She sank to her knees, sobbing, as Khal-Had showed us the horrid fruits of his corruption with the foulest of smirks. "Too late, She-Elf," he hissed. "Your father is gone."

"No!" she cried out, averting her eyes, clawing at the rock floor.

"It is justice," Khal-Had spat, "the return of this domain to its rightful owner."

I raised my staff, its light burning brightly. "We will cleanse this sacred place of your foul presence, Khal-Had," I cried. "We will return you to the darkness."

Khal-Had laughed, revealing blackened fangs in bleeding gums, then leered at us. "But you are mistaken, outsider. *You* are the invaders; *you* are the ones that shall be *cleansed*."

"Are you too blind to see the filth you set to work?" I asked. "You are hurting this place, deforming it. If there ever was anything right and pure about you and your Beastfolk kin, then you must now recognize that—"

"Pah!" Khal-Had sneered. "Speak of virtue and purity all you will, pitiful Mage of Mouse and Key; *I* know the truth of you. Isn't it so easy? To play with our lives using your mechanical gadgets, assuming always to be the arbiter of right and wrong?

"But this is no experience designed around *you*—not some challenge for you to overcome. Nor is this a bespoke *game* crafted for you and your miserable fellows by some cellar-dwelling, fat outcast seeking to make the coin he believes he needs to win the affections of the fairer sex." Khal-Had snickered. "Oh no, *Oram Ludwickson, this* is your life and your death; the former you shall give up to me, and the latter shall fuel my purpose, for I wish *death* upon you and your allies—death upon Humans, death upon Elves. May your blood feed the trees of Liandrenn restored to its proper owners, and may a generation of my kin feast on your flesh as your races dwindle into nothingness under the stroke of our axes, the piercing jab of our spears, and the vindicating fire of our magic…"

An icy hand of fear gripped my heart as I saw the abomination hover before me, gloating. The hunger in his eyes told me that this creature had long since sold himself to the darkness, giving up whatever peace, empathy, and wisdom his heart may once have held in return for the chance to exact revenge upon those who had wronged him.

There is only one way this can end.

I felt the warmth of Anuina's shoulder under my palm, and I willed strength into her, squeezed her tightly. "Gather your strength," I said softly, but loud enough for her to hear. "We need you now beside us." Next to me, fearless Roswitha took her position.

"Now," Khal-Had continued. "My work is just begun, and you are but vermin chewing at my roots." His black eyes shone with malicious light. "And I have ways of dealing with *vermin*."

He raised his hands, floating over the pool, and uttered a dark phrase.

A moment later, the world shimmered, as if a veil had been drawn back.

Fuck… invisibility.

Dozens upon dozens of Corrupted Elves surrounded us. They flooded from tunnels that had been concealed by Khal-Had's magic and climbed out of shafts above us and under us, scampering across the walls and ceilings as if they were spiders. As they moved, they watched us with black eyes and hissed their hatred at us.

Khal-Had's cracked and deformed lips curled into a fell smile. "Take them now, my children," he said. "Eat them alive."

With deafening shrieks, it began.

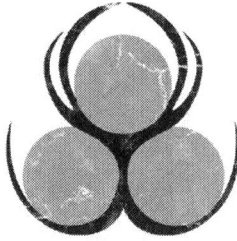

CHAPTER 15

We stood side by side, the three of us, backs to the water so that the Corrupted Elves would not attack us from that side, as the horde descended on us.

"We cannot win this," I cried out. "Focus on Khal-Had! If we destroy him, we will at least save the Willow." I gave him a quick glance over my shoulder to glean his stats.

Khal-Had
Level 10 (Boss)
Stamina: 55(82), Health: 5, Mana: 99(119),
Sanity: 9

Damn... This was going to be tough.

Raising my staff, I cast my Windward spell and quickened it through my Meta-Magic. Gusting winds enveloped all three of us.

Elemental Check result: (87 + 6 Cunning + 21 Elemental =) 114.

There... so long as we can defend ourselves, it will be near-impossible to hit us.

Then, speaking a word to invoke the element of water while splashing some from my jug, I cast Iceplane and created a frozen plane between us and nearly half of the Corrupted Elves. Unfortunately, the RNG gave me a 4, resulting in a 31... Most Corrupted Elves would not be stopped by that.

I gave Khal-Had a quick glance. "Anuina," I said. "Begin shooting at him!"

Anuina focused her keen eye on Khal-Had and nocked an arrow. She drew back, but then a whimper escaped her. "Father," she whispered.

Fuck...

I exchanged a glance with Roswitha, and she looked as worried as I did as she touched the amulets around her neck and muttered a prayer to the Tribunal. A soft glow emanated from her, its effect wholesome and reinvigorating.

You are under the effect of an Aura of Invigoration spell. You restore 6 Stamina per round so long as you remain within a 5-meter radius of the caster.

Then, she battered the iron rim of her shield with her sword and waited for the flood of enemies to crash into us.

The next moment, the horde was upon us.

Staff raised, I began swatting at their clawed hands and feet, seeking to deflect their furious attacks. I was overcome with dread and fear for my life, and my efforts were clumsy and poor. But whenever a raking claw or a pair of rotted fangs came close, a gale rebuffed the attacker, forcing them to relent and draw back behind the barrier of my Windward spell, where they snarled at me and regarded me with black eyes full of hate. When the dust settled, I had parried three attacks, costing me 3 Stamina, but none had gone through.

Thank the Tribunal for Windward.

It was the same with Roswitha. She fought with the visceral fury that I knew of her; effortlessly, she parried every blow, aided by my Windward where needed.

Anuina was less lucky… Holding no weapon to parry with, she only dodged the first attack, but the other two Corrupted Elves that attacked her struck true. Claws tore at her skin-tight leather armor, ripping pieces of it to reveal the soft, pale skin underneath, which the Corrupted Elves regarded with a filthy hunger as she cried out in pain and fear.

She will not last long.

Hovering over the pond, far out of our reach, Khal-Had shrieked words of fury. From his outstretched hands flew tendrils of black energy, as harmful and corrupting as the rot that infested the Willow. There was nothing to do but dodge or let my armor take it, and I knew that dodging would force me on the defensive. We'd be dead in seconds…

Hoping for the best, I let the armor from my Barkskin take it.

Medium Armor Check result: (77 + 4 Endurance + 8 Medium Armor =) 89 versus opponent's 21.

Your armor absorbs 12 Physical damage (dark) and suffers 1 Breach. You receive 2 Physical damage (dark)!

That was a serious blast. From the corner of my eyes, I saw the last shreds of Anuina's skimpy armor coil and break under the corrupting energy. It fell away, and she stood there half naked, only one full breast still covered in shreds of leather. Her ivory skin was scratched and raw, and the foul Corrupted Elves barked their filthy hunger as they saw her enticing flesh.

Khal-Had chuckled. "Ah... the Warden of the Willow's daughter unfettered by her attire," he hissed, voice laden with degenerate desire. "Such pleasures we will force onto you. By the end, you will shriek yourself hoarse under raking claw and ravishing tongue." He licked his lips. "Perhaps we shall have you bear our children... Fitting, that your father's body shall be made to force such a depraved load upon you, is it not?"

The wicked smirk on his face, Anuina in such a dire and shameful state... it made me furious.

With a frenzied cry, I pointed my staff at Khal-Had. Tendrils of dun energy shot out as I cast my new Ground spell on the floating wretch, using my Meta-Magic to render the casting instant. The smirk on Khal-Had's face vanished as he tried to dodge my spell.

Elemental Check result: (62 + 6 Cunning + 21 Elemental =) 89 versus opponent's 83.

I veered my tendrils of arcane might to latch onto him, and they enveloped him and pulled him down into the pond.

"Fool!" he cried. "Do you think that—"

I cast an upgraded Freeze/Thaw spell the moment his hands broke the surface of the pool.

His expression froze when he realized what I had done.

I allowed myself a smirk as I froze the water, sealing him in the ice from the elbows down. He was unable to move. In this state, he could not cast any spells with somatic components, and I had yet to run into a spell that had none.

The expression on his face became one of impotent fury as he jerked his arms. But like any good mage, Strength was probably his dump stat.

Dumbass…

"To him!" I called out to Roswitha and Anuina. "Tear him apart. I'll hold off these wretches."

The smirk that I so loved returned to Roswitha's face. Anuina's expression remained one of sorrow, but determination set her jaw. The two women ran away from the melee and left me with the horde of shrieking and clawing Corrupted Elves. Luckily, Roswitha's aura restored me to full Stamina before she moved, and my potent Windward would assure that I stood a good chance of parrying these creatures' efforts to bring me low.

Bellowing rage, Roswitha discarded her shield and brought her sword to bear two-handedly. It cut into Khal-Had, blade bursting into flame even as it descended. He could neither dodge nor parry, for his hands were caught in the ice. But as Roswitha's blade struck him, an armor made of purple force sprang to life; it absorbed her strike, and Khal-Had cackled madly.

But Anuina was beside her, stopping but two meters away from Khal-Had, her nimble and nearly naked body a flash of ivory lightning. Again, she hesitated as she gazed upon the face that had been her father's, but then she fired her volley without fear. Again, the armor lit up, but three mighty arrows all pierced it, and the third shattered the armor into a thousand pieces even as Khal-Had gave a cry of fury and rage. "Kill them, you fools!" he shrieked.

She had brought him down to 62 Stamina already!

That was all I had time to see before the wave of leering and snarling faces engulfed me. At Khal-Had's command, three shot past me toward Anuina and Roswitha, and I was unable to stop them, but the rest brought their fury to bear. Nine attacks to parry, costing me as much Stamina. None of them matched the might of my Windward spell, but my efforts of tapping away their attacks, however much the gusts of wind aided, cost me energy—of which I, as a feeble mage, had precious little. I stood there, panting as the sea of snarling faces shifted and thrummed around me, each one eager to get their claws on me.

It's only a matter of time until they do.

Despite my trick, Khal-Had was not yet done: he drew his head back even as my women tried to beat him into submission, and then released a sharp cry. The effect was like that of a thunderclap rolling out from him, and I saw Anuina and Roswitha stumble and waver under his attack, unwilling to waste their Action dodging. Anuina's Stamina went down by 10 to 22. At the same time, the three Corrupted Elves that had passed by me attacked Anuina and Roswitha. Thanks to my Windward, Roswitha easily parried their attacks, but Anuina gritted her teeth and suffered them, and she was left with 7 Stamina at the end of it.

We were on a slippery slope…

"Keep it up!" I cried out. Then, even as I tapped away a claw, I raised my staff, spoke a word of arcane command, and with a splash of water unleashed an overcharged Frostbite spell on Khal-Had. Since he was bound by ice, the frost descended on him unerringly, dealing 23 damage, reducing him to 39.

Just before I faced the clawing, biting horde again, I cried out: "He's almost done for!"

Roswitha raised her flaming brand and struck Khal-Had, dealing 28 damage. I was about to cry victory, but then I saw.

The glowing heat of her blade melted the ice, and Khal-Had's clawed hand came free.

Fuck...

A smirk appeared on his twisted face. "Now, it is time for you all to—"

"*Die*," Anuina finished.

She had her Action still; she had chosen to endure the attacks of her enemies to keep her own Action to fire her arrows. She stood there as a half-naked goddess, an image of the pure and unspoiled beauty and might of Elvenkind.

The arrow on her bow was sharp and swift, and her hands were quick and nimble enough to fire two in rapid succession. With all of her abilities in play, she could deal triple damage against a foe she had marked and who had lost Stamina this round.

Shrieking hell-fury, Khal-Had attempted to dodge, but the arrows struck without fault.

The first arrow dealt 42 damage. It took Khal-Had full in the chest, and his shriek ended in a pitiful cough. Anuina did not falter, merciless now against the creature that had absorbed and killed her father, and the second arrow landed in Khal-Had's throat with a thunk. He gave her one last look of surprise, then collapsed, his body still held upright in the ice.

It was done.

***

The cave shook as Khal-Had's body slumped, and for a moment I saw a dark shade flit away from the twisted body of the Elf that had once been Anuina's father. It lingered for a moment, then was caught on a current of air and dissipated. A moment later, icons began flashing, informing me I had completed my quests and received 3,000 XP.

Hopefully, that was the end of Khal-Had.

But he has cheated death before, if the stories are true...

Swiftly, I turned back to the horde of Corrupted Elves. I would die here, but I would be born again. But my death didn't need to be in vain; perhaps it could buy my women the time—

There was fear in the Corrupted Elves' black eyes— *doubt.*

Holding out my staff, I took a step back.

One by one, they fell. In blind panic, some tried to run, but the effect that was slaying them did not emanate from me. Khal-Had's dark magic had bound them to him in life, and now that his magic was gone, the scarred and twisted bodies succumbed to the wounds and mutations that should have killed them the moment Khal-Had possessed and altered them. Fell magic had kept death at bay, and now that its source was gone, death came to claim what was due.

It gave me no pleasure to watch them die. Their last moments were full of fear and terror as they clawed over each other toward the exit, trampling one another in animal fury. Even though they were creatures of the dark, they had been Elves once, and I did not doubt that the promises and trickery with which Khal-Had bound them to him had played on their desire to do good.

For a while, their cries echoed in the cavern, until the place was strewn with their corpses. Only the three of us stood alive still.

Slowly, as if every muscle now ached, Roswitha and Anuina—her eyes wet with tears—crossed the cracked and battered ice my magic had created and made their way over to me, the bond calling us together.

I held them close, and we stood there for a long time, finding solace in each other's presence, in each other's strength, and even in each other's weaknesses.

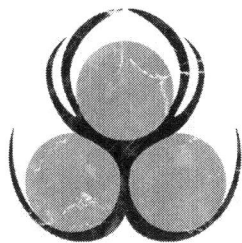

CHAPTER 16

Mesmerized, I took a deep breath of forest air.

"Come… or we'll be late."

I was standing on one of the Willow's branches, overlooking the sea of silver and golden leaves that was the heart of Elvendom in Liandrenn under a perfect nebulae-streaked sky. It was hard to turn away. But when I glanced over my shoulder at Anuina, dressed in a gauzy white robe that left no illusions about the supple and perfect body underneath, I relented.

I gave the forest a last look, then turned to follow her, my eyes fixed on her luscious backside as it swayed.

It had been three weeks since Khal-Had fell.

After Khal-Had's defeat, we found the Woodland Folk who had survived the corruption he had wrought. Since Anuina had defeated Khal-Had and was the descendant of the Warden of the Willow—her sister was still lost—the Elves of Liandrenn had taken to Anuina as their leader. I knew her as an intelligent and bashful woman, but the admiration and veneration of her people awoke something inside her; she matured.

The Woodland Folk wreathed and laureled us, and their Council of Elders asked Anuina to take up residence in the palace in the moonlit city of Mith-Ahannan, the capital of Liandrenn perched on a high hill among the mighty trees. At first, she had been hesitant, but the Council of Elders— many of whom she still knew from her days among her kin—pleaded with her; she had saved the Willow, and it was only fitting that she would become its next Warden.

And so she would.

We walked down the thick branch to where it joined the mighty trunk, and I watched with pleasure as Anuina's limber form jumped down from branch to branch. More than once did her supple movements cause her flimsy robes to lift, showing me the beautiful body underneath. My desire for her was strong indeed; during the three weeks that had passed, she found no time to meet with me as she organized the Sylvan Folk into driving the last of the Beastfolk from Liandrenn, and I pined for a night with her.

It didn't help that Roswitha had left for Wealdhaven to bring news of our victory to Jarl Strumma Hardenkson Life-Tree.

Once Anuina was down to the leaf-covered forest floor, I used my Windwalk spell to teleport from branch to branch until I was with her. In silence, we rounded the trunk until we came again to the cave entrance. Here, I felt her waver through our bond, her mind doubtlessly dwelling on the massacre within that had seen the end of so many of her kinfolk, her father among them and at her own hand no less.

I reached out and took her slender hand in mine. She was cool to the touch. With a wistful smile, she looked up at me, and her face at that moment was the very image of beauty. Unable to resist, I leaned in and kissed her on her full, ruby-red lips. When I drew back, she looked at me with a melancholy glow in her emerald eyes.

"Shall we go in?" I asked.

She took a deep breath. "I am afraid."

"You have proven that fear is no obstacle to you," I said, squeezing her hand. "But what are you afraid of?"

Her eyes were big and serious as she studied me. "Losing you."

I smiled. The fear had been unspoken until now, and I sensed it too. "You're not *losing* me," I said. "I am here."

"But you *will* leave," she said, and it was not a question.

"Maybe," I said. "I am no Elf. I can't live out my days in the forest and derive pleasure from that. This whole world is still open to me, and I feel a compelling desire to explore it."

She set her jaw. "Then I shall come with."

I reached up and ran my hand over her smooth cheek. "And what will happen to Liandrenn if you do?"

She sighed, a wet sheen forming on her eyes.

"You are brave, beautiful, and stronger than I am," I said. "Your place is here because this is where you are needed most. Besides," I added, brushing a beautiful golden lock behind her pointy ear, "I will not leave just yet." I grinned. "You owe me at least one night."

She laughed at that, even though a tear rolled down her perfect cheek. "You are a hound!" she exclaimed.

"We are both," I said. "I just conceal it poorly."

I took her hand in mine and gestured for her to enter.

***

Gathered in a circle around the pool that fed the roots of the Willow stood the Council of Elders. The oily rot had faded from the Willow, and the scent in the cave was now crisp and pure like a summer morning. Colorful, glowing orbs danced among the roots—Sprites, or so I had learned; diminutive Fae charged with tending to the Willow. Khal-Had's dark magic had all but chased them off, but they returned when the pool became pure once more. The light they shed was more than enough to illuminate the cave.

Flanking the path from the cave entrance to the pool stood the highest and most honored of the Sylvan Folk, and even though I was not of Elven blood, the great honor had been bestowed upon me that I may be present as well.

It was the first time a Human would see a Willow of the Sylvan Folk accept a new Warden.

First came a long speech in Elven, held by Ulindran, head of the Council of Elders. Although my grasp of the Elven tongue was improving, I could not follow a word of this, and I assumed it to be some dialect or archaic form. It took a long while, but I did not mind; my eyes were fixed on Anuina.

She kneeled by the edge of the pool, head solemnly bowed, the silky robe flowing about her. She was like a dream, and I still had trouble believing that I had bonded with her—that I had *possessed* her—and seeing her this way only made me want her more. I suspected every soul in this gathering shared my desire.

When the last echo of Ulindran's speech faded away, he bade Anuina to enter the pool. With a graceful shrug, she let her robe slip to the floor, and my body stirred at the sight of her alabaster form, golden hair swaying long and clean down to her enchanting hips.

She waded in, one elegant step at a time.

As her foot first touched the water, a humming mounted in the caves, and it took me a moment before I realized it came from the Sprites. And even as she went deeper into the water, tendrils of living and hopeful energy shot over the surface of the pool like lightning crackling. It lit up the cave, and in between the flashes of light, I saw the roots of the Willow stir. Then, Anuina raised her slender arms and lifted her chin to look up at the Willow, and the very ground shook.

It was as if the earth sighed with delight.

Then, quiet returned to the cave. Ulindran spoke a single word, and never had I heard a word that contained so much hope and joy, and even though I knew not what the word meant, I joined the Elves as they began cheering and clapping.

The Willow had a new Warden.

***

The feast that followed the ceremony was full of song and dance. Elven minstrels played beautiful music and sang with a purity and beauty that I had never heard before. In the pleasant and learned company of the Woodland Folk, I drank and ate delights that by far outshone anything I ever enjoyed in my previous life—although my craving for a Big Mac remained a real and palpable thing.

Yet through it all, I watched Anuina at the head of the table. She was majestic here, in this hall where the pillars were tree trunks, the vaulted ceiling a canopy of golden leaves and ivory branches. And although I enjoyed the purest music, the finest food and drink, the most intellectual and entertaining conversation—it all paled compared to her.

"Greetings, Oram Ludwickson."

I looked up, startled, then gave a broad smile; Roswitha stood beside me, and there was a knowing grin on her face.

"You have returned," I said.

She nodded as she settled her rump on the table between me and the Elf I had been speaking with, earning herself an indignant glance. "I have," she said.

"And? What news of Jarl Strumma?"

She shrugged. "He is an Askil... he will wait and see. But he seemed pleased when I told him that the Woodland Folk were hunting down the last of the Beastfolk."

"Any news of Anuina's sister?"

"None," she said. "But I did learn that Captain Ydbrad Ydbradson spoke true and told the jarl of the aid we gave him. If we return to Wealdhaven, we'll be his honored guests."

I nodded, looking again at the radiant Elven beauty.

Roswitha chuckled. "I see you are not sure yet if you will leave."

"No," I said. "It's... it's difficult." I looked back at the redhead and studied her beautiful, toned body in her skimpy armor. "I am happy that you are with me."

She dipped a finger into my goblet of wine, tasted it, and made a face before she focused her icy eyes on me. "I will be with you, Oram Ludwickson. I will be with you always."

I smiled and patted her on her shapely thigh. "Go speak to Anuina," I said. "She'll want to know what news of Wealdhaven."

"I already spoke to her," Roswitha said. "She wishes to meet you after the feast to discuss my findings."

I frowned and turned to look at Anuina. She was deep in conversation, but I could have sworn her eyes were on me for a moment.

"Very well," I said. "After the feast."

***

For the rest of the evening, my mind was in overdrive.

On the one hand, I wanted to stay here for a while; on the other, I wanted to see more of Aerda. Now that I had chosen this world over my own, a desire entered my mind to explore it and to grow more powerful as I did so. I also felt a need to find more of my kind; my encounter with Rahandi had been pleasant enough, and his idea of establishing a base of operations resonated with me.

I was still pondering these things as I made my way through the winding hallways of the palace of moonlit Mith-Ahannan. A world of adventure was waiting, and I wanted to answer the call.

The door to Anuina's chambers was arched, wrought of the silvery wood that grew in the Elven forest, and adorned with braided and knotted patterns. I knocked twice, then pushed it open.

"Oram Ludwickson…"

My mouth fell open.

The chamber was lofty, with arched windows that rose from the floor to the vaulted ceiling, offering a beautiful view of a peaceful and quiet stretch of Liandrenn forest. The air was clean and soft, and at the center of the room, a four-poster bed fit for a king stood on a high dais. On its white sheets sat Anuina, legs folded under her, clad in the light gauzy robe she had worn during the ceremony. Her ruby-red lips were curled into a smile as she looked up at me, her slender fingers playing with the stem of the goblet of wine she had been drinking.

"Welcome," she said.

I stepped inside, my eyes fixed on every lovely curve, every rise and fall of that perfect young body. A jolt shot straight down to my manhood, stirring a deep desire within me.

She rose to her knees. "I have spoken to Roswitha," she said. "I know her desire, and I know yours."

I took a step closer. "Anuina…" I said.

"You are staying here for me," she said. "And I love you for it. But I have thought of what you said earlier today. This is no farewell, dear Oram, we *shall* meet again, and our fire will burn just as bright when we do."

I grinned, eyes roving over her body. "It will," I said.

She laughed lightly, then placed her slender hands on the collar of her robe. "You must know that it was not easy to convince Roswitha to give me a night alone with you," she said. "She drives a hard bargain."

My staff clattered as I dropped it to the floor. "I wouldn't have her any other way," I said.

Anuina bit her lower lip as she opened the robe, revealing the perfect rise of her chest to me, her puffy pink nipples already erect. The sight sent a jolt of electricity through my body, and I was with her with five great strides, my tunic already on the floor by the fifth.

She chuckled as she pulled away the robe, and the beauty that it revealed to me was breathtaking: the long and slender body, the perfect inward curve of her smooth midriff, the cute strip of blond pubic hair, and the pink folds beneath.

A thrill shot through my veins as I crawled onto the bed. The bond between us burned like lightning crackling. She smiled coyly, inching away from me as if to postpone that entrancing moment when our bodies would touch.

I would have none of that teasing.

I lunged, grabbed hold of her beautiful, shapely leg, and she yelped. "You are mine," I said, my eyes burning on her. "Whether you are Warden of a thousand Willows or queen of a hundred Elven realms."

She bit her lip, eyes growing hazy with lust.

I picked up her leg, placed her foot on my shoulder, and inhaled the intoxicating wildberry scent of her. Placing a passionate kiss on her ankle, I looked up. "Say that it's true," I said.

"I am yours," she said, echoing her vow to me. "And you are mine, Oram Ludwickson."

My name on her lips was like wine, and our connection blazed, dazzling me even as I planted my hungry kisses on her slender leg. She giggled as my beard pricked her, but the giggling only lasted until the molten heat bubbled up in her, and a lustful moan escaped her lips that told of long days of pent-up desire.

I was going to fuck her hard to make sure she wouldn't forget me until I stood hungering at her door again.

She threw her head back, giving little sighs of pleasure as I ran my tongue over her smooth calf. Her scent intoxicated me, and I was powerless to resist the temptation of her fiery presence. The taste of her sent a bolt of desire through my veins—a lustful and wanton wish to taste all of her.

With a visceral grunt, I picked up her other leg and draped it over my shoulder. My hands rested lightly on her velvet thighs as I left a burning trail of kisses on her legs, going ever up and up.

"Hmm," she moaned. "I have wanted this."

"I know," I said, voice buzzing against the delicate skin of her thighs and making her giggle and jerk her leg. "So have I."

Her skin rippled with goosebumps as I crept up and up, her warm hands reached down, fingers digging into my hair. I sucked in a sharp breath, catching the intoxicating musk of her womanhood; it made my cock stand to hard attention, eager to plow into her and flood her womb with my seed.

But I was going to make myself wait, if only for a while.

I extended my tongue, licking all along the outside of her thigh, then curving over her smooth and flat stomach. She jerked at the touch, and I gazed up longingly to the swell of her breasts rising and falling with every fast, heated breath.

"Oram…" she sighed, almost pleading as my mouth went lower and lower. I explored the rise of her mons pubis with my lips, teeth nipping for a moment at her inviting tuft of blond hair. As I teased and played, her grip on my hair tightened until she began pushing me down, arching herself up for me, wanting me to taste her.

Her need turned me on beyond reason; my feverish hot blood hummed through my veins and set my heart to pounding. Burning bright, my eyes settled on her inviting flower, open and wet for me, and her soft sighs drove me along.

Like a starving hound, I ran my tongue over her, causing her to squirm and quake like a wanton harlot. Her taste was ambrosia, and I lapped up her wetness eagerly, gently blowing against her pulsing clit, then teasingly pricking her pining lips with my tongue, stealing a sweet sample of her. Her breath came quicker as her body rippled with pleasure, both hands massaging my hair with an urgency that resonated in my loins.

I could no longer resist—I didn't want to.

Burying my face between her thighs, her legs still draped over my shoulders, I slaked my hunger for her, licking, sucking, and leaving no part of her untouched with my eager tongue. Breathy sounds came from her lips as I made her relinquish control to the rhythm of my tongue. It could not last long enough for me, but Anuina's desire had her body burning for release. Her voice a desperate whisper, she urged me on and on until I was drunk on her, licking her slick heat as her entire body tensed.

A soft cry escaped her lips, and then her hips shot up, bucking wildly against my lips as I drove her on. She called out my name even as her orgasm overwhelmed her, and in those blazing whispers a thousand-and-one promises of loyalty and love lay. Unceasing, I gave her pleasure, until at length I coaxed a final wave out of her, causing her body to shiver once more, then lay still, chest heaving with short, burning breaths.

I came up, wanting to say something clever and sweet, but Anuina's orgasm had made her lose grip of the last vestige of control. With the thin veneer of civilization away, she was once again the primal Elf—born to nature, to be free and naked as the flowers, fickle as the wind, and passionate as the suns of Aerda. She jumped up, pupils diluted in pure lust, and pushed me down before I could utter a single word. I heard fabric rip as she tore the hose from my body.

A moment later, she palmed my throbbing cock, looking up at me with lust out of this world, a fantastic desire that could only come from a race born of the Fae. My heart raged in my chest, liquid heat pumping through my veins, and I had not an ounce of control in me—resistance and composure long dead and burned to ashes. I grabbed a fistful of her hair and pulled her down, then gave a primal grunt as she took me in her mouth.

By the Gods, but those lips were silk made flesh!

I fell back into the sheets, moaning and twisting as my alabaster Elven beauty writhed on her hands and knees, pleasing me with her mouth. I was close to exploding the moment she began, and it took every ounce of my considerable willpower to postpone the moment. The bittersweetness of it all was there in the back of my mind, and I wanted this to last.

I fought her. I fought her plump and pleasing lips and her wet and deft tongue for control over my body, but by the throbbing in my veins and from the almost painfully erect shaft she worked so expertly, I could tell it was a battle I would lose.

And *soon...*

With a feral snarl, I pulled her up by her luscious blond locks. She whimpered at the rough and sudden move, but from the way her eyes ate me up and her teeth sank into her lower lip, I knew she loved it. I grinned at her as I pulled her to her knees, planted a fiery kiss on her lips, tongues intertwining for a heated moment, our sweaty, burning bodies connecting...

Then I pushed her over.

She laughed as she fell on her back and sank into the soft mattress. Within a breath, I was on her. I ran my nose along the elegant slope of her neck, kissed her shoulder as she let out a soft moan and wrapped her arms around me.

"You are mine," I breathed into her neck, and my lips trailed a searing-hot path to her pointed Elven ear, nipping on it.

"I am yours," she said, her voice hoarse with passion.

She guided me in before I could stop her—even if I had wanted to—and the fire of my longing took over as I cradled her in my arms and slipped into her ready wetness. She urged me on with an airy moan, legs wrapping around me, and unchecked lust mastered us.

There was no gentle beginning—no sweet easing into it. We wanted to consume each other raw. Our lips found each other in the tangle, and I drank greedily from her, every nerve in my body basking in the warm glow of our union as—with inevitable strength—my pleasure rose from the depths of my body, wrapping around my core, building up.

I was in Anuina's hold as she urged me on—legs, arms wrapped around me, her hot lips kissing my neck, my cheeks, nipping at my ears as she pleaded with me to fill her with my love.

It was impossible to hold back. I silenced her moans with a deep kiss, and she arched her body, ready to receive. I let loose inside her, filling her with my seed even as the sweet scent of wildberry, mingled with her intoxicating sweat, swirled around my head, the soft sensation of her perfect skin against mine.

She held me close as I came, coaxing my pleasure from me as I lay clamped between her thighs. With every ripple of my body, she moaned softly, until finally we lay still, panting, our thirst quenched for now.

Kissing her sleek neck, giving one of her beautiful Elven ears a last playful nip, I pulled back. She slid her hands over my shoulders, fingers leaving a prickling delight in their wake.

I sighed, deeply contented.

She gave me a lopsided grin, kissed me on the cheek, and sidled up against me, her body glowing and warm.

As we lay there, in a perfect union that would not last, my mind wandered…

To tomorrow… to what may come.

A world was ripe for the taking.

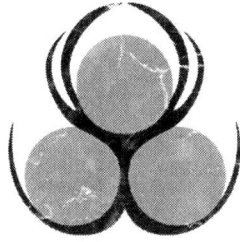

From the Author

THANK YOU FOR READING!

If you liked this book, check out the preview for **DEMON TAMER, the second volume of Aerda Online,** on the following pages. If you want to receive a notification when I release it, head on over to jackbryce.nl. My website is also where you can contact me; I love getting in touch with my readers and hearing what they'd like to read about next!

Finally, be sure to **leave me a review** to let me know if you liked this book! Like most independent authors, I use the feedback from your review to improve my work and to decide what to focus on next, so your review can make a difference.

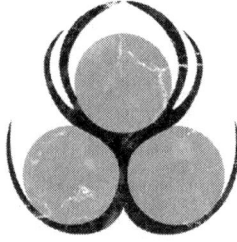

PREVIEW FOR DEMON TAMER

I came to the city of Chevalec wrapped in an old fur cloak, caked with dust and dirt, leaning on my trusty Pyromancer's Staff.

And I came alone, just as the letter had requested.

I sat down by the roadside for a moment, no longer caring that my cloak would get muddier and dirtier still. Travelers passed me by—farmers with their handcarts, warriors in breastplates of iron, and young ones with minds of revelry. None gave me a second look.

Just another weary wretch seeking a fortune in illustrious Chevalec.

As I sat, I reached into the folds of my cloak and retrieved the letter. I had read it perhaps twenty times over, and by now the delicate parchment was close to tearing along its creases. In many places, the ink had been stained by rain and drink.

To Oram Ludwickson:

Phylomancer, your coming to Aerda is like the Rains of Autumn, a vanguard of the Storms of Winter.

Your striving in the north among the Askils has not gone unnoticed, nor has the defeat of the Beastfolk spirit of Khal-Had by your hands. Yet you do not know the full truth behind Khal-Had's actions or the consequences of what you have done.

Such truths are not to be entrusted to parchment; couriers have their follies, and the Enemy is ever watchful and looking for us. Travel to the Caerolian city of Chevalec if you wish to truly rise to the defense of Aerda. Travel as a pilgrim—travel unseen and alone—and do not speak your true name, for more know it than you may think. Seek the Temple of the Severed Hand and pray to the statue of the Salved One for no shorter than an hour's candle burns.

I will find you there.

Yours,

Marcatus

Unease rose from the pits of my stomach as I read the letter again. Something about it rang true; an—albeit friendlier—echo of the words Khal-Had had spoken to me in the cave below the Willow of Liandrenn.

You have no idea what your foolish meddling may bring about.

"This is a trap," Roswitha had said.

"I'm inclined to agree," Anuina had added.

Even I was forced to admit it sounded an awful lot like someone was luring me to the Caerolian Kingdom under false pretenses. But still, the letter raised questions of the kind that I struggled to leave unanswered.

And if it is a trap, then why? Who would want to trap me? I knew of no enemies apart from the ones brought low at Liandrenn, and while I suspected that Khal-Had was not as easily defeated and that his spirit may have survived, there was no sense in the Beastfolk luring me to Chevalec, one of the largest and most civilized cities of Aerda; they wielded no power there.

I folded the letter and stuck it back in my cloak as I eyed the nebula-streaked sky above.

A lot of questions.

I took a piece of bread and a jug of water from my Vault, and I ate and drank as I studied the large, earth-like moon and the cloudless sky.

"So, you're just going to walk into this trap?" Roswitha had said, arms crossed, her full bosom heaving with anger at the foolishness she perceived.

"Oram, please," Anuina had said. "Reconsider! This sounds foolish."

I grinned. My two women were hard to resist, but the letter had one last ace up its sleeve.

Reading it started a quest.

I focused on the question mark icon, always in my field of vision, and a text popped up.

The Truth
Challenge level: 7 (difficult)

You received a mysterious letter from a stranger by the name of Marcatus. In his letter, Marcatus writes that your victory at Liandrenn had unforeseen consequences, and that you do not know the truth behind Khal-Had's actions. He wishes to meet with you in the Caerolian city of Chevalec to discuss these matters.

Objective: Travel to the Temple of the Severed Hand in Chevalec and pray at the statue of the Salved One for at least an hour.
Bonus objective: Travel in disguise and do not let anyone recognize you.
Reward: 2,000 XP and 500 XP per bonus objective completed.

How can I say no to that?

I willed away the text and smiled as I chewed on my stale bread, then washed it away with flat-tasting water.

"If you insist on this folly," Roswitha had said. "I'm coming with you."

"This Marcatus guy is asking me to come alone," I had retorted.

She had given me that impish smirk I so loved. "And you will... we will *both* travel alone."

I wonder if she's here yet or if I beat her to it...

I rose to my feet and, slouching slightly and head buried under my hood, I joined the file of shuffling and jostling men and women making their way to Chevalec.

On to adventure...

Want to receive a notification when this book comes out? Head on over to jackbryce.nl and subscribe to my newsletter!

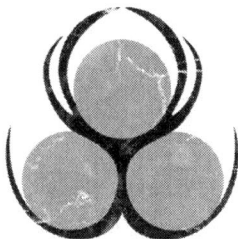

SPELLBOOK

Barkskin
Spell type: Rote
Spell level: 2
Mana: 5
Casting time: 1 Action
Target: Self, Creature
Range: Touch
Duration: 1 Hour
Components: Somatic, Vocal, Material (a piece of bark)
Skill: Protection
Element: Life
Description: Through an incantation and a symbol of life, you create a solid armor made of flexible bark that protects the chest, shoulders, back, and upper arms. This vest has Encumbrance 1, Armor 6, and 2 maximum Breaches. This armor uses the Medium Armor skill.
Upgrades: By spending 2 additional Mana, you may increase the spell level by 1 and increase the Armor of the vest by 6, its maximum Breaches by 1, and its Encumbrance by 1.

Befriend Animal
Spell type: Rote
Spell level: 1
Mana: 3
Casting time: 1 Action
Target: Creature (Animal)
Range: 20 Meters
Duration: 10 Rounds
Components: Somatic, Vocal, Material (an item of food)
Skill: Illusion
Element: Life
Description: With an incantation and a token of friendship, you cause animals to heel and befriend you. Animals may resist with the Intuition skill. If your Check result equals or beats the animal's, it becomes charmed by you. Charmed animals will not attack you or your allies unless provoked. Provoking a creature will break the spell's effect.
Upgrades: By spending 2 additional Mana, you may increase the spell level by 1 and increase its duration by 10 rounds.

***

Bond Animal
Spell type: Ritual
Spell level: 1
Mana: 3
Casting time: 1 Minute

Target: Creature (Animal)
Range: Touch
Duration: Instant
Components: Somatic, Vocal, Material (an item of food)
Skill: Druidcraft
Element: Life
Description: You speak a solemn incantation of the beasts to enrapture an animal, then offer a token of friendship to it, turning the animal into your bonded animal. Animals that are unfriendly toward you may resist with the Intuition skill. If your Check equals or beats the animal's, it becomes your bonded animal. Bonded animals level with you, obey your simple commands, remain close to you, and have a telepathic link with you that allows you to communicate simple messages back and forth. The animal will not become smarter, and its choice of words will be limited by its intelligence and knowledge. You can only have one bonded animal.

***

Boulder
Spell type: Rote
Spell level: 1
Mana: 3
Casting time: 1 Action
Target: Creature
Range: 10 Meters
Duration: 5 Rounds
Components: Somatic, Vocal, Material (any stone)
Skill: Elemental

Element: Earth
Description: With a word of elemental force and a mighty sigil drawn in the air, you turn any stone into a mighty boulder that you catapult at your enemy. The boulder deals 1-2 + Intellect Physical damage (earth) and will also crush your target, pinning them under it for the duration of the spell. Creatures pinned under a rock must succeed at an Athletics Check that equals or defeats the result of your Elemental Check or be unable to do anything, wasting their Action, and suffer another 1-2 Physical damage (earth).
Upgrades: By spending 2 additional Mana, you may increase the spell level by 1 and deal an additional 1-2 Physical damage (fire).

***

Cascade
Spell type: Rote
Spell level: 2
Mana: 5
Casting time: 1 Action
Target: Up to 3 creatures, no more than 5 meters apart
Range: 20 Meters
Duration: Instant
Components: Somatic, Material (any stone)
Skill: Elemental
Element: Earth
Description: With a gesture of power, you change any stone into an overwhelming cascade of rock that batters your foes. Three such cascades plummet onto a maximum of 3 creatures that are no more than 5 meters apart from each

other. You make only one Check. Every creature that you successfully strike receives 2-4 + Intellect Physical damage (earth).

Upgrades: By spending 2 additional Mana, you may increase the spell level by 1 and deal an additional 2-4 Physical damage (earth) per cascade.

***

Create/Destroy Water
Spell type: Rote
Spell level: 2
Mana: 5
Casting time: 1 Action
Target: Area
Range: 50 Meters
Area of effect: 10-Meter radius
Duration: Instant
Components: Somatic, Vocal
Skill: Elemental
Element: Water
Description: At your arcane call, you create or destroy water. With a single casting, you may either create or destroy 20 liters' worth of water in the area of effect or in designated containers. Water you create is potable. Any liquids other than pure water that you target will be unaffected. Alternatively, you may destroy fog or steam in the area of effect.
Upgrades: By spending 2 additional Mana, you may increase the spell level by 1 and create or destroy an

additional 10 liters' worth of water and increase the area of effect by 5 meters.

***

Enrich Soil
Spell type: Rote
Spell level: 0
Mana: 1
Casting time: 1 Action
Target: Area
Range: 10 Meters
Area of effect: 5-Meter radius
Duration: Instant
Components: Somatic, Vocal
Skill: Druidcraft
Element: Earth
Description: With a simple incantation and a symbol of fertility, you enrich the earth in a 5-meter radius to become fertile and optimal for the growth of the crop you have in mind at the time of casting. The spell does not work on a floor that has been worked or made by intelligent creatures.
Upgrades: By spending 2 additional Mana, you may increase the spell level by 1 and increase the radius of its area of effect by 5 meters.

***

Ensnare

Spell type: Rote
Spell level: 1
Mana: 3
Casting time: 1 Action
Target: Creature
Range: 10 Meters
Duration: 10 Rounds
Components: Somatic, Vocal, Material (a branch or vine)
Skill: Druidcraft
Element: Life
Description: From a small branch or vine, a sigil, and an arcane incantation, you call forth powerful vines to ensnare your target. Ensnared targets cannot move and suffer a -50 penalty on any Checks that require use of their arms or legs. Creatures attempting to break free must succeed at an Athletics Check that equals or defeats the result of your Druidcraft Check or be unable to move and waste their Action.
Upgrades: By spending 2 additional Mana, you may increase the spell level by 1 and increase its range by 10 meters.

***

Entangle
Spell type: Rote
Spell level: 1
Mana: 3
Casting time: 1 Action
Target: Creature
Range: 50 Meters

Area of effect: 5-Meter radius
Duration: 10 Rounds
Components: Somatic, Vocal, Material (a branch or vine)
Skill: Druidcraft
Element: Life
Description: At your beckon, vines and plant tendrils cover an area in a 5-meter radius. The vines and tendrils seek out and grope targets with intelligence, entangling anyone caught in them. Creatures attempting to traverse the area must succeed at an Acrobatics Check that equals or defeats the result of your Druidcraft Check or be unable to move and waste their Action.
Upgrades: By spending 2 additional Mana, you may increase the spell level by 1 and increase the radius of its area of effect by 5 meters.

***

Fire Sprout
Spell type: Rote
Spell level: 1
Mana: 3
Casting time: 1 Action
Target: Creature
Range: 20 Meters
Duration: Instant
Components: Somatic
Skill: Elemental
Element: Fire
Description: A gout of flame bursts from your outstretched hand, dealing 1-6 + Intellect Physical damage (fire).

Flammable objects that are not worn or carried will burst into flame when hit by Flame Sprout.

Upgrades: By spending 2 additional Mana, you may increase the spell level by 1 and deal an additional 1-6 Physical damage (fire).

***

Fog
Spell type: Rote
Spell level: 1
Mana: 3
Casting time: 1 Action
Target: Area
Range: 50 Meters
Area of effect: 5-Meter radius
Duration: 1 Minute or until dispersed
Components: Somatic, Vocal, Material (a splash of water)
Skill: Elemental
Element: Water
Description: From a splash of water, you create a thick cloud of fog in the shape of a rough circle with a 5-meter radius. In the fog cloud, visibility is limited to 1 meter. The fog cloud can be dispersed by a moderate wind.

Upgrades: By spending 2 additional Mana, you may increase the spell level by 1 and either increase the radius of its area of effect by 5 meters or its duration by 1 minute.

***

Freeze/Thaw
Spell type: Rote
Spell level: 1
Mana: 3
Casting time: 1 Action
Target: Area
Range: 50 Meters
Area of effect: 5-Meter radius
Duration: Instant
Components: Somatic, Vocal
Skill: Elemental
Element: Water
Description: You draw a sign of power and speak an incantation to instantly freeze or thaw a body of liquids in the shape of a circle with a 5-meter radius.
Upgrades: By spending 2 additional Mana, you may increase the spell level by 1 and increase the radius of its area of effect by 5 meters.

***

Frost Ray
Spell type: Rote
Spell level: 1
Mana: 3
Casting time: 1 Action
Target: Creature
Range: Self
Area of effect: 10-Meter cone
Duration: Instant
Components: Somatic, Vocal

Skill: Elemental
Element: Water
Description: A gust of frosty air blasts forth from your outstretched hand, dealing 1-4 + Intellect Physical damage (water) to all creatures it strikes within the area of effect. You make only one Check.
Upgrades: By spending 2 additional Mana, you may increase the spell level by 1 and deal an additional 1-4 Physical damage (water).

***

Frost Shield
Spell type: Rote
Spell level: 1
Mana: 3
Casting time: 1 Action
Target: Self, Creature
Range: 10 Meters
Duration: 1 Round
Components: Somatic, Vocal
Skill: Elemental
Element: Water
Description: You speak a word of power and trace a sigil in the air to summon a thin and flexible barrier of ice around your target's chest. The ice does not harm your target or feel cold to the touch. For the duration of the spell, the subject receives half damage from sources of Physical damage (water) or Physical damage (fire) after your choice.

Upgrades: By spending 2 additional Mana, you may increase the spell level by 1 and change the casting time to Instant (Interruption).

***

Frost Ward
Spell type: Rote
Spell level: 0
Mana: 1
Casting time: 1 Action
Target: Self, Creature
Range: Touch
Duration: 1 Round
Components: Somatic
Skill: Elemental
Element: Water
Description: You trace a sigil in the air to create a shimmering barrier around your target to defend it against cold. For the duration of the spell, the subject receives half damage from sources of Physical damage (water).
Upgrades: By spending 2 additional Mana, you may increase the spell level by 1 and change the casting time to Instant (Interruption).

***

Frost Wave
Spell type: Rote

Spell level: 1
Mana: 3
Casting time: 1 Action
Target: Creature
Range: Self
Area of effect: 5-Meter radius
Duration: Instant
Components: Somatic, Vocal
Skill: Elemental
Element: Water
Description: A wave of icy air emanates from your body, dealing 1-2 + Intellect Physical damage (water) to all creatures it strikes within the area of effect. You make only one Check.
Upgrades: By spending 2 additional Mana, you may increase the spell level by 1 and deal an additional 1-2 Physical damage (water).

***

Frostbite
Spell type: Rote
Spell level: 2
Mana: 5
Casting time: 1 Action
Target: Creature
Range: 20 Meters
Duration: Instant
Components: Somatic
Skill: Elemental
Element: Water

Description: Harrowing frost descends at your beckoning, freezing and biting and dealing 2-12 + Intellect Physical damage (water).
Upgrades: By spending 2 additional Mana, you may increase the spell level by 1 and deal an additional 1-6 Physical damage (water).

***

Ghost Touch
Spell type: Rote
Spell level: 0
Mana: 1
Casting time: 1 Action
Target: Other (see description)
Range: 10 Meters
Duration: Concentration
Components: Somatic, Vocal
Skill: Psionic
Element: Force
Description: Exert your will on an object in range to manipulate it from a distance. You cannot control an object with Encumbrance above 1, and you cannot control objects that are worn or carried. You may throw the object at others or attack with it. In either case, you use your Psionic skill to resolve the Check and add your Intellect to damage dealt.
Upgrades: By spending 2 additional Mana, you may increase the spell level by 1 and manipulate an object of 0.5 more Encumbrance.

***

Ground
Spell type: Rote
Spell level: 2
Mana: 5
Casting time: 1 Action
Target: Creature
Range: 50 Meters
Duration: 10 Rounds
Components: Somatic
Skill: Elemental
Element: Earth
Description: With a single jerk of your hand, you weigh down a flying creature with raw elemental power and force it to descend. Any flying creature you successfully strike is safely lowered to the ground and cannot fly for the duration of the spell.
Upgrades: By spending 2 additional Mana, you may increase the spell level by 1 and increase its duration by 10 rounds.

***

Ice Shield
Spell type: Rote
Spell level: 2
Mana: 5
Casting time: 1 Action
Target: Self, Creature

Range: 10 Meters
Duration: 1 Round
Components: Somatic, Vocal
Skill: Elemental
Element: Water
Description: You speak a word of power and draw a powerful symbol to create a sturdy but flexible barrier of ice around your target. The ice does not harm your target or feel cold to the touch. For the duration of the spell, the subject receives no damage from sources of Physical damage (water) or Physical damage (fire) after your choice.
Upgrades: By spending 2 additional Mana, you may increase the spell level by 1 and change the casting time to Instant (Interruption).

***

Ice Spikes
Spell type: Rote
Spell level: 1
Mana: 3
Casting time: 1 Action
Target: Up to 3 creatures, no more than 5 meters apart
Range: 20 Meters
Duration: Instant
Components: Somatic
Skill: Elemental
Element: Water
Description: Three icy spikes fly from your outstretched hand at up to 3 creatures that are no more than 5 meters apart from each other. You make only one Check. Every

creature that is successfully struck, receives 1-2 + Intellect Physical damage (water)

Upgrades: By spending 2 additional Mana, you may increase the spell level by 1 and deal an additional 1-2 Physical damage (water) per spike.

***

Ice Vest
Spell type: Rote
Spell level: 1
Mana: 3
Casting time: 1 Action
Target: Self, Creature
Range: Touch
Duration: 1 Hour
Components: Somatic, Vocal, Material (a splash of water)
Skill: Elemental
Element: Water
Description: From a splash of water, a few signs of power, and an incantation, you create a solid armor of ice that protects the shoulders and chest. This vest has Encumbrance 1, Armor 4, and 1 maximum Breach. This armor uses the Medium Armor skill.
Upgrades: By spending 2 additional Mana, you may increase the spell level by 1 and increase the Armor of the vest by 4, its maximum Breaches by 1, and its Encumbrance by 1.

***

Iceplane
Spell type: Rote
Spell level: 2
Mana: 5
Casting time: 1 Action
Target: Area
Range: 50 Meters
Area of effect: 10-Meter radius
Duration: 10 Rounds
Components: Somatic, Vocal, Material (a splash of water)
Skill: Elemental
Element: Water
Description: From a splash of water, an arcane sigil, and an ancient incantation, you create a slippery plane of ice with a 10-meter radius within range. Creatures attempting to traverse the plane of ice must succeed at an Acrobatics Check that equals or defeats the result of your Elemental Check or be unable to move and waste their Action.
Upgrades: By spending 2 additional Mana, you may increase the spell level by 1 and increase the radius of its area of effect by 10 meters.

***

Icy Hand
Spell type: Rote
Spell level: 0
Mana: 1
Casting time: 1 Action
Target: Creature
Range: Touch

Duration: Instant
Components: Somatic
Skill: Elemental
Element: Water
Description: Agonizing cold radiates from your hand. If you successfully touch your target, you deal 1-6 + Intellect Physical damage (water). This spell may freeze up to 1 cubic meter of liquid that is not worn or carried.
Upgrades: By spending 2 additional Mana, you may increase the spell level by 1 and deal an additional 1-6 Physical damage (water).

***

Light
Spell type: Rote
Spell level: 0
Mana: 1
Casting time: 1 Action
Target: Other (see description)
Range: Touch
Area of effect: 5-Meter radius
Duration: 1 Hour or until dismissed
Components: Somatic
Skill: Illusion
Element: Light
Description: An object you touch sheds light of any color you choose in a 5-meter radius. The object can be no larger than 2 meters in any dimension. Casting this spell on a worn or carried object counts as an attack. Use your Illusion

skill to resolve the Check; if successful, it does not deal damage.

Upgrades: By spending 2 additional Mana, you may increase the spell level by 1 and increase the radius of the area of effect by 5 meters.

***

Mold Earth
Spell type: Rote
Spell level: 0
Mana: 1
Casting time: 1 Action
Target: Area
Range: 10 Meters
Area of effect: 5-Meter radius
Duration: Instant
Components: Somatic, Vocal
Skill: Druidcraft
Element: Earth
Description: Through a word of power and a symbol of elemental earth, you may manipulate dirt or stone in a 5-meter radius in any of the following ways: 1) make it into uneven, difficult terrain so that creatures cannot charge across it; 2) dig it up and place it right beside the excavated hole; 3) sculpt its surface into any semblance you like.

Upgrades: By spending 2 additional Mana, you may increase the spell level by 1 and increase the radius of its area of effect by 5 meters.

***

Reinvigorate
Spell type: Rote
Spell level: 1
Mana: 3
Casting time: 1 Action
Target: Self, Creature
Range: Touch
Duration: Instant
Components: Somatic, Vocal, Focus
Skill: Healing
Element: Life
Description: You call upon the grace of your god to renew the vigor of your target, restoring 1-6 + Intellect Stamina.
Upgrades: By spending 2 additional Mana, you may increase the spell level by 1 and restore an additional 1-6 Stamina.

***

Spikes
Spell type: Rote
Spell level: 2
Mana: 5
Casting time: 1 Action
Target: Area
Range: 50 Meters
Area of effect: 10-Meter radius
Duration: 10 Rounds

Components: Somatic, Vocal, Material (any stone)
Skill: Elemental
Element: Earth
Description: Using an arcane sigil and an ancient incantation, you make a single stone into rock-hard, deathly sharp spikes that cover an area in a 10-meter radius. Creatures attempting to traverse the spikes must succeed at an Acrobatics Check that equals or defeats the result of your Elemental Check or suffer 1-6 + Intellect Physical damage (earth).
Upgrades: By spending 2 additional Mana, you may increase the spell level by 1 and increase the radius of its area of effect by 10 meters.

***

Summon Beast
Spell type: Rote
Spell level: 2
Mana: 5
Casting time: 1 Action
Range: 20 Meters
Duration: 1 Minute
Components: Somatic, Vocal
Skill: Summoning
Element: Life
Description: You call forth your Spirit Animal. Your Spirit Animal is level 4. Your Spirit Animal does your bidding, obeying simple mental commands, and may act in the round after it was summoned.

Upgrades: By spending 2 additional Mana, you may increase the spell level by 1 and increase the duration by 1 hour.

***

Summon Lesser Ice Imp
Spell type: Rote
Spell level: 1
Mana: 3
Casting time: 1 Action
Range: 20 Meters
Duration: 1 Minute
Components: Somatic, Vocal, Material (a splash of water)
Skill: Summoning
Element: Water
Description: From a splash of water, a few words of power, and a sigil drawn in the air, you call forth a small Ice Elemental. The Ice Elemental does your bidding, obeying simple mental commands, and may act in the round after it was summoned.
Upgrades: By spending 2 additional Mana, you may increase the spell level by 1 and increase the duration by 1 hour.

***

Summon Lesser Rock Man
Spell type: Rote

Spell level: 1
Mana: 3
Casting time: 1 Action
Range: 20 Meters
Duration: 1 Minute
Components: Somatic, Vocal, Material (any stone)
Skill: Summoning
Element: Earth
Description: From a simple stone and a sigil of arcane might, you summon an Earth Elemental. The Earth Elemental does your bidding, obeying simple mental commands, and may act in the round after it was summoned.
Upgrades: By spending 2 additional Mana, you may increase the spell level by 1 and increase the duration by 1 hour.

***

Sustenance
Spell type: Ritual
Spell level: 1
Mana: 3
Casting time: 10 Minutes
Target: Self, Creature
Range: Touch
Duration: 1 Hour
Components: Somatic, Vocal, Material (a seed, nut, or any edible item)
Skill: Druidcraft
Element: Life

Description: Through words of secret druidic power and a symbol of might, you cause an entire meal to grow from a single sprout. The magical meal provides sustenance to 1 creature for 24 hours. It must be consumed within 1 hour or it will disappear.
Upgrades: By spending 2 additional Mana, this spell creates food for 1 additional creature.

***

Trackless Step
Spell type: Ritual
Spell level: 1
Casting time: 1 Minute
Target: Self and up to 4 other creatures
Range: 10 Meters
Duration: 1 Hour
Components: Somatic, Vocal, Material (a handful of dirt)
Skill: Illusion
Element: Earth
Description: You make a series of secret signs of shadow and, using a handful of dirt, obscure the tracks of you and up to 4 others for the duration of the spell. Anyone tracking you or those affected by this spell receive a penalty to their Check to do so equal to the result of your Illusion Check.

***

Tremor

Spell type: Rote
Spell level: 1
Mana: 3
Casting time: 1 Action
Target: Area
Range: 10 Meters
Area of effect: 5-Meter radius
Duration: Instant (Interruption)
Components: Somatic
Skill: Elemental
Element: Earth
Description: A single gesture of power from you, and the earth begins to shake in a 5-meter radius, destabilizing all within it. Creatures in the area of effect must succeed at an Acrobatics Check that equals or defeats the result of your Elemental Check or be unable to move and waste their Action. You may only cast this spell once per Round.
Upgrades: By spending 2 additional Mana, you may increase the spell level by 1 and increase the radius of its area of effect by 5 meters.

***

Windwalk
Spell type: Rote
Spell level: 2
Mana: 5
Casting time: 1 Action
Target: Self
Range: 50 Meters
Duration: Instant

Components: Somatic
Skill: Teleportation
Element: Air
Description: Gusting winds briefly envelop you as you teleport to anywhere within range. You must be able to see your destination.
Upgrades: By spending 2 additional Mana, you may increase the spell level by 1 and increase its range by 20 meters.

***

Windward
Spell type: Rote
Spell level: 2
Mana: 5
Casting time: 1 Action
Target: Self, Creature
Range: Touch
Duration: 10 Rounds
Components: Somatic, Vocal
Skill: Elemental
Element: Air
Description: You draw an arcane symbol in the air and speak the words that command the elements to envelop yourself in fierce gusts and gales of wind. Anyone attempting to target you with an effect that deals Physical damage suffers a penalty to their Check equal to your Elemental Check result. However, if you do not respond to an attack, it will still strike true.

Upgrades: By spending 2 additional Mana, you may increase the spell level by 1 and change the casting time to Instant (Interruption).

***

Word of Invigoration
Spell type: Rote
Spell level: 2
Mana: 5
Casting time: 1 Action
Target: Self, Creature
Range: 50 Meters
Duration: Instant
Components: Somatic, Vocal, Focus
Skill: Healing
Element: Life
Description: You call upon the grace of your god to renew the vigor of your target at a distance, restoring 1-6 + Intellect Stamina.
Upgrades: By spending 2 additional Mana, you may increase the spell level by 1 and restore an additional 1-6 Stamina.

Printed in Great Britain
by Amazon